"Merry Christmas 2003"

999

Huck Finn & Tom Sawyer
Among the Indians

Huck Finn & Tom Sawyer
Among the Indians

by

Mark Twain
&
Lee Nelson

COUNCIL·PRESS™

Springville, Utah

ISBN: 1-55517-680-1
e.1
Published by Council Press
Imprint of Cedar Fort Inc.
www.cedarfort.com
Distributed by:

Typeset by Kristin Nelson
Cover design by Barry Hansen
Cover design © 2003 by Lyle Mortimer
Printed in the United States of America
10 9 8 7 6 5 4 3 2 1
Printed on acid-free paper

Library of Congress Cataloging-in-Publication Data

Twain, Mark, 1835-1910.
 Huck Finn & Tom Sawyer among the Indians / by Mark Twain & Lee Nelson.

    p. cm.
Unfinished novel by Mark Twain, completed by Lee Nelson.
 ISBN 1-55517-680-1 (pbk. : alk. paper)
 1. Finn, Huckleberry (Fictitious character)--Fiction. 2. Sawyer, Tom (Fictitious character)--Fiction. 3. Indians of North America--Fiction.
I. Title: Huck Finn and Tom Sawyer among the Indians. II. Nelson, Lee.
III. Title.
 PS1322 .H84 2003
 813'.4--dc21

                        2002154248

Author's Note

Mark Twain (Samuel Clemens) began this story in 1885, long before his death, shortly after the publication of *The Adventures of Huckleberry Finn*. I first read it in the Brigham Young University barbershop in 1968 when it was published for the first time in *Life Magazine*. I remember how enthralled I was with the story. Huck, Tom and Jim were heading west to live with the Indians, meeting and joining up with the Mills family. A group of Sioux warriors befriended the emigrants before slaughtering the older boys and parents, and carrying off the two girls and Jim. Huck and Tom joined up with Brace Johnson, the fiancé of the older girl, Peggy, to catch up with the Indians and rescue the girls and Jim. As they approach the Indian camp, preparing for a daring rescue, the story suddenly ends, right in the middle of a sentence (where the three periods are located on page 62). Although Mark Twain wrote and published a number of books and stories after 1885, he never finished this one.

Early in 2002, while watching a documentary on Mark Twain on the local PBS station, I remembered reading *Among the Indians* in the barbershop. A little research on the web led me to the University of California Press which now holds the copyright to the unfinished story. I approached the legal counsel handling copyrights on Mark Twain's writings, with the idea of me finishing the story. They were agreeable to my proposition, the terms simple and straight forward. UCPress would receive royalties on the portion of the final text authored by Mark Twain, and Lee Nelson would receive royalties on the portion of the text which he composed.

With this agreement in place, I went to work.

As the work progressed, and I would tell friends what I was doing, a frequent response was that the critics would rip me to pieces, "How dare you presume to finish a work begun by possibly the father of American literature, and the best-selling author of the nineteenth century!" My response was to say that I do not presume to know how Mark Twain wanted to finish the story. In fact, I'm not sure he knew himself how he wanted to end it, or he probably would have done it himself. Maybe he had trouble writing about the delicate subject of sexual abuse; a white girl being raped by Indians. We don't know what he was thinking, only that he never finished it. I did know, however, how I wanted to finish it, having researched and written a dozen or so historical novels with settings in the western landscape and Native American culture of the mid-1800s.

While writing my part of the story I tried to maintain at least in part the style of the Huck Finn first person narrative with its blatant disregard for the rules and niceties of the English language. Mark Twain began the story:

That other book which I made before, was named Adventures of Huckleberry Finn. Maybe you remember about it. But if you don't, it don't make no difference, because it ain't got nothing to do with this one. The way it ended up, was that me and Tom Sawyer and the nigger Jim, that used to belong to old Miss Watson, was away down in Arkansaw at Tom's Aunt Sally's and Uncle Silas's. Jim warn't a slave no more, but free; because—but never mind about that: how he become to get free, and who done it, and what a power of work and danger it was, is all told about in that other book.

The reader should keep in mind that the Mark Twain portion of the story is a rough draft that never went through the normal editing and proofreading processes. With Mark Twain unavailable to approve changes and corrections, I chose to leave his portion of the story as he wrote it, as it appeared in *Life Magazine* in 1968.

I am certain that Mark Twain would not have used the word *nigger* as much as he did if readers in his day found it as offensive as they do today. I tried to substitute words like *slave* and *black*. Also, I'd like to remind the more critical readers, who might notice my style at times drifting into a more correct and easy-flowing narrative, that Mark Twain did that too. Some of his paragraphs seem a lot smoother and *correct* than others. Both styles switch back and forth between the present and past tense. I look at this work as a journey into the American west of the mid-1800s, through the eyes of Mississippi River river rat Huck Finn, began by Huck's creator, Mark Twain, and finished by one of his ardent fans, Lee Nelson. No more, no less. And if you'd ruther it be something else, it don't make no difference to me, and I ain't going to argue about it.

Chapter 1

That other book which I made before, was named Adventures of Huckleberry Finn. Maybe you remember about it. But if you don't, it don't make no difference, because it ain't got nothing to do with this one. The way it ended up, was that me and Tom Sawyer and the nigger Jim, that used to belong to old Miss Watson, was away down in Arkansaw at Tom's Aunt Sally's and Uncle Silas's. Jim warn't a slave no more, but free; because—but never mind about that: how he become to get free, and who done it, and what a power of work and danger it was, is all told about in that other book.

Well then, pretty soon it got dull there on that little plantation, and Tom he got pisoned with a notion of going amongst the Injuns for a while, to see how it would be; but about that time Aunt Sally took us off up home to Missouri and then right away after that she went away across the state, nearly to the west border, to stay a month or two months with some of her relations on a hemp farm out there, and took Tom and Sid and Mary; and I went along because Tom wanted me to, and Jim went too, because there was white men around our little town that was plenty mean enough and ornery enough to steal Jim's papers from him and sell him down the river again; but they couldn't come and do that if he staid with us.

Well, there's liver places than a hemp farm, there ain't no use to deny it, and some people don't take to them. Pretty soon, sure enough, just as I expected, Tom he begun to get in a sweat to have something going on. Somehow, Tom Sawyer couldn't ever stand much lazing around; though as for me, betwixt lazing around and pie, I hadn't no choice, and wouldn't know which to take, and just as soon have them both as not, and druther. So he rousted out his Injun notion again, and was dead set on having us run off, some night, and cut for the Injun country and go for adventures. He said it was getting too dull on the hemp farm, it give him the fan-tods.

But me and Jim kind of hung fire. Plenty to eat and nothing to do. We was very well satisfied. We hadn't ever had such comfortable times before, and we reckoned we better let it alone as long as Providence warn't noticing; it would get busted up soon enough, likely, without our putting in and helping. But Tom he stuck to the thing, and pegged at us every day. Jim says:

"I doan' see de use, Mars Tom. Fur as I k'n see, people dat has Injuns on day han's ain' no better off den people dat ain't got no Injuns. Well den: we ain't got no Injuns, we doan' need no Injuns, en what does we want to go en hunt 'em up f'r? We's gitt'n along jes' as well as if we had a million un um. Dey's a powerful ornery lot, anyway?"

"Who is?"

"Why, de Injuns."

"Who says so?"

"What do you know about it?"

"What does I know 'bout it? I knows dis much. Ef day ketches a body out, dey'll take en skin him same as day would a dog. Dat's what I knows 'bout 'em."

"All fol-de-rol. Who told you that?"

"Why, I hear ole Missus say so."

"Ole Missus! The Widow Douglas! Much she knows about it. Has she ever been skinned?"

"Course not."

"Just as I expected. She don't know what she's talking about. Has she ever been amongst the Injuns?"

"No."

"Well, then, what right has she got to be blackguarding them and telling what ain't so about them?"

"Well, anyway, old Gin'l Gaines, he's ben amongst 'm, anyway."

"All right, so he has. Been with them lots of times, hasn't he?"

"Yes—lots of times."

"Been with them years, hasn't he?"

"Yes sir! Why, Mars Tom, he . . ."

"Very well, then. Has he been skinned? You answer me that."

Jim see Tom had him. He couldn't say a word. Tom Sawyer was the keenest boy for laying for a person and just leading him along by the nose without ever seeming to do it till he got him where he couldn't budge and then bust his arguments all to flinders I ever see. It warn't no use to argue with Tom Sawyer—a body never stood any show.

Jim he hem'd and haw'd, but all he could say was, that he had somehow got the notion that Injuns was powerful ornery, but he reckoned maybe—then Tom shut him off.

"You reckon maybe you've been mistaken. Well, you have. Injuns ornery! It's the most ignorant idea that ever—why, Jim, they're the noblest human beings that's ever been in the world. If a white man tells you a thing, do you know it's true? No, you don't; because generally it's a lie. But if an Injun tells you a thing, you can bet on it every time for the petrified fact; because you can't get an Injun to lie, he would cut his tongue out first. If you trust to a white man's honor, you better look out; but you trust to an Injun's honor, and nothing in the world can make him betray you—he would die first, and be glad to. An Injun is all honor. It's what they're made of. You ask a white man to divide his property with you—will he do it? I think I see him at it; but you go to an Injun, and he'll give you everything he's got in the world. It's just the difference between an Injun and a white man. They're just all generousness and unstingeableness. And brave? Why, they ain't afraid of anything. If there was just one Injun, and a whole regiment of white men against him, they wouldn't stand the least show in the world–not the least. You'd see that splendid gigantic Injun come war-whooping down on his wild charger all over paint and feathers waving his tomahawk and letting drive with his bow faster than anybody could count the arrows and hitting a soldier in any part of his body he wanted to, every time, any distance, and in two minutes you'd see him santering off with a wheelbarrow-load of scalps and the rest of them stampeding for the United States the same as if the menagerie was after them. Death?–an Injun don't care shucks for death. They prefer it. They sing when they're dying–sing their death-song. You take an Injun and stick him full of arrows and splinters, and hack him up with a hatchet, and skin him, and start a slow fire under him, and do you reckon he minds it? No sir; he will just set there in the hot ashes, perfectly comfortable, and sing, same as if he was on salary. Would a white man? You know he wouldn't. And they're the most gigantic magnificent creatures in the whole world, and can knock a man down with a barrel of flour as far as they can see him. They're awful strong, and fiery, and eloquent, and wear beautiful blankets, and war-paint, and moccasins, and the buckskin clothes, all over beads, and go fighting and scalping every day in the year but Sundays, and have a noble good time, and they love friendly white men, and just dote on them, and can't do too much for them, and would ruther die than let any harm come to them, and they think just as much of niggers as they do of anybody, and the young squaws are the most be-utiful maidens that was ever in the whole world, and they love a white hunter the minute their eye falls on him, and from that minute nothing can ever shake their love loose again, and they're always on the watch-out to protect him from danger and get themselves killed in the place of him–look at Pocahontas!–and an Injun can see as far as a telescope with the naked eye, and an enemy can't slip around anywhere, even in the dark, but he knows it; and if he sees one single blade of grass bent down, it's all he wants, he knows which way to go to find the enemy that done it, and he can read all kinds of trifling little signs just the same way with his eagle eye which you wouldn't ever see at all, and if he sees a little whiff of smoke going up in the air thirty-five miles off, he knows in a second if it's a friend's camp fire or an enemy's, just by the smell of the smoke, because they're the most giftedest people in the whole world, and the hospitablest and the happiest, and don't ever have anything to do from year's end to year's end but have a perfectly supernatural good time and piles and piles of adventures! Amongst the Injuns, life is just simply a circus, that's what it is. Anybody that knows, will tell you you can't praise it too high and you can't put it too strong."

Jim's eyes was shining, and so was mine, I reckon, and he was excited, and it was the same with both of us, as far as that was concerned. Jim drawed a long breath, and then says:

"Whoosh! Dem's de ticket for Jim! Bust ef it doan' beat all, how rotten ignorant a body kin be 'bout Injun s w'en 'e hain't had no chance to study um up. Why, Mars Tom, ef I'd a knowed what Injuns reely is, I pledges you my word I'd—well, you jes count me in, dat's all; count me in on de Injun-country business; I's ready to go, I doan' want no likelier folks aroun' me d'n what dem Injuns is. En Huck's ready, too—hain't it so, Huck?"

Course I warn't going to stay behind if they went, so I said I was.

Chapter 2

So we went to making preparations; and mighty private and secret, too, because Tom Sawyer wouldn't have nothing to do with a thing if there warn't no mystery about it. About three mile out in the woods, amongst the hills, there was an old tumble-down log house that used to be lived in, some time or other when people cut timber there, and we found it on a coon hunt one night, but nobody ever went there, now. So we let on it was infested with pirates and robbers, and we laid in the woods all one rainy night, perfectly still, and not showing fire or a light; and just before dawn we crept up pretty close and then sprung out whooping and yelling, and took it by surprise, and never lost a man, Tom said, and was awful proud of it, though I couldn't see no sense in all that trouble and bother, because we could a took it in the day time just as well, there warn't nobody there. Tom called the place a cavern, though it warn't a cavern at all, it was a house, and a mighty ornery house at that.

Every day we went up to the little town that was two mile from the farm, and bought things for the outfit and to barter with the Injuns–skillets and coffee pots and tin cups, and blankets, and three sacks of flour, and bacon and sugar and coffee, and fish hooks, and pipes and tobacco, and ammunition, and pistols, and three guns, and glass beads, and all such things. And we hid them in the woods; and nights we clumb out of the window and slid down the lightning rod, and went and got the things and took them to the cavern. There was an old Mexican on the next farm below ours, and we got him to learn us how to pack a pack-mule so we could do it first rate.

And last of all, we went down fifteen or twenty mile further and bought five good mules, and saddles, because we didn't want to raise no suspicions around home, and took the mules to the cavern in the night and picketed them in the grass. There warn't no better mules in the State of Missouri, Tom said, and so did Jim.

Our idea was to have a time amongst the Injuns for a couple of months or so, but we had stuff enough to last longer than that I reckon, because Tom allowed we ought to be fixed for accidents. Tom bought a considerable lot of little odds and ends of one kind and another which it ain't worth while to name, which he said they would come good with the Injuns.

Well, the last day that we went up to town, we laid in an almanac, and a flask or two of liquor and struck a stranger that had a curiosity and was peddling it. It was little sticks about as long as my finger with some stuff like yellow wax on the ends, and all you had to do was to rake the yellow end on something, and the stick would catch fire and smell like all possessed, on account of part of it being brimstone. We hadn't ever heard of anything like that, before. They were the convenientest things in the world, and just the trick for us to have; so Tom bought a lot of them. The man called them lucifer matches, and said anybody could make them that had brimstone and phosphorus to do it with. So he sold Tom a passel of brimstone and phosphorus, and we allowed to make some for ourselves some time or other.

We was already, now. So we waited for full moon, which would be in two or three days. Tom wrote a letter to his aunt Polly to leave behind, telling her good bye, and saying rest easy and not worry, because we would be back in two or three weeks, but not telling her anything about where we was going.

And then, Thursday night, when it was about eleven and everything still, we got up and dressed, and slid down the lightning rod, and shoved the letter under the front door, and slid by the nigger-quarters and give a low whistle, and Jim come gliding out and we struck for the cavern, and packed everything onto two of the mules, and put on our belts and pistols and bowie knives, and saddled up the three other mules and rode out into the big moonlight and started west.

By and by we struck level country, and a pretty smooth path, and not so much woods, and the moonlight was perfectly splendid, and so was the stillness. You couldn't hear nothing but the kreaking of the saddles. After a while there was that cool and fresh feeling that tells you day is coming; and then the sun come up behind us, and made the leaves and grass and flowers shine and sparkle, on account of the dew, and the birds let go and begun to sing like everything.

So then we took to the woods, and made camp, and picketed the mules, and laid off and slept a good deal of the day. Three more nights we traveled that way, and laid up daytimes, and everything was mighty pleasant. We never run across anybody, and hardly ever see a light. After that, we judged we was so far from home that we was safe; so then we begun to travel by daylight.

The second day after that, when we was hoping to begin to see Injun signs, we struck a wagon road, and at the same time we struck an emigrant wagon with a family aboard, and it was near sundown, and they asked us to camp with them, and we done it. There was a man about fifty-five and his wife, named Mills, and three big sons, Buck and Bill and Sam, and a girl that said she was seventeen, named Peggy, and her little sister Flaxy, seven year old. They was from down in the lower end of Missouri and said they was bound for Oregon—going to settle there. We said we was bound for Injun country, and they said they was going to pass through it and we could join company with them if we would like to.

They was the simple-heartedest good-naturedest country folks in the world, and didn't know anything hardly—I mean what l you call learning. Except Peggy. She had read considerable many books, and knowed as much as most any girl, and was just as pretty as ever she could be, and live. But she warn't no prettier than she was good, and all the tribe doted on her. Why, they took as much care of her as if she was made out of sugar or gold or something. When she'd come to the camp fire, any of her brothers would get up in a minute and give her the best place. I reckon you don't see that kind of brothers pretty often. She didn't have to saddle her own mule, the way she'd have to do in most society, they always done it for her. Her and her mother never had anything to do but cook, that is all; the brothers got the wood, they built the fires, they skinned the game; and whenever they had time they helped her wash up the things. It ain't often you see a brother kiss his own sister; fact is, I don't know as I'd ever seen such a thing before; but they done it. I know, because I see them do it myself; and not just once, but plenty of times. Tom see it too, and so did Jim. And they never said a cross word to her, not one. They called her Dear. Plenty of times they called her that; and right before company, too; they didn't care; they never thought nothing of it. And she didn't, either. They'd say "Peggy dear," to her, just in the naturalest off-handedest way, it didn't make no difference who was around; and it took me two or three days to get so I could keep from blushing, I was so ashamed for them, though I knowed it warn't the least harm, because they was right out of the woods and didn't know no better. But I don't wish to seem to be picking flaws in them, and abusing them, because I don't, they was the splendidest people in the world; and after you got that fact stowed in your mind solid, you was very well satisfied, and perfectly willing to overlook their manners; because nobody can't be perfect, anyway.

We all got to be uncommon friendly together; it warn't any trouble at all. We traveled with them, and camped with them every night. Buck and Bill and Sam was wonderful with a lasso, or a gun, or a pistol, or horseback riding, and they learned us all these things so that we got to be powerful good at them, specially Tom; and though he couldn't throw a lasso as far as a man could, he could throw it about as true. And he could cave in a squirrel's or a wild turkey's or a prairie chicken's head any fair distance; and could send both loads from his pistol through your hat on a full gallop, at twenty yards, if you wanted him to. There warn't ever any better people than the Millses; but Peggy she was the cap-sheaf of the lot, of course; so gentle, she was, and so sweet, and whenever you'd done a little thing for her it made you feel so kind of all over comfortable and blessed to see her smile. If you ever felt cut, about anything, she never asked about the rights of it, or who done it, but just went to work and never rested til she had coaxed the smart all out and made you forget all about it. And she was that kind of a girl that if you ever made a mistake and happened to say something that hurt her, the minute you saw by her face what you had done, you wanted to get down on your knees in the dirt you felt so mean and sorry. You couldn't ever get tired looking at her, all day long, she was so dear and pretty; and mornings it warn't ever sun-up to me till she come out.

One day, about a couple of weeks after we had left the United States behind, and was ever so far away out on the Great Plains, we struck the Platte river and went into camp in a nice grassy place a couple of hours before sun-down, and there we run across a camp of Injuns, the first ones we had been close enough to, yet, to get acquainted with. Tom was powerful glad.

Chapter 3

It was just the place for a camp; the likeliest we had found yet. Big stream of water, and considerable many trees along it. The rest of the country, as far as you could see, any which-way you looked, clear to where the sky touched the earth, was just long levels and low waves–like what I reckon the ocean would be, if the ocean was made out of grass. Away off, miles and miles, was one tree standing by itself, and away off the other way was another, and here and yonder another and another scattered around; and the air was so clear you would think they was close by, but it warn't so, most of them was miles away.

Old Mills said he would stop there and rest up the animals. I happened to be looking at Peggy, just then, because I mostly always happened to be looking at her when she was around, and her cheeks turned faint red and beautiful, like a nigger's does when he puts a candle in his mouth to surprise a child; she never said nothing, but pretty soon she got to singing low to herself and looking happy. I didn't let on; but next morning when I see her slip off to the top of one of them grass-waves and stand shading her eyes with her hands and looking away off over the country, I went there and got it all out of her. And it warn't no trouble, either, after she got started. It looked like the mainest trouble was going to be to stop her again.

She had a sweetheart–that was what was the matter of her. He had staid behind, to finish up things, and would be along when he got done. His name was Brace Johnson; big, and fine, and brave, and good, and splendid, and all that, as near as I could make out twenty-six years old; been amongst the Injuns ever since he was a boy, trapping, hunting, scouting, fighting; knowed all about Injuns, knowed some of the languages, knowed the plains and the mountains, and all that whole country, from Texas to Oregon; and now he was done with all that kind of life, and her and him was going to settle down in Oregon, and get married, and go to farming it. I reckon she thought she only loved him; but I see by her talk it was upwards of that, she worshiped him. She said we was to stay where we was till he come, which might be in a week, and then we would stay as much longer as her pap thought the horses needed to.

There was five of the Injuns, and they had spry little ponies, and was camped tolerable close by. They was big, strong, grand looking fellows, and had on buckskin leggings and moccasins, and red feathers in their hair, and knives and tomahawks, and bows and arrows, and one of them had an old gun and could talk a little English, but it warn't any use to him, he couldn't kill anything with it because it hadn't any flint–I mean the gun. They was naked from the waist up, when they hadn't on their blankets.

They set around our fire till bedtime, the first night, and took supper with us, and passed around the pipe, and was very friendly, and made signs to us, and grunted back, when we signed anything they understood, and pretty much everything they see that they liked, they wanted it. So they got coffee, sugar, and tobacco, and a lot of little things.

They was there to breakfast, next morning, and then me and Tom went over to their camp with them, and we all shot at a mark with their bows and arrows, and they could outshoot anything I ever see with a bow and arrow, and could stand off a good ways and hit a tree with a tomahawk every time.

They come back with us at noon and eat dinner, and the one with the gun showed it to Peggy, and made signs would she give him a flint, and she got one from her father, and put it in the gunlock and fixed it herself, and the Injun was very thankful, and called her good squaw and pretty squaw, and she was ever so pleased; and another one named Hog Face that had a bad old hurt on his shin, she bandaged it up and put salve on it, and he was very thankful too.

Tom he was just wild over the Injuns, and said there warn't no white men so noble; and he warn't by himself in it, because me and Jim, and all the rest of us got right down fond of them; and Peggy said she did wish Brace was here, he would change his notions about Injuns, which he was down on, and hated them like snakes, and always said he wouldn't trust one any how or any where, in peace time or war time or any other time. She showed me a little dirk-knife which she got out of her bosom, and asked me what I reckoned it was for, and who give it to her.

"I don't know," says I. "Who did give it to you?"

"Brace." Then she laughed, gay and happy, and says, "You'll never guess what it's for."

"Well, what is it for?" says I.

"To kill myself with!"

"O, good land!" says I, "how you talk."

"Yes," she says, "it's the truth. Brace told me that if I ever fell into the hands of the savages, I mustn't stop to think about him, or the family, or anything, or wait an hour to see if I mightn't be rescued; I mustn't waste any time, I mustn't take any chances, I must kill myself right away."

"Goodness," I says, "and for why?"

"Of course; I teased him to tell me, but he wouldn't. He kept trying to get me to promise, but I laughed him off, every time, and told him if he was so anxious to get rid of me he must tell my why I must kill myself, and then maybe I would promise. At last he said he couldn't tell me. So I said, very well, then I wouldn't promise; and laughed again, but he didn't laugh. By and by he said, very serious and troubled, 'You know I wouldn't ask you to do that or any other thing that wasn't the best for you–you can trust me for that, can't you?' That made me serious, too, because that was true; but I couldn't promise such a thing, you know, it made me just shudder to think of it. So then he asked me if I would keep the dirk, as his gift and keepsake; and when I said I would, he said that would do, it was all he wanted."

One of the Injuns, named Blue Fox, come up, just then, and the minute he see the dirk he begun to beg for it; it was their style–they begged for everything that come in their way. But Peggy wouldn't let him have it. Next day and the next he come teasing around her, wanting to take it to his camp and make a nice new sheath and a belt for her to wear it in, and so she got tired at last and he took it away. But she never let him have it till he promised he would take good care of it and never let it get out of his hands. He was that pleased, that he up and give her a necklace made out of bears' claws; and as she had to give him something back, of course, she give him a Bible, and tried to learn him some religion, but he couldn't understand, and so it didn't do him no particular good–that is, it didn't just then, but it did after a little, because when the Injuns go to gambling, same as they done every day, he put up his Bible against a tomahawk and won it.

They was a sociable lot. They wrassled with Buck and Bill and Sam, and learned them some new holts and throws that they didn't know before; and we all run foot races and horse races with them, and it was prime to see the way their ornery little ponies would split along when their pluck was up.

And they danced dances for us. Two or three times they put on all their fuss and feathers and war paint and danced the war dance, and whooped and jumped and howled and yelled, and it was lovely and horrible. But the one with the gun, named Man-afraid-of-his-Mother-in-law, didn't ever put on any paint and finery, and didn't dance in the war dances, and mostly he didn't come around when they had them, and when he did he looked sour and glum and didn't stay.

Yes, we was all stuck after the Injuns, kind of in love with them, as you may say, and I reckon I never had better times than I had then. Peggy was as good to them as if she was their sister or their child, and they was very fond of her. She was sorry for the one with the gun, and tried to encourage him to put on his war paint and dance the war dance with the others and be happy and not glum; and it pleased him to have her be so friendly, but he never done it. But pretty soon it struck her what maybe the matter was, and she says to me:

"He's in mourning—that's what it is; he has lost a friend. And to think, here I have been hurting him, and making him remember his sorrows, when I wouldn't have done such a thing for the whole world if I had known."

So after that, she couldn't do too much for him, nor be sorry enough for him. And she wished more than ever that Brace was here, so he could see that Injuns was just like other people, after all, and had their sorrows and troubles, and knowed how to love a friend and grieve for him when he was gone.

Tom he was set on having the Injuns take me and him and Jim into their band and let us travel to their country and live in their tribe a week or two; and so, on the fourth day, we went over to their camp, me an Tom did, to ask them. But they was fixing for a buffalo hunt next morning, to be gone all day, and maybe longer, and that filled Tom so full of excitement, he couldn't think about anything else, for we hadn't ever seen a buffalo yet. They had a plan for me and Jim and Tom to start before daylight with one Injun and go in one direction, and Buck in another with another Injun, and Bill with another and Sam with another, and leave the other Injun in their camp because he was so lame with his sore leg, and whichever gang found the buffaloes first was to signal the other. So it was all fixed.

Then we see Peggy off there on one of them grass-waves, with Flaxy, looking out over the country with her hand over her eyes, and all the Injuns noticed her at once and asked us what she was looking for. I said she was expecting a lot of friends. The Injun that spoke a little English asked me how many. It's always my disposition to stretch, so I said seven. Tom he kind of smiled, but let it go at that. Man-afraid-of-his-Mother-in-law says:

"Little child (meaning Flaxy, you know) say only one."

I see I was ketched, but in my opinion a body don't ever gain anything by weakening, in them circumstances, so I says:

"Seven," and said it firm, and stuck to it.

The Injuns talked amongst themselves a while, then they told us to go over and ask Bill and Buck and Sam to come and talk about the hunt. We done it, and they went over, and we all set down to wait supper till they come back; they said they reckoned they would be back inside of half an hour. In a little while four of the Injuns come and said the boys was staying behind to eat supper with Hog Face in their camp. So then we asked the Injuns to eat supper with us, and Peggy she passed around the tin plates and things, and dished out the vittles, and we all begun. They had put their war-paint and feathers and fixings on since we left their camp—all but the one with the gun—so I judged we would have another good time. We eat, and eat, and talked, and laughed, till by and by we was all done, and then still we set there talking.

By and by Tom shoved his elbow into my side, soft and easy, and then got up and took a bucket and said he would fetch some water for Peggy, and went santering off. I said I would help; so I got a bucket and followed along. As soon as we was behind some trees, Tom says:

"Somehow everything don't seem right, Huck. They don't smoke; they've always smoked, before. There's only one gun outside the wagon, and a minute or two ago one of them was meddling with it. I never thought anything of it at the time, but I do now, because I happened to notice it just a minute ago, and by George the flint's gone! There's something up, Huck—I'm going to fetch the boys."

Away he went, and what to do I didn't know. I started back, keeping behind the trees, and when I got pretty close, I judged I would watch what was going on, and wait for Tom and the boys. The Injuns was up, and sidling around, the rest was chatting, same as before, and Peggy was gathering up the plates and things. I heard a trampling like a lot of horses, and when it got pretty near, I see that other Injun coming on a pony, and driving the other ponies and all our mules and horses ahead of him, and he let off a long wild whoop, and the minute he done that, the Injun that had a gun, the one that Peggy fixed, shot her father through the head with it and scalped him, another one tomahawked her mother and scalped her, and then these two grappled Jim and tied his hands together, and the other two grabbed Peggy, who was screaming and crying, and all of them rushed off with her and Jim and Flaxy, and as fast as I run, and as far as I run, I could still hear her, till I was a long, long ways off.

Soon it got dark, and I had to stop, I was so tired. It was an awful long night, and I didn't sleep, but was watching and listening all the time, and scared at every little sound, and miserable. I never see such a night for hanging on, and stringing out, and dismalness.

When daylight come, I didn't dast to stir, at first, being afraid; but I got so hungry I had to. And besides, I wanted to find out about Tom; so I went sneaking for the camp, which was away off across the country, I could tell it by the trees. I struck the line of trees as far up as I could, and slipped along down behind them. There was a smoke, but by and by I see it warn't the camp fire, it was the wagon; the Injuns had robbed it and burnt it. When I got down pretty close, I see Tom there, walking around and looking. I was desperate glad; for I didn't know but the other Injun had got him.

We scratched around for something to eat, but didn't find it, everything being burnt; then we set down and I told Tom everything, and he told me everything. He said when he got to the Injun camp, the first thing he see was Buck and Sam and Bill laying dead–tomahawked and scalped, and stripped; and each of them had as much as twenty-five arrows sticking in him. And he told me how else they had served the bodies, which was horrible, but it would not do to put it in a book. Of course the boys' knives and pistols was gone.

Then Tom and me set there a considerable time, with our jaws in our hands, thinking, and not saying anything. At last I says:

"Well?"

He didn't answer right off, but pretty soon he says:

"I've thought it out, and my mind's made up; but I'll give you the first say, if you want it."

I says:

"No, I don't want it. I've tried, but I can't seem to strike any plan. We're here, and that's all there is to it. We're here, as much as a million miles from any place, I reckon; and we haven't got any where but just to hoof it, and I reckon we'd play out and die before we got there that way. We're in a fix. That's all I know about it; we're just in a fix, and you can't call it by no lighter name. Whatever your plan is, it'll suit me; I'll do whatever you say. Go on. Talk."

Chapter 4

So he says:

"Well, this is my idea, Huck. I got Jim into this scrape, and so of course I ain't going to turn back towards home till I've got him out of it again, or found out he's dead; but you ain't in fault, like me, and so if we can run across any trappers bound for the States . . ."

"Never mind about that, Tom," I says, "I'm agoing with you, I want to help save Jim, if I can, and I want to help save Peggy, too. She was good to us, and I couldn't rest easy if I didn't. I'll go with you, Tom."

"All right," he says, "I hoped you would, and I was certain you would; but I didn't want to cramp you or influence you."

"But how are we going?" says I, "walk?"

"No," he says. "Have you forgot about Brace Johnson?"

I had. And it made the cold misery go through me to hear his name; for it was going to be sorrowful times for him when he come.

So we was to wait there for him. And maybe two or three days, without anything to eat; because the folks warn't expecting him for about a week from the time we camped. We went off a half a mile to the highest of them grass-waves, where there was a small tree, and took a long look over the country, to see if we could see Brace or anybody coming, but there wasn't a living thing stirring, anywhere. It was the biggest, widest, levelest world—and all dead; dead and still; not a sound. The lonesomest place that ever was; enough to break a body's heart, just to listen to the awful stillness of it. We talked a little sometimes—once an hour, maybe; but mostly we took up the time thinking, and looking, because it was hard to talk against such solemnness. Once I said: "Tom, where did you learn about Injuns–how noble they was, and all that?"

He gave me a look that showed me I had hit him hard, very hard, and so I wished I hadn't said the words. He turned away his head, and after about a minute he said "Cooper's novels," and didn't say anything more, and I didn't say anything more, and so that changed the subject. I see he didn't want to talk about it, and was feeling bad, so I let it just rest there, not ever having any disposition to fret or worry any person.

We had started a camp fire in a new place further along down the stream, with fire from the burnt wagon, because the Injuns had burnt the bodies of old Mr. Mills and his wife along with the wagon, and so that place seemed a kind of graveyard, you know, and we didn't like to stay about it. We went to the new fire once in a while and kept it going, and we slept there that night, most starved.

We turned out at dawn, and I jumped up brash and gay, for I had been dreaming I was home; but I just looked around once over that million miles of gray dead level, and my soul sucked back that brashness and gayness again with just one suck, like a sponge, and then all the miserableness come back and was worse than yesterday.

Just as it got to be light, we see some creatures away off on the prairie, going like the wind; and reckoned they was antelopes or Injuns, or both, but didn't know; but it was good to see some life again, anyway; it didn't seem so lonesome after that, for a while.

We was so hungry we couldn't stay still; so we went loafing off, and run across a prairie-dog village–little low mounds with holes in them, and a sentinel, which was a prairie dog, and looked like a Norway rat, standing guard. We had long cottonwood sticks along, which we had cut off of the trees and was eating the bark for breakfast; and we dug into the village, and rousted out an owl or two and a couple of handfuls of rattlesnakes, and hoped we was going to get a dog, but didn't, nor an owl, either; but we hived as bully a rattlesnake as ever I see, and took him to camp and cut his head off and skinned him and roasted him in the hot embers, and he was prime; but Tom was afraid, and wouldn't eat any, at first, but I knowed they was all right, because I had seen hogs and niggers eat them, and it warn't no time to be proud when you are starving to death, I reckoned. Well, it made us feel a powerful sight better, and nearly cheerful again; and when we got done we had snake enough left for a Sunday School blowout, for he was a noble big one. He was middling dry, but if we'd a had some gravy or butter or something, it wouldn't a been any slouch of a picnic.

We put in the third day that we was alone talking, and laying around, and wandering about, and snaking, and found it more and more lonesomer and drearier than ever. Often, as we come to a high grass-wave, we went up and looked out over the country, but all we ever saw was buzzards or ravens or something wheeling round and round over where the Injun camp was—and knowed what brought them there. We hadn't been there, and hadn't even been near there.

When we was coming home towards evening, with a pretty likely snake, we stopped and took another long look across country, and didn't see anything at first, but pretty soon we thought we did; but it was away off yonder against the sky, ever so far, and so we warn't certain. You can see an awful distance there, the air is so clear; so we calculated to have to wait a good while. And we did. In about a half an hour, I reckon, we could make out that it was horses or men or something, and coming our way. Then we laid down and kept close, because it might be Injuns, and we didn't want no more Injun then, far from it. At last Tom says;

"There's three horses, sure."

And pretty soon he says:

"There is only one man; he's driving three pack mules ahead of him; and coming along mighty brisk. He's got a wide slouch hat on, and I reckon he's white. It's Brace Johnson, I guess; I reckon he's the only person expected this year. Come—let's creep along behind the grass-waves and get nearer. If it's him, we want to stop him before he gets to the old camp, and break it to him easy."

But we couldn't. He was too fast for us. There he set, on his horse, staring. The minute we showed ourselves he had his gun leveled on us; then he notice we warn't Injuns, and dropped it, and told us to come on, and we did.

"Boys," he says, "by the odds and ends that's left, I see that this was the Mills's camp. Was you with them?"

"Yes."

"What happened?"

I never said nothing; and Tom he didn't, at first; then he said: "Injuns."

"Yes," he says, "I see that, myself, by the signs; but the folks got away, didn't they?"

We didn't answer. He jumped off of his horse, and come up to us quick, looking anxious, and says:

"Where are they?—quick, where are they? Where's Peggy?"

Well, we had to tell him—there warn't no other way. And it was all he could do to stand it; just all he could do. And when we come to tell about Peggy, he couldn't stand it; his face turned as white as milk, and the tears run down his cheeks, and he kept saying "Oh, my God, oh my God." It was so dreadful to see him, that I wanted to get him away from that part of it, and so I worked around and got back onto the other details, and says:

"The one with the gun, that didn't have no war paint, he shot Mr. Mills, and scalped him; and he bloodied his hands, then, and made blood stripes across his face with his fingers, like war paint, and then begun to howl war-whoops like the Injuns does in the circus. And poor old Mrs. Mills, she was down on her knees, begging so pitiful when the toma-hawk . . ."

"I shall never never see her again–never never any more–my poor little darling, so young and sweet and beautiful–but thank God, she's dead!"

He warn't listening to me.

"Dead?" I says; "if you mean Peggy, she's not dead."

He whirls on me like a wild-cat, and shouts:

"Not dead! Take it back, take it back, or I'll strangle you! How do you know?"

His fingers was working, and so I stepped back a little out of reach, and then says:

"I know she ain't because I see the Injuns drag her away; and they didn't strike her nor offer to hurt her."

Well, he only just groaned; and waved out his hands, and fetched them together on top of his head. Then he says:

"You staggered me, and for a minute I believed you, and it made me most a lunatic. But it's all right–she had the dirk. Poor child, poor thing–if I had only been here!"

I just had it on my tongue's end to tell him she let Blue Fox have the dirk for a while and I didn't know whether he give it back to her or not–but I didn't say it. Some kind of instinct told me to keep it to myself, I didn't know why. But this fellow was the quickest devil you ever see. He see me hesitate, and he darted a look at me and bored into mine like he was trying to see what it was I was keeping back in my mind. But I held my face quiet, and never let on. So then he looked considerable easier, but not entirely easy, and says:

"She had a dirk–didn't you see her have a dirk?"

"Yes," I says.

"Well, then, it's all right. She didn't lose it, nor give it way, nor anything, did she? She had it with her when they carried her away, didn't she?"

Of course I didn't know whether she did or not, but I said yes, because it seemed the thing to say.

"You are sure?" he says.

"Yes, perfectly sure," I says, "I ain't guessing, I know she had it with her."

He looked very grateful, then, and drawed a long sigh, and says:

"Ah, the poor child, poor friendless little thing—thank God she's dead."

I couldn't make out why he wanted her to be dead, nor how he could seem to be so thankful for it. As for me, I hoped she wasn't, and I hoped we would find her, yet, and get her and Flaxy away from the Injuns alive and well, too, and I warn't going to let myself be discouraged out of that thought, either. We started for the Injun camp; and when Tom was on ahead a piece, I up and asked Brace if he actually hoped Peggy was dead; and if he did, why he did. He explained it to me, and then it was all clear.

When we got to the camp, we looked at the bodies a minute, and then Brace said we would bury them presently, but he wanted to look around and make some inquiries, first. So he turned over the ashes of the fire, examining them careful, and examining any little thing he found amongst them, and the tracks, and any little rag or such like matter that was laying around, and pulled out one of the arrows, and examined that, and talked to himself all the time, saying "Sioux—yes, Sioux, that's plain"—and other remarks like that. I got to wandering around, too, and once when I was a step or two away from him, lo and behold, I found Peggy's little dirk-knife on the ground! It just took my breath, and I reckon I made a kind of a start, for it attracted his attention, and he asked me if I had found something, and I said yes, and dropped on my knees so that the knife was under my leg; and when he was coming, I let some moccasin beads drop on the ground that I had found before, and pretended to be looking at them; and he come and took them up, and whilst he was turning them over in his hand examining them, I slipped the dirk into my pocket; and presently, as soon as it was dark, I slipped out of our camp and carried it away off about a quarter of a mile and throwed it amongst the grass. But I warn't satisfied; it seemed to me that it would be just like that fellow to stumble on it and find it, he was so sharp. I didn't even dast to bury it, I was so afraid he'd find it. So at last I took and cut a little hole and shove it in betwixt the linings of my jacket, and then I was satisfied I was glad I thought of that, for it was like having a keepsake from Peggy, and something to remember her by, always as long as I lived.

Chapter 5

That night, in camp, after we had buried the bodies, we set around and talked, and me and Tom told Brace all about how we come to be there, on account of Tom wanting us to go with him and hunt up some Injuns and live with them a while, and Brace said it was just like boys the world over, and just the same way it was with him when he was a boy; and as we talked along, you could see he warmed to us because we thought so much of Peggy and told him so many things she done and said, and how she looked. And now and then, as we spoke of the Injuns, a most wicked look would settle into his face, but at these times he never said nothing.

There was some things which he was a good deal puzzled about; and now and then he would bust into the middle of the talk with a remark that showed us his mind had been wandering to them things. Once he says:

"I wonder what nation put 'em on the war path. It was perfectly peaceable on the Plains a little while back, or I wouldn't a had the folks start, of course. And I wonder if it's general war, or only some little private thing."

Of course we couldn't tell him, and so had to let him puzzle along. Another time, he busted in and says:

"It's the puzzlingest thing!—there's features about it that I can't seem to make head nor tail of, no way. I can understand why they fooled around here three or four days, because there warn't no hurry; they knowed they had from here to Oregon to do the job in, and besides, an Injun is patient; he'd ruther wait a month till he can make sure of his game without any risk to his own skin than attempt it sooner where there's the least risk. I can understand why they planned a buffalo hunt that would separate all the whites from each other and make the mastering of them easy and certain, because five warriors, not yet fifteen, won't tackle five men and two boys, even by surprise when they're asleep at dawn, when there's a safer way. Yes, I can understand all that—it's Injun, and easy. But the thing that gits me, is, what made them throw over the buffalo plan and act in such a hurry at last—for they did act in a hurry. You see, an Injun don't kill a whole gang, that way, right out and out, unless he is mighty mad or in a desperate hurry. After they had got the young men safe out of the way, they would have saved at least the old man for the torture. It clear beats me, I can't understand it."

For a minute, I couldn't help him out any; I couldn't think of anything to make them in a hurry. But Tom he remembered about me telling the Injuns the Millses was expecting seven friends, and they looked off and see Peggy and Flaxy on the watchout for them. So Brace says:

"That's all right, then; I understand it, now. That's Injun—that would make 'em drop the buffalo business and hurry up things. I know why they didn't kill the nigger, and why they haven't killed him yet, and ain't going to, nor hurt him; and now if I only knowed whether this is general war or only a little private spurt, I would be satisfied and not bother any more. But—well, hang it, let it go, there ain't any way to find out."

So we dropped back on the details again, and by and by I was telling how Man-afraid-of-his-Mother-in-law streaked his face all over with blood after he killed Mr. Mills, and then—

"Why, he done that for war-paint!" says Brace Johnson, excited; "warn't he in war-outfit before?—warn't they all painted?"

"All but him," I says. "He never wore paint nor danced with the rest in the war-dance."

"Why didn't you tell me that before; it explains everything."

"I did tell you," I says, "but you warn't listening."

"It's all right, now, boys," he says, "and I'm glad it's the way it is, for I wasn't feeling willing to let you go along with me, because I didn't know but all the Injuns was after the whites, and it was a general war, and so it would be bad business to let you get into it, and we couldn't dare to travel except by night, anyway. But you are all right, now, and can shove out with me in the morning, for this is nothing but a little private grudge, and like as not this is the end of it. You see, some white man has killed a relation of that Injun, and so he had hunted up some whites to retaliate on. It wouldn't be the proper thing for him to ever appear in war fixings again till he had killed a white man and wiped out that score. He was in disgrace till he had done that; so he didn't lose any time about piling on something that would answer for war paint; and I reckon he got off a few war-whoops, too, as soon as he could to exercise his throat and get the taste of it in his mouth again. They're probably satisfied, now, and there won't be any more trouble."

So poor Peggy guessed right; that Injun was "in mourning;" he had "lost a friend;" but it turns out that he knowed better how to comfort himself than she could do it for him.

We had breakfast just at dawn in the morning, and then rushed our arrangement through. We took provisions and such like things as we couldn't get along without, and packed them on one of the mules, and cached the rest of Brace's truck—that is, buried it—and then Brace struck the Injun trail and we all rode away, westward. Me and Tom couldn't have kept it; we would have lost it every little while, but it warn't any trouble to Brace, he dashed right along like it was painted on the ground before him or paved.

He was so sure Peggy had killed herself, that I reckoned he would be looking out for her body, but he never seemed to. It was so strange that by and by I got into a regular sweat to find out why; and so at last I hinted something about it. But he said no, the Injuns would travel the first twenty-four hours without stopping, and then they would think they was far enough ahead of the Millses'; seven friends to be safe for a while—so then they would go into camp; and there's where we'd find the body. I asked him how far they would go in that time, and he says:

"The whole outfit was fresh and well fed up, and they had the extra horses and mules besides. They'd go as much as eighty miles—maybe a hundred."

He seemed to be thinking about Peggy all the time, and never about anything else or anybody else. So I chanced a question, and says:

"What'll the Injuns do with Flaxy?"

"Poor little chap, she's all right, they won't hurt her. No hurry about her—we'll get her from them by and by. They're fond of children, and so they'll keep her or sell her; but whatever band gets her, she'll be the pet of that whole band, and they'll dress her fine and take good care of her. She'll be the only white child the most of the band ever saw, and the biggest curiosity they ever struck in their lives. But they'll see 'em oftener, by and by, if the whites ever get started to emigrating to Oregon, and I reckon they will."

It didn't ever seem to strike him that Peggy wouldn't kill herself whilst Flaxy was a prisoner, but it did me. I had my doubts; sometimes I believed she would, sometimes I reckoned she wouldn't.

We nooned an hour, and then went on, and about the middle of the afternoon Brace seen some Injuns away off, but we couldn't see them. We could see some little specks, that was all; but he said he could see them well enough, and it was Injuns; but they warn't going our way, and didn't make us any bother, and pretty soon they was out of sight. We made about forty or fifty miles that day, and went into camp.

Well, late the next day, the trail pointed for a creek and some bushes on its bank about a quarter of a mile away or more, and Brace stopped his horse and told us to ride on and see if it was the camp; and said if it was, to look around and find the body; and told us to bury it, and be tender with it, and do it as good as we could, and then come to him a mile further down the creek, where he would make camp—just come there, and only tell him his order was obeyed, and stop at that, and not tell him how she looked, nor what the camp was like, nor anything; and then he rode off on a walk, with his head down on his bosom, and took the pack mule with him.

It was the Injun camp, and the body warn't there, nor any sign of it, just as I expected. Tom was for running and telling him, and cheering him up. But I knowed better. I says:

""No, the thing has turned out just right. We'll stay here about long enough to dig a grave with bowie knives, and then we'll go and tell him we buried her."

Tom says:

"That's mysterious and crooked, and good, and I like that much about it; but hang it there ain't any sense in it, nor any advantage to anybody in it, and I ain't willing to do it."

So I looked like I'd got to tell him why I reckoned it would be better, all around, for Brace to think we found her and buried her, and at last I come out with it, and then Tom was satisfied; and when we had staid there three or four hours, and all through the long twilight till it was plumb dark, we rode down to Brace's camp, and he was setting by his fire with his head down, again, and we only just said, "It's all over—and done right," and laid down like we wanted to rest; and he only says, in that deep voice of his'n, "God be good to you, boys, for your kindness," and kind of stroked us on the head with his hand, and that was all that anybody said.

Chapter 6

After about four days, we begun to catch up on the Injuns. The trail got fresher and fresher. They warn't afraid, now, and warn't traveling fast, but we had kept up a pretty good lick all the time. At last one day we struck a camp of theirs where they had been only a few hours before, for the embers was still hot. Brace said we would go very careful, now, and not get in sight of them but keep them just a safe distance ahead. Tom said maybe we might slip up on them in the night, now, and steal Jim and Flaxy away; but he said no, he had other fish to fry, first, and besides it wouldn't win, anyway.

Me and Tom wondered what his other fish was; and pretty soon we dropped behind and got to talking about it. We couldn't make nothing out of it for certain, but we reckoned he was meaning to get even with the Injuns and kill some of them before he took any risks about other things. I remembered he said we would get Flaxy "by and by," and said there warn't no hurry about it. But then for all he talked so bitter about Injuns, it didn't look as if he could actually kill one, for he was the gentlest, kindest-hearted grown person I ever see.

We killed considerable game, these days; and about this time here comes an antelope scampering towards us. He was a real pretty little creature. He stops, about thirty yards off, and sets up his head, and arches up his neck, and goes to gazing at us out of his bright eyes as innocent as a baby. Brace fetches his gun up to his shoulder, but waited and waited, and so the antelope capered off, zig-zagging first to one side and then t'other, awful graceful, and then stretches straight away across the prairie swift as the wind, and Brace took his gun down. In a little while here comes the antelope back again, and stopped a hundred yards off, and stood still, gazing at us same as before, and wondering who we was and if we was friendly, I reckon. Brace fetches up his gun twice, and then the third time; and this time he fired, and the little fellow tumbled. Me and Tom was starting for him, seeing Brace didn't. But Brace says:

"Better wait a minute, boys, you don't know the antelope. Let him die, first. Because if that little trusting, harmless thing looks up in your face with its grieved eyes when it's dying, you'll never forget it. When I'm out of meat, I kill them, but I don't go around them till they're dead, since the first one."

Tom give me a look, and I give Tom a look, as much as to say, "his fish ain't revenge, that's certain, and so what the mischief is it?"

According to my notions, Brace Johnson was a beautiful man. He was more than six foot tall, I reckon, and had broad shoulders, and he was as straight as a jack staff, and built as trim as a race-horse. He had the steadiest eye you ever see, and a handsome face, and his hair hung all down his back, and how he ever could keep his outfit so clean and nice, I never could tell, but he did. His buckskin suit looked always like it was new, and it was all hung with fringes, and had a star as big as a plate between the shoulders of his coat, made of beads of all kinds of colors, and had beads on his moccasins, and a hat as broad as a barrel-head, and he never looked so fine and grand as he did a-horseback; and a horse couldn't any more throw him than he could throw the saddle, for when it come to riding, he could lay over anything outside the circus. And as for strength, I never see a man that was any more than half as strong as what he was, and a most lightning marksman with a gun or a bow or a pistol. He had two long-barreled ones in his holsters, and could shoot a pipe out of your mouth, most any distance, every time, if you wanted him to. It didn't seem as if he ever got tired, though he stood most of the watch every night himself, and let me and Tom sleep. We was always glad, for his sake, when a very dark night come, because then we all slept all night and didn't stand any watch; for Brace said Injuns ain't likely to try to steal your horses on such nights, because if you woke up and managed to kill them and they died in the dark, it was their notion and belief that it would always be dark to them in the Happy Hunting Grounds all through eternity, and so you don't often hear of Indians attacking in the night, they do it just at dawn; and when they do ever chance it in the night it's only moonlight ones, not dark ones.

He didn't talk very much; and when he talked about Injuns, he talked the same as if he was talking about animals; he didn't seem to have much idea that they was men. But he had some of their ways, himself, on account of being so long amongst them; and moreover he had their religion. And one of the things that puzzled him was how such animals ever struck such a sensible religion. He said the Injuns hadn't only but two Gods, a good one and a bad one, and they never paid no attention to the good one, nor ever prayed to him or worried about him at all, but only tried their level best to flatter up the bad god and keep on the good side of him; because the good one loved them and wouldn't ever think of doing them any harm, and so there warn't any occasion to be bothering him with prayers and things, because he was always doing the very best he could for them, anyway, and prayers couldn't better it; but all the trouble come from the bad god, who was sitting up nights to think up ways to bring them bad luck and bust up all their plans, and never fooled away a chance to do them all the harm he could; and so the sensible thing was to keep praying and fussing around him all the time, and get him to let up. Brace thought more of the Great Spirit than he did of his own mother, but he never fretted about him. He said his mother wouldn't hurt him, would she?—well then, the Great Spirit wouldn't, that was sure.

Now as to that antelope, it brought us some pretty bad luck. When we was done supper, that day, and was setting round talking and smoking, Brace begun to make some calculations about where we might be by next Saturday, as if he thought this day was a Saturday, too—while it wasn't. So Tom he interrupted him and told him it was Friday. They argued over it, but Tom turned out to be right. Brace set there awhile thinking, and looking kind of troubled; then he says:

"It's my mistake, boys, and all my fault, for my carelessness. We're in for some bad luck, and we can't get around it; so the best way is to keep a sharp look-out for it and beat it if we can—I mean make it come as light as we can, for of course we can't beat it altogether."

Tom asked him why he reckoned we would have bad luck, and it come out that the Bad God was going to fix it for us. He didn't say Bad God, out and out; didn't mention his name, seemed to be afraid to; said "he" and "him," but we understood. He said a body had got to perpetuate him in all kinds of ways. Tom allowed he said propitiate, but I heard him as well as Tom, and he said perpetuate. He said the commonest way and the best way to perpetuate him was to deny yourself something and make yourself uncomfortable, same as you do in any religion. So one of his plans was to try to perpetuate him by vowing to never allow himself to eat meat on Fridays and Sundays, even if he was starving; and now he had gone and eat it on a Friday, and he'd druther have cut his hand off than done it if he had knowed. He said "he" has got the advantage of us, now, and you could bet he would make the most of it. We would have a run of bad luck, now, and no knowing when it would begin or when it would stop.

We had been pretty cheerful, before that, galloping over them beautiful plains, and popping at Jack rabbits and prairie dogs and all sorts of things, and snuffing the fresh air of the early mornings, and all that, and having a general good time; but it was all busted up, now, and we quit talking and got terrible blue and uneasy and scared; and Brace he was the bluest of all, and kept getting up, all night, and looking around, when it wasn't his watch; and he put out the camp fire too and several times he went out and took a wide turn around the camp to see if everything was right. And every now and then he would say:

"Well, it hain't come yet, but it's coming."

It come the next morning. We started out from camp, just at early dawn, in a light mist, Brace and the pack mule ahead, I next, and Tom last. Pretty soon the mist begun to thicken, and Brace told us to keep the procession closed well up. In about a half an hour it was a regular fog. After a while Brace sings out:

"Are you all right?"

"All right," I says.

By and by he sings out again:

"All right, boys?"

"All right," I says, and looked over my shoulder and see Tom's mule's ears through the fog.

By and by Brace sings out again, and I sings out, and he says:

"Answer up, Tom," but Tom didn't answer up. So he said it again, and Tom didn't answer up again; and come to look, there warn't anything there but the mule—Tom was gone.

"It's come," says Brace, "I knowed it would," and we faced around and started back, shouting for Tom. But he didn't answer.

Chapter 7

When we had got back a little ways we struck wood and water, and Brace got down and begun to unsaddle. Says I:

"What you going to do?"

"Going to camp,"

"Camp," says I, "why what a notion. I ain't going to camp, I'm going for Tom."

"Going for Tom! Why, you fool, Tom's lost," he says, lifting off his saddle.

"Of course he is," I says, "and you may camp as much as you want to, but I ain't going to desert him, I'm going for him."

"Huck, you don't know what you're talking about. Get off of that mule."

But I didn't. I fetched the mule a whack, and started; but he grabbed him and snaked me off like I was a doll, and set me on the ground. Then he says:

"Keep your shirt on, and maybe we'll find him, but not in the fog. Don't you reckon I know what's best to do?" He fetched a yell, and listened, but didn't get any answer. "We couldn't find him in the fog; we'd get lost ourselves. The thing for us to do is to stick right here till the fog blows off. Then we'll begin the hunt, with some chance."

I reckoned he was right, but I most wanted to kill him for eating that antelope meat and never stopping to think up what day it was and he knowing so perfectly well what confounded luck it would fetch us. A body can't be too careful about such things.

We unpacked, and picketed the mules, and then set down and begun to talk, and every now and then fetched a yell, but never got any answer. I says:

"When the fog blows off, how long will it take us to find him, Brace?"

"If he was an old hand on the Plains, we'd find him pretty easy; because as soon as he found he was lost he would set down and not budge till we come. But he's green, and he won't do that. The minute a greeny finds he's lost, he can't keep still to save his life—tries to find himself, and gets lost worse than ever. Loses his head; wears himself out, fretting and worrying and tramping in all kinds of directions; and what with starving, and going without water, and being so scared, and getting to mooning and imagining more and more, it don't take him but two or three days to go crazy, and then . . ."

"My land, is Tom going to be lost as long as that?" I says, "it makes the cold shudders run over me to think of it."

"Keep up your pluck," he says, "it ain't going to do any good to lose that. I judge Tom ain't hurt; I reckon he got down to cinch up, or something, and his mule got away from him, and he trotted after it, thinking he could keep the direction where the fog swallowed it up, easy enough; and in about a half a minute he was turned around and trotting the other way and didn't doubt he was right, and so didn't holler till it was too late—it's the way they always do, confound it. And so, if he ain't hurt . . ."

He stopped; and as he didn't go on, I says:

"Well? If he ain't hurt, what then?"

He didn't say anything, right away; but at last he says:

"No, I reckon he ain't hurt, and that's just the worst of it; because there ain't no power on earth can keep him still, now. If he'd a broken his leg—but of course he couldn't, with this kind of luck against him."

We whooped, now and then, but I couldn't whoop much, my heart was most broke. The fog hung on, and on, and on, till it seemed a year, and there we set and waited; but it was only a few hours, though it seemed so everlasting. But the sun busted through it at last, and it begun to swing off in big patches, and then Brace saddled up and took a lot of provisions with him, and told me to stick close to camp and not budge, and then he cleared out and begun to ride around camp in a circle, and then in bigger circles, watching the ground for signs all the time; and so he circled wider and wider, till he was far away, and then I couldn't see him any more. Then I freshened up the fire, which he told me to do, and throwed armfuls of green grass on it to make a big smoke; it went up tall and straight to the sky, and if Tom was ten mile off he would see it and come.

I set down, blue enough, to wait. The time dragged heavy. In about an hour I see a speck away off across country, and begun to watch it; and when it got bigger, it was a horseman, and pretty soon I see it was Brace, and he had something across the horse, and I reckoned it was Tom, and he was hurt. But it wasn't; it was a man. Brace laid him down, and says:

"Found him out yonder. He's been lost, nobody knows how long–two or three weeks, I judge. He's pretty far gone. Give him a spoonful of soup every little while, but not much, or it will kill him. He's as crazy as a loon, and tried to get away from me, but he's all used up, and he couldn't. I found Tom's trail in a sandy place, but I lost it again in the grass."

So away he started again, across country, and left me and this fellow there, and I went to making soup. He laid there with his eyes shut, breathing kind of heavy, and muttering and mumbling. He was just skin and bones and rags, that's all he was. His hands was all scratched up and bloody, and his feet the same and all swelled up and wore out, and a sight to look at. His face–well, I never see anything so horrible. It was baked with the sun, and curled, like old wall paper that's rotted on a damp wall. His lips was cracked and dry, and didn't cover his teeth, so he grinned very disagreeable, like a steel trap. I judged he had walked till his feet give out on him, and then crawled around them deserts on his hands and knees; for his knees hadn't any flesh or skin on them.

When I got the soup done, I touched him, and he started up scared, and stared at me a second, and then tried to scramble away; but I catched him and held him pretty easy, and he struggling and begging very pitiful for me to let him go and not kill him. I told him I warn't going to hurt him, and had made some nice soup for him; but he wouldn't touch it at first, and shoved the spoon away and said it made him sick to see it. But I persuaded him, and told him I would let him go if he would eat a little, first. So then he made me promise three or four times, and then he took a couple of spoonfuls; and straight off he got just wild and ravenous, and wanted it all. I fed him a cup full, and then carried the rest off and hid it; and so there I had to set, by the hour, and him begging for more; and about every half an hour I give him a little, and his eyes would blaze at the sight of it, and he would grab the cup out of my hands an take it all down at a gulp, and then try to crowd his mouth into it to lick the bottom, and get just raging and frantic because he couldn't.

Between times he would quiet down and doze; and then start up wild, and say "Lost, my God, lost!" and then see me, and recollect, and go to begging for something to eat again. I tried to get something out of him about himself, but his head was all wrong, and you couldn't make head nor tail of what he said. Sometimes he seemed to say he had been lost ten years, and sometimes it was ten weeks, and once I judged he said a year; and that is all I could get out of him, and no particulars. H had a little gold locket on a gold chain around his neck, and he would take that out and open it and gaze and gaze at it and forget what he was doing, and doze off again. It had a most starchy young woman in it, dressed up regardless, and two little children in her arms, painted on ivory, like some the widow Douglas had on her old anzesters in Scotland.

This kind of worry and sweat went on the whole day long, and was the longest day I ever see. And then the sun was going down, and no Tom and no Brace. This fellow was sound asleep, for about the first time. I took a look at him, and judged it would last; so I thought I would run out and water the mules and put on their side-lines and get right back again before he stirred. But the pack mule had pulled his lariat loose, and was a little ways off dragging it after him and grazing, and I walked along after him, but every time I got pretty close he throwed up his head and trotted a few steps, and first I knowed he had tolled me a long ways and I wished I had the other mule to catch him with, but I dasn't go back after him, because the dark would catch me and I would lose this one, sure; so I had to keep tagging along after him afoot, coming as near to cussing the antelope meat as I dast, and getting powerful nervous all the time and wondering if some more of us was going to get lost. And I would a got lost if I hadn't had a pretty big fire; for you could just barely see it, away back yonder like a red spark when I catched the mule at last, and it was plumb dark too, and getting black before I got home. It was that black when I got to camp that you couldn't see at all, and I judged the mules would get water enough pretty soon without any of my help; so I picketed them closer than they was before, and put on their side-lines, and groped into the tent, and bent over this fellow to hear if he was there, yet, and all of a sudden it busted on me that I had been gone two or three hours, I didn't know how long, and of course he was out and gone, long ago, and how in the nation would I ever find him in the dark, and this awful storm coming up, and just at that minute I hear the wind begin to shiver along amongst the leaves, and the thunder to mumble and grumble away off, and the cold chills went through me to think of him again in the dark and the rain, dad fetch him for making all this trouble, poor pitiful rat, so far from home and lost, and I so sorry for him, too.

So I held my breath, and listened over him, and by Jackson he was there yet, and I hear him breathe—about once a minute. Once a week would a done me, though, it sounded so good to hear him and I was so thankful he hadn't sloped. I fastened the flap of the tent and then stretched out snug on my blankets, wishing Tom and Brace was there; and thinks I, I'll let myself enjoy this about five minutes before I sail out and freshen up the camp fire.

The next thing that I knowed anything about, was no telling how many hours afterwards. I sort of worked along up out of a solid sleep, then, and when I come to myself the whole earth was rocking with the smashingest blast of thunder I ever heard in my life and the rain was pouring down like the bottom had fell out of the sky. Says I, now I've done it! The camp fire's out, and no way for Tom or Brace to find the camp. I let out, and it was so; everything drenched, not a sign of an ember left. Of course nobody could ever start a new fire out there in the rain and wind; but I could build one inside and fetch it out after it got to going good. So I rushed in and went to bulging around in the dark, and lost myself and fell over this fellow, and scrambled up off of him, and begged his pardon and asked if I hurt him; but he never said a word and didn't make a sound. And just then comes one of them blind-white glares of lightning that turns midnight to daytime, and there he laid, grinning up at me, stone dead. And he had hunks of bread and meat around, and I see in a second how it all was. He had got at our grub whilst I was after the mule, and over-eat himself and died, and I had been sleeping along perfectly comfortable with his relics I don't know how long, and him the gashliest sight I ever struck. But I never waited there to think all that; I was out in the public wilderness before the flash got done quivering, and I never went back no more. I let him have it all to his own self; I didn't want no company.

I went off a good ways, and staid the rest of the night out, and got most drownded; and about an hour or more after sun-up Tom and Brace come, and I was glad. I told them how things had went, and we took the gold locket and buried the man and had breakfast, and Brace didn't scold me once. Tom was about used up, and we had to stay there a day or two for him to get straightened up again. I asked him all about it, and he says:

"I got down to cinch up, and I nearly trod on a rattlesnake which I didn't see, but heard him go bzzz! Right at my heel. I jumped most a rod, I was so scared and taken so sudden, and I run about three steps, and then looked back over my shoulder and my mule was gone—nothing but just white fog there. I forgot the snake in a second, and went for the mule. For ten steps I didn't hurry, expecting to see him all the time; but I picked up my heels, then, and run. When I had run a piece I got a little nervous, and was just going to yell, though I was ashamed to, when I thought I heard voices ahead of me, bearing to the right, and that give me confidence, knowing it must be you boys; so I went heeling it after you on a short-cut; but if I did hear voices I misjudged the direction and went the other way, because you know you can't really tell where a sound comes from in a fog. I reckon you was trotting in one direction and me in the other, because it warn't long before I got uneasy and begun to holler, and you didn't hear me nor answer. Well, that scared me so that I begun to tremble all over, and I did wish the fog would lift, but it didn't, it shut me in, all around, like a thick white smoke. I wanted to wait, and let you miss me and come back, but I couldn't stay still a second; it would a killed me, I had to run, and I did. And so I kept on running, by the hour, and listening, and shouting; but never a sound did ever I hear; and whenever I stopped just a moment and held my breath to listen, it was the awfulest stillness that ever was, and I couldn't stand it and had to run on again.

"When I got so beat out and tired I couldn't run any more, I walked; and when the fog went off at last and I looked over my shoulder and there was a tall smoke going up in the sky miles across the plain behind me, I says to myself if that was ahead of me it might be Huck and Brace camping and waiting for me; but it's in the wrong direction, and maybe it's Injuns and not whites; so I wouldn't take any chances on it, but kept right on, and by and by I thought I could see something away off on the prairie, and it was Brace, but I didn't know it, and so I hid. I saw him, or something, twice more before night, and I hid both times; and I walked, between times, further and further away from that smoke and stuck to ground that wouldn't leave much of a track, and in the night I walked and crawled, together, because I couldn't bear to keep still, and was so hungry, and so scratched up with cactuses, and getting kind of out of my head besides; but the storm drove me up onto a swell to get out of the water, and there I staid, and took it. Brace he searched for me till dark, and then struck for home, calculating to strike for the campfire and lead his horse and pick his way; but the storm was too heavy for that, and he had to stop and give up that notion; and besides you let the fire go out, anyway. I went crawling off as soon as dawn come, and making a good trail, the ground was so wet; and Brace found it and then he found me; and the next time I get down to cinch up a mule in the fog I'll notify the rest of you; and the next time I'm lost and see a smoke I'll go for it, I don't care if it comes out of the pit."

Chapter 8

We was away along up the North Fork of the Platte, now. When we started again, the Injuns was two or three days ahead of us, and their trail was pretty much washed out, but Brace didn't mind it, he judged he knowed where they was striking for. He had been reading the signs in their old camps, all these days, and he said these Sioux was Ogillallahs. We struck a hilly country, now, and traveled the day through and camped a few miles up a nice valley late in the afternoon on top of a low flattish hill in a grove of small trees. It was an uncommon pretty place, and we picked it out on account of Tom, because he hadn't stood the trip well, and we calculated to rest him there another day or two. The valley was a nearly level swale a mile or a mile and a half wide, and had a little river-bed in it with steep banks, and trees along it—not much of a river, because you could throw a brick across it, but very deep when it was full of water, which it wasn't now. But Brace said we would find puddles along in its bed, so him and me took the animals and a bucket, and left Tom in camp and struck down our hill and rode across the valley to water them. When we got to the river we found new-made tracks along the bank, and Brace said there was about twenty horses in that party, and there was white men in it because some of the horses had shoes on, and likely they was from out Fort Laramie way.

There was a puddle or two, but Brace couldn't get down the banks easy; so he told me to wait with the mules, and if he didn't find a better place he would come back and rig some way to get up and down the bank here. Then he rode off down stream and pretty soon the trees hid him. By and by an antelope darts by me and I looked up the river and around a corner of the timber comes two men, riding fast. When they got to me they reined up and begun to ask me questions. They was half drunk, and a mighty rough looking couple, and their clothes didn't help them much, being old greasy buckskin, just about all black with dirt. I was afraid of them. They asked me who I was, and where I come from, and how many was with me, and where we was camped; and I told them my name was Archibald Thompson, and says:

"Our camp's down at the foot of the valley, and we're traveling for pap's health, he's very sick, we can't travel no more till he gets better, and there ain't nobody to take care of him but me and aunt Mary and Sis, and so we're in a heap of troub . . ."

"It's all a lie!" one of them breaks in. "You've stole them animals."

"You bet he has," says the other. "Why, I know this one myself; he belongs to old Vaskiss the trader, up at the Fort, and I'm dead certain I've seen one of the others somewheres."

"Seen him? I reckon you have. Belongs to Roubidou the blacksmith, and he'll be powerful glad we've found him again. I knowed him in a minute. Come, boy, I'm right down sorry for your sick pap, and poor aunt Mary and Sis, but all the same you'll go along back to our camp, and you want to be mighty civil and go mighty careful, or first you know you'll get hung."

First I didn't know what to do; but I had to work my mind quick, and I struck a sort of an idea, the best I could think of, right off, that way. I says to myself, it's two to one these is horse thieves, because Brace says there's a plenty of them in these regions; and so I reckon they'd like to get one or two more while they're at it. Then I up and says:

"Gents, as sure as I'm here I never stole the animals; and if I'll prove it to you you'll let me go, won't you?"

"How're you going to prove it?"

"I'll do it easy if you'll come along with me, for we bought two mules that's almost just like these from the Injuns day before yesterday, and maybe they stole 'em, I don't know, but we didn't, that's sure."

They looked at each other, and says:

"Where are they—down at your camp?"

"No; they're only down here three or four hundred yards, Sister Mary she . . ."

"Has she got them?"

"Yes."

"Anybody with her?"

"No."

"Trot along, then, and don't you try to come any tricks, boy, or you'll get hurt."

I didn't wait for a second invite, but started right along, keeping a sharp lookout for Brace, and getting my yell ready, soon as I should see him. I edged ahead, and edged ahead, all I could, and they notified me a couple of times not to shove along so fast, because there warn't no hurry; and pretty soon they noticed Brace's trail, and sung out to me to halt a minute, and bent down over their saddles, and checked up their speed, and was mightily interested, as I could see when I looked back. I didn't halt, but jogged ahead, and kept widening the distance. They sung out again, and threatened me, and then I brushed by Brace's horse, in the trees, and knowed Brace was down the bank or close by, so I raised a yell and put up my speed to just the highest notch the mules could reach. I looked back, and here they come—and next comes a bullet whizzing by!! I whacked away for life and death, and looked back and they was gaining; looked back again, and see Brace booming after the hind one like a house afire, and swinging long coils of his lariat over his head; then he sent it sailing through the air, and as it scooped that fellow in, Brace reined back his horse and yanked him out of this saddle, and then come tearing ahead again, dragging him. He yelled to me to get out of range, and so I turned out sudden and looked back, and my man had wheeled and was raising his gun on Brace, but Brace's pistol was too quick for him, and down he went, out of his saddle.

Well, we had two dead men on our hands, and I felt pretty crawly, and didn't like to look at them; but Brace allowed it warn't a very unpleasant sight, considering they tried to kill me. He said we must hurry into camp, now, and get ready for trouble; so we shoved for camp, and took the two new horses and the men's guns and things with us, not waiting to water our animals.

It was nearly dark. We kept a watch-out towards up the river, but didn't see anything stirring. When we got home we still watched from the edge of the grove, but didn't see anything, and no sign of that gang's camp fire; then Brace said we was probably safe from them for the rest of the night, so we would rest the animals three or four hours, and then start out and get as well ahead as we could, and keep ahead as long as this blamed Friday-antelope luck would let us, if Tom could stand the travel.

It come on starlight, a real beautiful starlight, and all the world as still and lovely as Sunday. By and by Brace said it would be a good idea to find out where the thieves was camped, so we could give it a wide berth when we started; and he said I could come along if I wanted to; and he took his gun along, this time, and I took one of the thieves' guns. We took the two fresh horses and rode down across the valley and struck the river, and then went pretty cautious up it. We went as much as two mile, and not a sign of a camp fire anywheres. So we kept on, wondering where it could be, because we could see a long ways up the valley. And then all of a sudden we heard people laugh, and not very far off, maybe forty or fifty yards. It come from the river. We went back a hundred yards, and tied the horses amongst the trees, and then back again afoot till we was close to the place where we heard it before, and slipped in amongst the trees and listened, and heard the voices again, pretty close by. Then we crept along on our knees, slow and careful, to the edge of the bank, through the bush, and there was the camp, a little ways up, and right in the dry bed of the river; two big buffalo-skin lodges, a band of horses tied, and eight men carousing and gambling around a fire—all white men, and the roughest kind, and prime drunk. Brace said they had camped there so their camp couldn't be seen easy, but they might as well camped in the open as go and get drunk and make such a noise. He said they was horse thieves, certain.

We was interested, and stayed looking a considerable time. But the liquor begun to beat them, and first one and then another went gaping and stretching to the tents and turned in. And then another one started, and the others tried to make him stay up, because it was his watch, but he said he was drunk and sleepy and didn't want to watch, and said "Let Jack and Bill stand my watch, as long as they like to be up late—they'll be in directly, like as not."

But the others threatened to lick him if he didn't stand his watch; so he grumbled, but give in, and got his gun and set down, and when the others was all gone to roost, he just stretched himself out and went to snoring as comfortable as anybody.

We left, then, and sneaked down to where our horses was, and rode away, leaving the rapscallions to sleep it out and wait for Jack and Bill to come, but we reckoned they'd have to wait a most notorious long time first.

We rode down the river to where Brace was when I yelled to him when the thieves was after me; and he said he had dug some steps in the bank there with his bowie, and we could finish the job in a little while, and when we broke camp and started we would bring our mules there and water them. So we tied our horses and went down into the river bed to the puddle that was there, and laid down on our breasts to take a drink; but Brace says:

"Hello, what's that?"

It was as still as death before, but you could hear a faint, steady, rising sound, now, up the river. We held our breath and listened. You could see a good stretch up it, and tolerable clear, too, the starlight was so strong. The sound kept growing and growing, very fast. Then all of a sudden Brace says:

"Jump for the bank! I know what that is."

It's always my plan to jump first, and ask afterwards. So I done it. Brace says:

"There's a water-spout broke loose up country somewheres, and you'll see sights mighty soon, now."

"Do they break when there ain't no clouds in the sky?" I says, judging I had him.

"Ne'er you mind," he says, "there was clouds where this one broke. I've seen this kind of thing before, and I know that sound. Fasten your horse just as tight as you can, or he'll break loose presently."

The sound got bigger and bigger, and away up yonder it was just one big dull thundering roar. We looked up the river a piece, and see something coming down its bed like dim white snakes writhing along. When it went hissing and sizzling by us it was shallow foamy water. About twenty yards behind it comes a solid wall of water four foot high, and nearly straight up and down, and before you could wink it went rumbling and howling by like a whirlwind, and carrying logs along, and them thieves, too, and their horses and tents, and tossing them up in sight, and then under again, and grinding them to hash, and the noise was just awful, you couldn't a heard it thunder; and our horses was plunging and pitching, and trying their best to break loose. Well, before we could turn around the water was over the banks and ankle deep. "Out of this, Huck, and shin for camp, or we're goners!"

We was mounted and off in a second, with the water chasing after us. We rode for life, we went like the wind, but we didn't have to use whip or spur, the horses didn't need no encouragement. Half-way across the valley we meet the water flooding down from above; and from there on, the horses was up to their knees, sometimes, yes, and even up to their bellies towards the last. All hands was glad when we struck our hill and sailed up it out of danger.

Chapter 9

Our little low hill was an island, now, and we couldn't a got away from it if we had wanted to. We all three set around and watched the water rise. It rose wonderful fast; just walked up the long, gradual slope, as you may say, it come up so fast. It didn't stop rising for two or three hours; and then that whole valley was just a big level river a mile to a mile and a half wide, and deep enough to swim the biggest ship that was ever built, and no end of dim black drift logs spinning around and sailing by in the currents on its surface.

Brace said it hadn't took the water-spout an hour to dump all that ocean of water and finish up its job, but like enough it would be a week before the valley was free of it again; so Tom would have considerable more time than we bargained to give him to get well in.

Me and Tom was down-hearted and miserable on account of Jim and Peggy and Flaxy, because we reckoned it was all up with them and the Injuns, now; and so at last Tom throwed out a feeler to see what Brace thought. Tom never said anything about the others, but only about the Injuns; said the water-spout must a got the Injuns, hadn't it? But Brace says:

"No, nary an Injun. Water-spouts don't catch any but white folks. There warn't ever a white man that could tell when a water-spout's coming; and how the nation an Injun can tell is something I never could make out, but they can. When it's perfectly clear weather, and other people ain't expecting anything, they'll say, all of a sudden, 'heap water coming,' and pack up in a hurry and shove for high ground. They say they smell it. I don't know whether that's so or not; but one thing I do know, a water-spout often catches a white man, but it don't ever catch an Injun."

Next morning there we was, on an island, same as before; just a level, shining ocean everywheres, and perfectly still and quiet, like it was asleep. And awful lonesome.

Next day the same, only lonesomer than ever.

And next day just the same, and mighty hard work to put in the time. Mostly we slept. And after a long sleep, wake up, and eat dinner, and look out over the tiresome water, and go to sleep again; and wake up again, by and by, and see the sun go down and turn it into blood, and fire, and melted butter, and one thing or another, awful beautiful, and soft, and lovely, but solemn and lonesome till you couldn't rest.

We had eight days of that, and the longer we waited for that ocean to play out and run off, the bigger the notion I got of a water-spout that could puke out such a mortal lot of water as that in an hour.

We left, then, and made a good day's travel, and by sundown begun to come onto fresh buffalo carcases. There was so many of them that Brace reckoned there was a big party of Injuns near, or else white from the fort.

In the morning we hadn't gone five miles till we struck a big camp where Injuns had been, and hadn't gone more than a day or two. Brace said there was as many as a hundred of them, altogether; men, women and children, and made up from more than one band of Sioux, but Brulés mostly, as he judged by the signs. Brace said things looked like these Injuns was camped here a considerable time.

Of course we warn't thinking about our Injuns, or expecting to run across any signs of them or the prisoners, but Tom he found an arrow, broke in two, which was wound with blue silk thread down by the feather, and he said he knowed it was Hog Face's, because he got the silk for him from Peggy and watched him wind it. So Brace begun to look around for other signs, and he believed he found some. Well, I was ciphering around in a general way myself, and outside of the camp I run across a ragged piece of Peggy's dress as big as a big handkerchief, and it had blood on it. It most froze me to see that, because I judged she was killed; and if she warn't, it stood to reason she was hurt. I hid the rag under a buffalo chip, because if Brace was to see it he might suspicion she wasn't dead after all the pains we had took to make him believe she was; and just then he sings out "Run here, boys," and Tom he come running from one way and I the other, and when we got to him, there in the middle of the camp, he points down and says:

"There—that's the shoe-print of a white woman. See—you can see, where she turned it down to one side, how thin the sole is. She's white, and she's a prisoner with this gang of Injuns. I don't understand it. I'm afraid there's general trouble broke out between the whites and Injuns; and if that's so, I've got to go mighty cautious from this out." He looks at the track again, and says, "Poor thing, it's hard luck for her," and went mumbling off, and never noticed that me and Tom was most dead with uneasiness, for we could see plain enough it was Peggy's print, and was afraid he would see it himself, or think he did, any minute. His back wasn't more than turned before me and Tom had tramped on the print once or twice—just enough to take the clearness out of it, because we didn't know but he might come back for another look.

Pretty soon we see him over yonder looking at something, and we went there, and it was four stakes drove in the ground; and he looks us very straight and steady in the eyes, first me and then Tom, and then me again, till it got pretty sultry; then he says, cold and level, but just as if he'd been asking us a question:

"Well, I believe you. Come along."

Me and Tom followed along, a piece behind; and Tom says:

"Huck, he's so afraid she's alive, that it's just all he can do to believe that yarn of ours about burying her. And pretty soon, now, like enough, he'll find out she ain't dead, after all."

"That's just what's worrying me, Tom. It puts us in a scrape, and I don't see no way out of it; because what can we say when he tackles us about lying to him?"

"I know what to say, well enough."

"You do? Well I wish you'd tell me, for I'm blamed if I see any way out—I wouldn't know a single word to say."

"I'll say this, to him. I'll say, suppose it was likely you was going to get knocked in the head with a club some time or other, but it warn't quite certain; would you want to be knocked in the head straight off, so as to make it certain, or wouldn't you ruther wait and see if you mightn't live your life out and not happen to get clubbed at all? Of course, he would say. Then I would put it at him straight, and say, wasn't you happier, when we made you think she was dead, than you was before? Didn't it keep you happy all this time? Of course. Well wasn't it worth a little small lie like that to keep you happy instead of awfully miserable many days and nights? Of course. And wasn't it like she would be dead before you ever run across her again?—which would make our lie plenty good enough. True again. And at least I would up and say, just you put yourself in our place, Brace Johnson: now, honor bright, would you have told the truth, that time, and broke the heart of the man that was Peggy Mills's idol? If you could you are not a man, you are a devil; if you could and did, you'd be lower and hard-hearteder than the devils, you'd be an Injun. That's what I'll say to him, Huck, if the time ever comes."

Now that was the cleanest and slickest way out that ever was; and who would ever a thought of it but Tom Sawyer? I never seen the likes of that boy for just solid gobs of brains and levelheadedness. It made me comfortable, right away, because I knowed very well Brace Johnson couldn't ever get around that, nor under it nor over it nor through it; he would have to answer up and confess he would a told that lie his own self, and would have went on backing it up and standing by it, too, as long as he had a rag of a lie left in him to do it with.

I noticed, but I never said anything, that Tom was putting the Injuns below the devils, now. You see, he had about got it through his noodle, by this time, that book Injuns and real Injuns is different.

Brace was unslinging the pack; so we went to him to see what he was doing it for, and he says:

"Well, I don't understand that white woman's being with this band of Injuns. Of course maybe she was took prisoner years ago, away yonder on the edge of the States, and has been sold from band to band ever since, all the way across the Plains. I say of course that may be the explanation of it, but as long as I don't know that that's the way of it, I ain't going to take any chances. I'll just do the other thing: I'll consider that this woman is a new prisoner, and that her being here means that there's trouble broke out betwixt the Injuns and the whites, and so I'll act according. That is, I'll keep shy of Injuns till I've fixed myself up a little, so's to fit the new circumstances."

He had got a needle and some thread out of the pack, and a little paper bag full of dried bugs, and butterflies, and lizards, and frogs, and such like creatures, and he sat down and went to sewing them fast to the lapels of his buckskin coat, and all over his slouch hat, till he was that fantastic he looked like he had just broke out of a museum when he got it all done. Then he says:

"Now if I act strange and foolish, the Injuns will think I'm crazy; so I'll be safe and all right. They are afraid to hurt a crazy man, because they think he's under His special persecution" (he meant the Bad God, you know) "for his sins; and they kind of avoid him, and don't much like to be around him, because they think he's bad medicine, as they call it—'medicine' meaning luck, about as near as you can put it into English.

I got this idea from a chap they called a naturalist.

"A war party of Injuns dropped onto him, and if he'd a knowed his danger, he'd a been scared to death; but he didn't know a war party from a peace party, and so he didn't act afraid; and that bothered the Injuns, they didn't know what to make of it; and when they see how anxious, and particular he was about his bugs, and how fond of them and stuck after them he seemed to be, they judged he was out of his mind, and so they let him go his own gait, and never touched him. I've gone fixed for the crazy line ever since."

Then he packed the mule again, and says:

"Now we'll get along again, and follow the trail of the Injuns."

But it bore nearly straight north, and that warn't what he was expecting; so he rode off on the desert and struck another trail which bore more to the west, and this one he examined very careful, and mumbled a good deal to himself; but said at last that this was our Injuns, though there was more horses in the party than there was before. He knowed it by signs, he said, but he didn't say what the signs was.

We struck out on this trail, and followed it a couple of days . . .

Each day we went a little slower. We warn't among the grass-waves no more, but in hilly country with rocky ledges along the tops of some of the ridges. It warn't the hills that made us go slow, but the constant stopping, with me and Tom holding the horses and mules while Brace clumb the nearest rise to look up ahead for signs of the Injun camp. One time he comes scrambling down to tell us he seen smoke. He say the Injun camp is just ahead. It be time to save Flaxy and Jim, and that other white woman.

When we finds some trees around a nice little spring of clear water, Brace says we got to hide our outfit and the horses and mules. After taking off the saddles and packs, we picket the animals amongst the trees with ropes tied to their front feet 'stead of their necks so they won't get tangled up. Brace figured the trees would make it hard for an Injun from the camp to see our outfit and stock, even if he clumb the highest hill.

Then we stuff our coat pockets with biscuits and dried meat because Brace don't know how long it will take to do the rescuin,' and we might get hungry. Tom and me carries the two rifles we took from the horse thieves. Brace has his own rifle, and the two pistols in his belt. We each have a bowie too. Seeing the serious look on Brace's face as he checks his powder, I know he means business.

"How's one man and two boys goin'a lick a whole band of Injuns?" I asks. "An' there might be more than the five who kilt Peggy's family, there bein' more horse tracks than before."

"Doan know," Brace says, simply. "Need to find them first, count them, count their animals. Look at the layout. Consider possibilities. Then we figure a way to do it." And off we went.

It warn't much of a plan, it seemed to me, for marching into the camp of a bunch of murdering Injuns. But what did I know? Just a boy who grew up on the river, and never knowed nothin' about Injuns no how? So I said nothin', and neither did Tom, which surprised me a lot. Tom always had a lot to say about everything, even when he didn't know nothin' about it. As I was wondering why he didn't want to talk now, it occurred to me that maybe he was scairt. That's it. I bet Tom was so scairt he lost his pluck. He'ud never admit it, at least not to Brace. So on we marched, up a little valley, and to the top of a hill covered with brush and stone ledges.

Brace, without saying a word, points his arm at us, palm open, a signal for us to lay low and not say nothing. He stands that way for a long time, like a dog pointing at a wild chicken in a bush, not moving, looking real careful up ahead. We darn't move. Finally, Brace motions for us to come up and follow him to a clump of thick bushes. When we gets there he says:

"They been hunting buffaloes. Bringing in the hides and meat. Unloading the horses." Tom and me moved forward a little so we could see the camp too. Five or six men were unloading skins and meat from nearly ten horses. From their size and the way they moved I reckoned two of them was Hog Face and He-who-fears- his-Mother-in-law. They was wearing the same red feathers, but no war paint. Blue Fox warn't with them, I was sure.

Then I sees Jim, no doubt about it, sitting cross-legged on the ground by a thick post. There is a long rope, one end tied to his neck, the other to the post. He's tied up like a dog. But he don't seem unhappy. He's smiling at the Injuns as they pile up skins in front of him. They is heavy and slick, smeared with red and black blood. Jim has a tool in each hand, for the scraping. He starts to clean the hides, and he doesn't seem too unhappy to do the work.

Two women and a child are moving around the packs of meat. They have black hair and are wearing skin dresses, so I don't reckon they be prisoners. I see no sign of Peggy or Flaxy. While I'm seeing all this Brace and Tom don't say a word. It's getting dark. The sun is already down. We won't be able to watch the camp much longer. Finally Brace says:

"They won't hurt Jim. They needs him to work the hides. They fetched up some family when the joined the other Injuns, where we saw all them dead buffaloes. The women moving the meat is Injun too. Maybe the white woman and Flaxy has been traded off."

Just then we see some people coming out of the brush hut, two girls scrambling to get to their feet, and a man with a stick close behind. He hits the bigger girl. She's wearing a skin covering, like an old elk hide with a hole in the middle for the head to fit through. Not much of a dress. The littler girl in front is wearing a cloth dress, tan in color, like the one Flaxy was wearing when they carried her off. I look closer. The light is no good. Her hair might be brown. I believe Flaxy is the one I am looking at. Then I looks closer at the one behind her. Her hair looks brown too. I thought she was Injun because she was wearing the skin. Now I thinks she is white too. I don't dare guess that it might be Peggy.

Pretty soon it's too dark to see, even with the Injuns building fires to cook up a mess of meat. We crawl back into the thickest part of the bushes to talk about what we seed. Brace is the first to talk.

"I think the first one who crawled from the hut is Flaxy."

"She was wearing a dress like that when they carried her off," I says.

"I think the second one was an Injun," Tom says, not wanting Brace to think the second girl might be Peggy.

"Her hair looked brown, not black," I argues.

"But she was wearing a skin dress," Tom says.

"The Injun hit her with a stick," Brace says. "Like she was his dog. She might be the white woman who made that track we saw. Her dress got tore up, so they gave her a skin, maybe."

I didn't say any more. I didn't care none where all this talk was taking us. It was time for someone to ask if the girl might be Peggy, and I warn't going to get it started. I looked at Tom, and nodded for him to talk. He shook his head and stayed quiet. Both of us reached in our pockets for some food and started chewing on dry meat. Brace didn't want to ask the next question either, so all three of us was quiet for a long time, chewing and looking into the night. I would like a fire, but with the Injun camp so near, we couldn't risk that. It warn't too cold anyways. After watching the Injuns cook meat over two or three fires, we just curled up in the bushes and tried to sleep while Brace figured out a plan. It was quiet until Brace says:

"You boys sure it was Peggy you buried back there?"

I was glad it was so dark that he warn't able to see my face. Tom was the one who could never stay quiet very long, so I guess if I says nothing, pretty soon Tom wouldn't be able to stand the silence, and have to talk.

Besides he'd already told me what he was going to say to explain it all.

Tom surprised me, saying something totally different that I didn't expect he'd say at all.

"'Course we thought it was Peggy, that woman we buried. We was the ones who saw Peggy dragged off by the Injuns, so it was only natural to think she were the dead woman. But the one we buried had her face gashed in by a tomahawk, and it had been that way for a couple of days, and was swollen something awful, and covered with maggots and flies. Didn't look like the face of Peggy or any other woman I ever saw, but I thought it was the tomahawk and the swelling that made her look different." Then Brace asks:

"What about the rest of her? Was she wearing Peggy's dress? Was she about the same shape, size, weight—you knows what I mean. Did the whole person look like Peggy?"

Tom didn't answer right off. In the dark I couldn't see his face, to know if he was stumped, or just thinking up something else to say. Finally he says:

"The Injuns stole her clothes. Even with her dead, it didn't seem decent to look at her. We was embarrassed when we seed her. So we looked away. After we digged the hole, we tied our shirts on our faces so we couldn't look at her while we lifted her in and pushed the dirt on top of her. We didn't look at her enough to know she warn't Peggy."

"Why didn't you tell me this before?" Brace asked, his voice all broken up and sobbing.

Tom didn't even hesitate before he says:

"You told us not to say anyting except we done it. We knowed how much you loved her. The more we says the more you'd hurt. We knowed you'd never forget anything we says, and if we tells what we saw you'd see pictures in your head that would never go away, so we says hardly nothing. We thought you would want to remember her the way you last saw her, not the way we last saw her."

Suddenly Brace was between us, squeezing us near to death with his splendid powerful arms, loving us, telling us we was wonderful boys and the best friends a man ever had. His cheeks was wet with smeared tears. He said he was sorrowful he had brung us to Injun country, and hoped we warn't going to die.

I hoped I warn't going to die either. And Tom too, because someday he would make a mighty fine lawyer. He could tell a lie better than all the folks I had ever met, and ever hoped to meet. I knew if I ever got in trouble with the law, I would want Tom to be my lawyer.

"What will we do?" I asked. Brace, he says:

"I thought of the three of us agoin' to Fort Laramie and fetching the soldiers."

"That's a splendid idea," Tom says. He was talking real fast.

"It would take maybe a week to get there," Brace explained. "Another week to get back. The Injuns would be gone by then, and if a storm rolled in, the tracks would be gone too. If that's Peggy down there I darsn't leave her again, even to fetch a gang of soldiers."

"A gang of soldiers might have a better chance to save her than one man and two boys," Tom argued.

"I can't leave her," Brace says.

"We will die," Tom says, his voice sounding awful scared.

"I might die, but you boys will stay here on the hill. If the Injuns ketches me, then you two skedadle back to the mules and race to Fort Laramie."

"We don't know where she is, Fort Laramie," I says. "Shouldn't we go back the way we come, to the United States?" Then Brace says:

"Laramie is closest. Easy to find. Ride southwest, the morning sun on the back of your left shoulder, the evening sun on your right cheek. When you reach the North Platte you'll see plenty of wagon tracks, signs of stock grazing. Don't cross the river. Just follow it up. Should take near a week. With the soldiers, you be safe. They'll help you get home."

"So you be thinkin' you can fight all them Injuns by yourself," I says.

"I hope not," Brace says. "I'm hoping the bucks will go hunting again, take some of the women and older children with them. Then I can just saunter in and fetch Peggy and Flaxy and Jim, and maybe shoot any Injun who has a different idea. When the men comes back from hunting their horses will be wore out, and we'll have us a twenty mile head start for Laramie."

"What if they don't go hunting?" Tom asks.

"If I knows anything about Injuns, they will hunt all they can, before the buffaloes move on. Once they finds a herd, they usually goes out every day until they can't find no more buffaloes. Only one thing bothers me . . ."

"Tell us," Tom says.

"They has just one bush hut, no skin lodges. This ain't no regular camp. Like they was going someplace, maybe taking Peggy and Flaxy and Tom to the home camp, but they comes on these buffaloes and decides to go hunting. This ways, they might be in a hurry to get home, and not go hunting again. If this happens, my plan won't work."

I noticed that Brace was no longer talking as if the white woman might be Peggy. He had decided the woman was Peggy. I hoped his plan would work.

We was tired, but sleep warn't easy to come by. We didn't know who might be dead or alive by the next time it got dark. Finally I just gives up trying to sleep, and looks up at the stars wondering what it might be like to be dead.

Chapter 10

At first light we crawls out of the bushes and hides behind some rocks on the ridge where we got a clear view of the camp and the grazing horses. When we was following the trail a few days earlier, Brace thought white men was traveling with the Injuns because some of the horses was wearing iron shoes. But that warn't so. There warn't no white men in the camp. The horses with shoes was the ones Peggy's family had brung with them, some mules too.

The squaws in the camp were the first to stir about, starting the fires, cooking meat to eat. One sauntered down by the stream, a big knife in her hand, and begun cutting willows. I asked Brace if she was cutting willows to whip the prisoners. He said no, that they was only going to tie the willow sticks together into racks so they could dry the meat they had brung in the night before.

One of the squaws took a side of ribs over to Jim, who was already awake and scraping the hides they had brung him the day before. He didn't seem very unhappy, though the rope from the post was still tied around his neck. It warn't like he was really a prisoner because he could easy cut the rope with the scraping tool in his hand. I knowed it was plenty sharp by the way he sliced the ribs away from each other. He seemed one happy slave with more ribs than a man could eat at one time.

Then I noticed someone coming out of the bush lodge. It was Blue Fox, and he was pulling someone else along with him. It was the white girl, the one who was wearing the skin, the girl we thought might be Peggy. Behind her the little girl followed, the one we thought was Flaxy. I just knowed it was them sisters, though we was too far a distance to see their faces.

Blue Fox dragged Peggy over to a big hind quarter of buffalo meat and shoved her to the ground. Then I thought my eyes was fooling me, because I could not believe what happened next. Old Blue Fox pulled a big skinning knife out of his belt, and aimed it right at Peggy's heart. At the same time Brace was scrambling for his rifle. We was too far away for a clean shot, but Brace wasn't about to let Peggy die without trying something.

Just as Brace were about to shoot, Blue Fox spins the knife around in his hand and hands it to Peggy. Now she has the knife. Brace lowers his rifle. In a glance I see big drops of sweat on his forehead, but I have to look back at Peggy. I no longer feel bad about her not having the dirk Brace gave her, when he tried to make her promise to stick it in her heart if the Injuns ketched her. I reckon now she could do it with the big knife, if she warn't too afraid. I kept thinking she should stick it in Blue Fox's heart instead, now she had the chance. She did neither one. She turned away from Blue Fox and starts cutting on the buffalo leg. Flaxy crouches down to help.

"She's cutting meat for drying," Brace whispered. He didn't say anything about the dirk and how he wanted Peggy to kill herself if she could. She could do it now, easy as stabbing a frog, and I sure hoped she wouldn't, but I didn't ask Brace if he still wanted her to do it. I figured if she was going to do that, she would have done it already. I didn't ask about it because now we had other fish to fry, like getting her and Flaxy and Jim out of there.

The Injuns didn't go to ketching the horses as we reckoned they would. Brace was wrong. They was not going hunting again. The men sat in a circle around a big slab of buffalo meat, talking and laughing and eating, while mending bows and arrows. The squaws pulled and cut strips of meat to dry on the racks. Jim looked like he was whistling a happy tune while scraping the flesh and fat off the hides, but I cain't hear none of it. Some children played by the creek.

I reckon the scene in front of us was just like in the pages of Tom's books. Splendid, happy savages putting up meat against the winter, innocent and happy as Adam and Eve in the Garden of Eden. But we knowed different. They murdered a whole family of fine, nice people, then stole the girls and mules. Ain't no way around it—Blue Fox, Hog Face, and Man-afraid-of-his-Mother-in-law were wicked men, and I hoped Brace would kill them all, except maybe the squaws and children. Then Tom says:

"What do we do now?"

"You and Huck shut up while I think up a new plan," Brace says.

So we be quiet, for maybe two hours. Seemed like two days. Brace didn't think as fast as Tom. It would be a mistake if Brace decided to be a lawyer. Finally he says:

"You boys go back to the mules. Saddle up. Load the packs. Then come back here. Keep out of sight of the Injuns. Come slow, so you get here about dark. Make sure the mules have plenty to eat and drink." We nodded that we understood. Then Brace says:

"As soon as it's too dark for the Injuns to see me coming down the hill, I'll go straight to their horses, cutting the hobbles and tether ropes, then whooping and hollering like I was other Injuns just wanting to steal horses. Then I'll hide in the bushes while they runs after their ponies.

Soon as they go by I'll run the other way, into camp to fetch the girls and Jim. We'll climb up here where you are waiting with the animals ready to go. We'll ride all night, straight for Laramie, hoping it takes that long for the Injuns to round up their ponies and plan what to do."

We left while Brace was sewing more bugs onto his shirt. Tom and I saddled the mules and went back to the top of the hill. Brace's plan seemed sensible enough. Tom couldn't think of anything better. I wondered why Brace was still sewing on more bugs. That didn't seem part of the plan. But he knew more about Injuns than me so I kept quiet.

The sun was already down now, and Brace wandered off down the hill. Pretty soon we couldn't see him no more. We supposed he were edging his way towards the grazing ponies. He had taken his guns with him. We tied the horses and mules in the brush patch then hurried to the rocky ledge so we could better see the Injun camp.

There were a whole lot of willow racks that the squaws had built during the day. Strips of meat, hanging to dry, were covering all the racks. Jim was still scraping happily away at his hides. Peggy and Flaxy had finished cutting up the big hind leg and were crouched by one of the fires cooking some pieces of meat to eat. Beyond the camp, we could see fifteen or sixteen horses and mules grazing quietly. Two more horses were tied to a tree near the brush hut, so the Injuns would have them to round up the others. When it was almost too dark to see, Blue Fox herded Peggy and Flaxy into the brush hut. He followed them inside.

Pretty soon all we could see was the fires, and bodies moving back and forth in front of them. There was a sliver of a moon over our heads so we can see the close stuff, like our mules and horses.

The fires are still burning while the Injuns cook more meat when we hear Brace whooping and hollering, way off beyond the fires. We can only guess that the horses are stampeding away from the camp because we can't see anything that far away. Pretty soon there are no more Injuns by the fires.

We reckon Brace and Peggy and Jim and Flaxy will come running up the hill any minute. We tighten the cinches on all the saddles. The mules are filled up with grass and water. We is ready to run all the way to Fort Laramie. We wait and wait and wait. We drink some water and chew on dried meat. We ain't sleepy, though it's night, just knowing Brace and the prisoners might be coming right along, and mad Injuns not far behind.

Tom he kept whispering this or that about all the things that might be happening in the Injun camp, or might could happen, but it was just talk, and I warn't listening, not much. Mostly I was just scared for Peggy and Flaxy, and what the Injuns might do to them if they ketched them trying to get away. I figured Brace would be safe with all them bugs sewed on his shirt, and they wouldn't hurt Jim as long as there was hides to clean. But I worried about Peggy and Flaxy, more than about me and Tom. We was just boys who had run away, and didn't count for anything in the world. We didn't go to school and we didn't work. Nobody would miss us if we didn't come back, though the Widow Douglas might wonder why we didn't say goodby when we sneaked away.

They didn't come, not through the whole night. When it begun to get light the squaws started fixing up the fires and cooking again like it was just any regular day. Nothing in the camp looks different. Jim is rustling through his hides, getting ready to go to work. We can't see Peggy and Flaxy, but reckon they're still in the hut. Then I sees the horses is back in the meadows, grazing just as happy as if they was in heaven. Tom and me, we are asking each other what has happened to Brace.

Then we see him, running through the willows along the stream. Three Injuns is chasing him. Three more is in front trying to cut him off. They is getting close on both ends. I reckon that if I was an Injun I wouldn't want to get too close because Brace has his big bowie in his hand. But they tackles him anyways and wrassles away the knife. He smacks a couple of them in the faces but pretty soon two big Injuns is holding his arms, and there is no getting away. They drags him out of the willows and onto a grassy flat next to the camp. Some of the squaws and children runs over to see what their men has ketched.

Brace, he's a squirming and wiggling and jerking to get free, but he ain't doing no good. The Injuns won't let go. When the squaws get there, they starts pointing at his shirt. I guess they sees the bugs he pinned there.

Then the men sees the bugs. Everybody's pointing, talking, laughing like they never seen nothing like that before. Then Tom says:

"Those is the dumbest Injuns I ever see. Downright stupid."

"How so?" I asks, without looking away.

"Don't they know only crazy men has bugs on their shirts? They is supposed to let him go. Any idiot knows that. What's wrong with these Injuns?"

I had no answer for Tom's questions. I believed Brace when he said Injuns wouldn't harm him if he sewed bugs on his shirt. But I also knowed if I was an Injun, and caught an enemy trying to run off my horses, I wouldn't let him go because he had a bug on his shirt, even if he had lots of bugs on his shirt, and it didn't look like these Injuns was going to let their man go either. But they did wrassle his shirt off, and hang it real careful over a bush so the bugs wouldn't be harmed, and where everybody could look it over.

While they do this, Brace is still squirming to get away. Finally they get tired of holding him up, so they pushes him down on the ground, his face in the dirt. While two of the big ones is holding his arms, the rest grab his legs and pull his boots off. When they is done with that the one that looks like Blue Fox grabs one of Brace's feet, and using the bowie they just wrassled away from Brace, he cuts through the big tendon behind his ankle, just above the heel. Then he does the same thing to the other foot. When he's done all the Injuns jump away.

Brace gits up and tries to run, but he falls down because his feet ain't connected to the muscles nomore. The Injuns laugh to have such fine sport. Brace gits up again. This time he don't try to run, he stumbles over to a dead tree at the edge of the grass and picks up a club, big enough to smash a man's head. The Injuns is all excited and runs to make a circle around their prisoner, out of reach of the big club. Then I says to Tom:

"Maybe if we starts shooting they will come after us so Brace can get away."

"I don't want to die," Tom says. He is sobbing so hard I can hardly understand his words. Big tears is washing his cheeks. I never seen Tom Sawyer cry afore. I never knowed he could do that. He don't give a hoot that I see him either. I see now that things change when you think you'se gonna die. Then Tom says:

"If we shoots at them, they'll kill us like they is doin' to Brace."

"Brace ain't dead yet."

"He will be, and us too if we don't leave right now and ride as fast as we can to Fort Laramie."

"I want to help Brace, but I don't know what to do," I says, beginning to cry too. "I don't care much about leaving Peggy and Flaxy either." Then Tom says:

"Maybe the soldiers can save them, if we rides fast enough. That's the only way." So I says:

"I can't leave Brace and Peggy like this."

"We can stay and fight," Tom explains, getting a better handle on his voice. "Or we can run. If we fights, we dies. If we runs, maybe the soldiers will save Peggy and Flaxy and Jim, and bury Brace. Besides, we is only boys, nobody expects us to fight a whole band of Injuns just so we can get killed and be heroes."

I don't know why it was that Tom was always right when he had a different idea on what to do. I suppose he was just a lot smarter than me. After listening to Tom, I knowed it was right to run to the fort, and to save ourselves, if we could, but when Tom crawled over to his mule to untie the reins I didn't go with him. I could not take my eyes off Brace, and the Injuns that were now trying to take away his club. He swung hard at the ones that got too close, but they always seemed quick enough to jump back so he would miss. I couldn't see how much his feet was bleeding, but I knowed they was. He didn't have no boots on, so I guessed his feet was pretty sore as he jumped around trying to hit the

Injuns with his club. It was a game he warn't agoin' to win. He couldn't run anywhere even if he clubbed half of them to death. If the Injuns got tired of their game they could shoot him full of arrows.

Then I saw some movement by the bush hut. Peggy and Flaxy were outside and running to Brace. Peggy was in front, running the fastest, and full of enough pluck to fight all the Injuns at one time. There was no knife or club or gun in her hands. So I guessed she was just going to save Brace with her bare hands. Flaxy was running as fast as she could just to keep up.

Here was Tom and me with enough guns and ammo for five or six men, and we was scared to do anything. Where did the world come off thinking boys was braver than girls? Peggy had more pluck than both of us together, then some. Tom would say she was brave because she was going to marry Brace, because he was her fiancé.

We didn't have to wait long to find out what the Injuns thought of Peggy. One of the bucks tackles her, grabs her by the hair, and begins dragging her back to her bush house. He walks so fast Peggy is stumbling along to keep from falling down. Flaxy is close behind, yelling and throwing rocks at the man who is dragging her sister. I don't know which of the girls is the bravest. Girls was supposed to be afraid of Injuns, but these two warn't one little bit.

About this time a couple more Injuns shows up, riding their ponies and swinging ropes. The horses has white man saddles so the riders can dally if they ketches something. One of them ropes Brace around the neck and shoulder. Before the white man can slip out of the loop, the Injun has dallied and spun his pony around. He jerks Brace to the ground and drags him across the grass. Brace lets go of his club. The second Injun rides in close behind Brace and throws down a loop so Brace can be dragged into it. When this Injun finally pulls his rope tight, all he ketches is a foot, but that is good enough. He dallies and gallops forward to race side by side with the first Injun, poor Brace between them, flip flopping like a fresh caught catfish just throwed up on the bank. They drags him over rocks and bushes as fast as their ponies can run.

When they finally brings him back, Brace has no more fight in him. He lays there, torn and bloody, between the two ponies. The two Injuns gets down to the ground and start cutting at the top of Brace's head, collecting his scalp. When they is done, one stands tall, holding Brace's hair high above his head, yelling a war cry, just like the Injuns in the circus. Suddenly Brace is on his feet, wrapping his arm around the neck of the Injun who has been yelling, pushing his head forward until the neck is busted. About this time, the other Injun sinks a tomahawk into the back of Brace's head. Now I guess he is dead, and so is the Injun whose neck he broke. Both go down and don't move no more.

The Injuns is fighting mad now. Brace has spoiled their party. He wasn't suppose to kill nobody. Brace is too dead for them to hurt him, but they have to try, so they jabs sticks into his eyes, then cuts off his ears and privates. Then they digs into his chest and gets his heart out. Blue Fox holds it high .... I can't watch no more. I falls on the ground feeling like I is going to lose my breakfast when I feel Tom pull at my shirt. He says:

"We must be gone now. Get on your mule."

"No, I won't go."

"You have to."

"Says who?"

"Tom Sawyer."

"Tom you ain't no boss of me. Two girls and Jim needs saving. I cain't go."

"You're only a boy. How can you save those girls, and Jim too?"

"Don't know."

"You'll die, just like Brace, and the rest of the Mills family."

"Might be so, but I stays."

"You can't do no good for Peggy now."

"Maybe I can."

"She's been violated," he says.

I don't know what that means. I reckon I never heard that word before. I knowed a cabin without chinking was ventilated, and that a delicate little purple flower was a violet, but I had never heard the word violated, so I says:

"What does that mean?"

"It means defiled," Tom says.

I didn't think this was a good time for Tom to be the smart boy, using words an ordinary person could not understand, but it was Tom's way when he wanted everybody to think he was smarter than them.

"I don't know what that means, either," I says, willing to be the dummy, maybe for the last time.

"It means them Injuns has ruined her, not once but maybe a hundred times. That's why Brace wished her dead, and gave her the dirk so she could kill herself if the Injuns ketched her. To be defiled is worse than being dead, so she ain't worth being saved no more."

"But what about Flaxy and Jim?" I asks.

"Brace hisself said they won't hurt Flaxy and Jim, so there's plenty of time to get to the fort and send the soldiers to save them."

By now I think I had figured out what them big words meant. I could see what Tom was saying, but I still couldn't reckon why Peggy warn't worth saving no more. We had seen her, walking around the camp, cutting up meat, taking care of Flaxy, fighting Blue Fox to save Brace. Tom reckoned that violating and defiling with Injuns made her worth no more than a three-legged dog, that she was no longer the Peggy we knew. None of it made sense to me.

I'd seen dogs, pigs and slaves doing Tom's violating and defiling business, but I couldn't see it made any difference in who they was or what they was worth. They was the same afterwards as before, although sometimes a baby or litter would come along, but the ones that done it was still the same.

"I'll leave your mule behind," Tom says, as he mounts up.

"No, one mule by hisself would make such a fuss the Injuns will ketch me for sure. I'll just keep this here rifle," I says, running my hand up and down the cold barrel of the .40 caliber Hawken I had loaded the night before. After throwing down some dried meat, powder, lead and a bunch of them Lucifer fire sticks wrapped in oil cloth, Tom rides off without saying goodby, and all the mules follows him. I turns away to look some more at the Injun camp.

The squaws is all crying over the dead Injun which I now thinks is Hog Face. To feel better some of them picks up sticks and starts whipping on Brace, but I don't reckon he cares now he is dead.

The men picks up stout sticks and starts scraping out a hole. If I was Brace I don't think I would want to be buried with Hog Face. The Injuns is only digging one hole, but a really big one, so I thinks both men will go in together, either side by side, or one on top of the other. But I is wrong again. When the hole is digged, they don't throw Brace in with the Injun. Instead they slit the throat of a fine black pony. When it finally falls down and stops kicking, they roll it to the bottom of the hole, then they rolls old Hog Face down next to its back.

I remembers Tom telling me how Injuns buries their dead on pole racks that looks like skinny beds with long legs, above the ground. I see again how these real Injuns don't do things the same as Tom's book Injuns. But I reasons if I was an Injun out in the middle of the great plains, where trees don't grow much, I wouldn't want to ride a thousand miles just so I could make a pole bed to hold up a dead man. And I would not want to make a tree bed to hold up a dead horse neither.

Once they puts Hog Face and his pony in the hole, they don't hurry to cover him up. The men wait while some of the squaws goes back to camp to gather up stuff to bury with Hog Face. They throws in his bow, and a quiver of arrows, a knife, a pipe and some tobacco, a parfleche of dried meat, a skin full of water, then covers all of it with a big sleeping robe. Then they throws on the dirt. They makes the top of the hole as smooth as they can, then leads horses back and forth to tramp it in, then wipes away the tracks with branches. No marker. If you warn't there when they covered him up, you would never know a man was buried there. But I knowed. If ever I wanted a bow and all them arrows, or that knife, I would know exactly where to dig to get them things. Maybe I would do that, when the Injuns moved on.

As for Brace, after they was done with the hacking and slicing, they just tied a rope on his leg. One of the Injuns got on a saddled horse and dragged Brace beyond one of the near hills, out of sight, and just left him there for the birds and wolves to finish him off. I knowed I ought to sneak down there at night and give him a proper burial. But I knowed if the body was suddenly gone, no more birds circling in the sky, the Injuns would want to know why. They would sniff around, and maybe track me to my hiding place. I hoped Brace would understand why I couldn't bury him, not now anyways.

Chapter 11

Now some of the men goes out in the meadow ketching horses. Women is packing up some of the dried meat in rawhide parfleches which lookes like big white envelopes like the ones Aunt Polly mails letters in. I think maybe the Injuns is getting ready to move camp, but it warn't so. Instead, the men is getting ready to go hunting for buffaloes again. I guess they seen some whiles they was out chasing the horses Brace had run off. Men are gathering up bows and arrows and smearing paint on their ponies after they ketches them. They draws red circles around the eyes, blue hand prints on the hips, and yellow wiggly lines in other places. I guess they is putting on the war paint for the buffaloes they want to kill.

After the men has rode off, the women gets together, gathers up a bunch of the hides, some of the ones Jim has been scraping, and spreads them out on the ground so the hairs is on the top. Then they takes ashes from the fires where they was cooking and scoops them into buffalo stomach buckets, then adds water so they can stir the ashes into a thick black soup, which they pours over the hair on the buffalo skins, then they rolls them up. They carries the rolled skins down to the creek and throws them in at the deepest place. I just can't figure why these Injuns is so dumb. After working so hard to clean up the skins, they just gets them all dirty again then throws them away in the river.

Jim is over by his post cleaning more hides, like he doesn't even care that the squaws are just going to get them dirty and throw them away. After a while Peggy and Flaxy comes out of their brush tepee. After going over in some bushes and squatting, they goes to one of the fires and starts cooking up some meat to eat. I cain't see if Peggy is still crying about what happened to Brace, but I guess she is, maybe Flaxy too. Still, they have the good sense to get something in their stomachs.

They looks fine to me, but I'm far away, and only guessing. I wishes I could talk to them, just for a minute. But if I could, I should have a plan to tell them about, how I am going to help them run away. But I don't have no plan. I wishes Tom didn't leave. He could think up a plan better than any boy I ever knowed. But Tom warn't around no more. So I decides I must talk to Peggy. Maybe she can help me think up a plan.

I remembers from watching the camp, that during the warmer times of the day, the squaws santers down to the creek to wash or to fetch water, sometimes to take baths. Peggy and Flaxy goes down there too some times. So I creeps down the back side of my hill, out of sight of the Injuns, and sneaks around to the back side of the little creek, and hides myself in some thick willow bushes. I find me a spot where I can see most of the parts of the stream where the women washes and gets their water.

I roust out an army of ornery mosquitos in the willows, but I dare not slap at them, fearful the Injuns might see me move or hear the slapping. With so many bugs wanting to suck my blood, I don't know how long I can wait for Peggy. Then I sees some wild onions, and remembers Jim telling me how slaves living by swamps rubs onion tops on their skins to keep the bugs away. I pulls up a handful of the green tops, crushes them in my hands, then smears them over the parts of my skin where the mosquitos wants to do their sucking. Pretty soon there are no more mosquitos around me, and the bonus is that the onions smells a might good, and make me feel hungry. So I chews on some dried meat while I watches for Peggy and Flaxy.

Pretty soon the squaws and children start coming down to the stream. The men are gone, and most of the chores is done, so it's now a lazy, hot, summer afternoon. Everybody wants to be by the cool water.

The children just runs in the water and starts playing, but when the squaws starts pulling off their dresses I feels mighty embarrassed and feels some blushes coming on. I knows some boys who likes to hide in the bushes to watch women change clothes or swim, but there's still enough boy in me that I feel more embarrassed than curious, except maybe when Peggy finally comes down to join the sqaws. Flaxy is with her. But these white girls is more civilized. When Flaxy pulls off her dress, and Peggy tosses aside the big skin that covers her, they both is wearing their white cotton underslips which they leaves on when they goes into the creek. Most of the squaws just sits around, rubbing sand on the parts they want to clean. The children are splashing and playing. Peggy isn't any closer than the rest to me, so I don't know how I can talk to her, so all I do is wait, trying not to enjoy the watching too much as the embarrassing feelings gradually go away.

What surprises me is that now I am close in, Peggy looks as gentle and sweet as she did before her folks was killed, except her eyes is a little red where she was rubbing them. She looks more sad than before, but even that makes her more pretty–like I can look at her all the day long and never get tired of it. She makes me feel like I could of just stay in them willows and look at her for the rest of my life. I reckon she might look a little older, because of the hard life with the Injuns, being outside a lot, and the defiling. But she's still the same Peggy, making me feel like the sun has not come up until I can see her face. I feel happy again for the first time since her folks was killed.

It's a relaxing, peaceful condition, watching Peggy and Flaxy, and them squaws and children playing and bathing in the cool water. Before I knows it I falls asleep. And I sleeps for hours because when I finally wakes up, most of the squaws and children are gone, and the sun is getting low in the sky. But Peggy and Flaxy is there, sitting on the grassy bank, still in their white underslips, trying to comb each other's hair with forked sticks.

The two squaws who are watching them, have their backs to me, so I stands up and waves at Peggy, hoping to catch her attention. When one of the squaws starts to turn around, I drops down behind the willows again, but Peggy, she sees me. After a time she gets up, telling Flaxy to stay put, then wanders into the stream, seeming not to go in any particular direction, but as she wanders around, she is getting closer and closer. One of the squaws leaves to go back to the camp. Now there's only one lookout, and she's sitting at the edge of the water, her back towards me.

Finally Peggy is close enough to talk. She whispers:

"Huckleberry Finn, what are you doing here? You must leave. They'll kill you too." Her voice is sad, but still it is angel music.

"Me and Tom came with Brace to save you," I whispers back. "Tom's gone to Fort Laramie to fetch soldiers. You and Flaxy and Jim can sneak away with me. We can go to the fort, maybe meet the soldiers before we gets there."

"Too late to save me," she says. "Too late, way too late. They'll kill you like they did Brace."

I wondered what she meant about it being too late to save her. She looked alive and well, and as pretty as ever, though maybe a little older. There was creases in her brow that I never seen before. Then she says:

"You should've left with Tom."

"Didn't want to leave you and Flaxy and Jim."

"Nobody wants to kill us," she says, a scolding sound her voice, like a mad school teacher. "But they will kill a boy like you in a second. Now get out of here. Shoo."

The squaw hears Peggy talking and turns around as I duck down, my heart hurting that a white girl called me a boy, and I can't reckon why. I knowed Jim hated being called a boy by white men, and never did understand that either. Plenty of folks called me boy, but it never did hurt until Peggy done it. Some things a boy just ain't about to understand—like why Peggy says it's too late to save her when she looks more alive and wonderful than she ever looked before.

"Shoo, you rascal, git," Peggy says, kicking at the water like she is trying to drive off a snake or a turtle. The squaw watches a minute, then turns back to her regular position.

"Which way's the Fort?" Peggy whispers.

"Southwest," I says, pointing in that direction. "When you strike the North Platte, follow the wagon tracks west."

"If the men don't come back, maybe we can sneak away when it gets dark," she says.

"I be up there," I says, pointing to the hill where Tom and me was hiding. "Bring some dried meat. It might take a week or more to find the soldiers. I reckon we can travel at night, and hide when it's light. No horses. We got to walk."

"Look for us after dark, on the hill," she says, turning and wading back to Flaxy. I wish she didn't have to go, but knowed it was best.

When the women was gone I sneaks out of the willows and goes back to the top of the hill, being real careful to keep out of sight of the village. The sun is still shining as I gathers up all my stuff so I will be ready the minute the girls and Jim comes up. I just hopes they can get away without somebody chasing them.

Chapter 12

The sun is just getting ready to go down when I sees a big cloud of dust beyond the little hill where they dragged Brace. I gets a sick feeling in my stomach, because I knows the Injuns is likely coming home early. I hopes the dust is being made by buffaloes, or wild horses, but I knows different, in my heart.

Pretty soon I sees the Injuns riding into sight, but they ain't alone. Two white men and a bunch of mules with packs is riding with them. The white men looks like trappers, dressed just like the Injuns in buckskin shirts and leggings, but I knows they is white because they both have bushy beards on their faces, and their clothes is dirtier than those of the Injuns. The whites is too far away to see real good, but one of them is wearing a black and white hat. My eyes can see that for sure. A skunk hat it is. It puzzles me why a man would want a skunk on his head–unless maybe he is a skunk hisself. The other white man doesn't have any hat at all, just long brown hair. Both men is taller than the Injuns, but one is fat and the other skin and bones. Both is carrying long rifles across the front of their saddles. The is herding the pack mules like cows with no lead ropes tied to their halters.

The Injuns is all excited, making circles around the white men. Some is yelling and waving their bows and arrows. These is the same Injuns that went hunting earlier. The painted horses tell me this. I guess when they found these white men, they changed their minds about hunting buffaloes. I don't know why the Injuns is so excited to be bringing home two white men. I just knows that with all these men around it will be harder, maybe impossible, for the girls and Jim to sneak away.

Pretty soon the whole camp is getting ready for a big party. Lots of wood is throwed on the fires. Women is cooking meat. The white men pull some bottles from one of their packs. The fat one with the skunk hat yanks the cork from one of the bottles, and lets the Injuns take turns swallering down the contents. I can see all the Injuns. Only Peggy and Flaxy is staying in the bush tepee. Jim is leaning against his pole, watching the party, maybe wondering if he will get a turn to suck from the bottle.

I cain't see much after it gets dark, but the fires keeps burning, and there's lots of noises, mostly yelling and laughing. Sometimes a gun is fired. I waits all night, sleeping in short dozes. The girls and Jim never come.

When it gets light I see the two white men and Blue Fox sitting in a tight circle, talking real serious. Other Injuns is standing back, watching their business. I cain't guess what their talk might be until some of the Injuns goes to the bush tepee and fetches Peggy. She don't want no part of this business as they drag her over to the white men. I reckon she knows they ain't come to save her, and I don't know how she knows that.

When the one with the skunk hat tries to lift up Peggy's skin to look underneath, she kicks him in the chest so he falls over backwards. Instead of getting mad, he just laughs and takes another drink from one of the bottles. He and Blue Fox start talking again, while the other Injuns holds onto Peggy. As I watch these white men do business with the Injuns, I thinks these are the kinds of men my pappy would want to ride with if he was still alive. I check my rifle. It's ready to fire. I don't know what to do, except watch.

Finally the white men gets up, and walks around like their business is done. The Injuns helps them ketch their horses and mules, except two mules which they leave in the meadow. When everything is ready for them to leave, they take Peggy away from the Injuns who is holding her, and try to put her on one of the mules, but she won't do it. My gentle, sweet Peggy, she bites one of them on the arm, then starts hitting and kicking like a wildcat. I cain't figure out why she wants so bad to stay with the Injuns who has killed her folks and Brace. These white men might even take her to Fort Laramie where she could get away from them and be safe.

Pretty soon they stops trying to put Peggy on the mule. Some Injuns hold onto her, while the two white men and Blue Fox starts another round of business talk, passing one of them bottles back and forth as they do it.

Then after a while one of the white men gets up and starts taking some more bottles out of one of the mule packs. He gives them to Blue Fox, who yells something towards the bush tepee. Pretty soon little Flaxy comes out of the tepee and runs to Peggy. They starts hugging. Now I figures out what is happening. Peggy warn't about to leave with the white men unless Flaxy could go with her. That's why she made all the fuss, and bit the man. That Peggy warn't about to leave her little sister behind.

Pretty soon the white men help Peggy and Flaxy get on a mule, Peggy in front. Then all of them leaves while the Injuns is opening up the new bottles and having a grand time passing them around. The white men warn't headed east towards the United States, but in a southwest-ward direction, towards Fort Laramie. The trail would be easy to follow, but without anything to ride, I guessed I would have a hard time keeping up with them.

After a while one of the Injuns takes a bottle over to old Jim who is sitting by his post, and gives Jim a sip. Jim nods his head and smiles like he is mighty grateful. Pretty soon the Injun unties Jim's tether rope and lets him come back to the main group. Jim struts around like he is mighty proud they let him leave his post. I watch him a long time. I want to be following Peggy and Flaxy, but Jim and me have been like brothers almost as long as I remembers. On the big river he saved me a time or two, and I saved him too. I warn't about to leave him with these mean Injuns, not without talking some. I decides as soon as it is dark again, I will sneak down to Jim's post, and ask him if he wants me to save him from the Injuns and let him run away with me. He can maybe help me save Peggy and Flaxy from the white men.

While waiting for dark to set in, I watch what is happening in the Injun camp, when not taking naps. I have plenty of meat and dried biscuits, stuff Tom had left for me, but I ain't much hungered. Usually a boy like me eats everything around, but not now. I reckon being scared makes me not want to eat. I wishes I could be brave like Brace, and stop thinking what these Injuns might do if they ketches me, the kind of thinking that makes my hands quiver like a hog's belly on a hot day. Then I think about Peggy, how she looks and talks, and how I feel when she talks to me, then I feel less scared, but I still ain't hungry. I wishes Tom was around so he could explain my feelings. Tom could explain most anything. He could tell me why I no longer felt like eating all the time.

As I watched the camp I see one of the squaws is near Jim, more than the rest. She is bringing him things to eat and drink, and sometimes she just sits by him as she cuts and sews on pieces of skin. Sometimes she holds a piece of skin against Jim's foot. I reckon she is making him his own moccasins. I guess Jim is real pleased that she is doing it.

I am glad in late afternoon when Jim returns to his post and starts cleaning skins again. I guess the Injuns stays away from there, mostly because the skins stink, it being summer and all. But that squaw still comes over and checks his feet once in a while. The rest of the Injuns seems to be going to bed early.

When it's dark I sneaks down the hill. I'm glad these Injuns has no dogs. They would see and smell me for sure and start barking, me crawling through the grass and getting close. But they don't have no dogs, so I don't worry about that.

"Jim," I whispers, when I's about a rod away.

"Who dat'?" he whispers back. There's still enough light from the fires that I can see him looking towards me, but he can't see me because I am holding still in the grass, flat on my belly.

"It's me, Huck," I says.

"If dat don' beat all," he sings.

I move in close so we don't have to talk so loud.

"Me thinked you's scalped with them Mills boys," he says as he wraps his powerful arms around me and squeezes so hard I can't hardly breathe.

"They warn't able to ketch me and Tom," I says. I tells him how we waited for Brace, then followed the Injuns to this camp.

"Tom here too?" he asks, gradually releasing his hold on me.

"Tom's went to fetch the soldiers."

"Dirty white men, dey tell Injuns 'bout soldier boys, they gits Miss Peggy."

"What?"

"Dey tell Injuns soldier boys kill all Blue Fox people, if dey finds white woman. Give 'm two mules too, so dey can take Miss Peggy. Den two bottles of white lightn'n for Flaxy girl, 'cause Miss Peggy won't go if she don't."

"They take them girls to Fort Laramie?" I asks.

"Na. Going trapping for beavers and other varments. All winter. Beyond Fort Laramie."

"Why do they want the girls?" I asks.

"Dey wants only Miss Peggy. Da reason men wants women everywheres."

"Defiling and violating," I says in a sober voice, feeling angry instead of scared for the first time since I can remember.

"Guess so, white mens calls it dat."

I's mad, and ready to go after the girls, but I got to ask Jim something first.

"Brace give Peggy a dirk to kill herself if them Injuns defiled her," I says. "He was sorry she hadn't done it. So was Tom, I thinks. I don't understand."

"Dey reads too many books," Jim says, without seeming to give my question much thought.

"I still don't understand," I says.

"Book women and real women ain't same," he says. "If all de dark women dat got violated by white boss mens stuck dirks in der hearts, no women be left over to haf de babes. No mo slaves to pick de cotton. No mo slaves fo ablutionists to set free. Real woman doan do dat. Dat's all."

Tom hadn't been to school like Huck and Brace, and didn't even know how to read. But he was the wisest man in the world that I knowed. Since leaving the United States I learned that real Injuns and book Injuns ain't the same. Now I knowed real women and book women warn't the same either.

"Run away with me, Jim," I says. "We got to save them girls."

"I stays right here," he says.

"These is mean, dangerous Injuns," I argues. "You can't want to stay here."

"I is, Huck, and dat's de solm' truth," he says.

"I don't understand," I says.

"Dese Injuns lets old Jim drink from de same bottle," he says. "No white man never done dat, 'cept maybe Huck Finn. Dey don't call me boy, and say do dis and do dat."

"You don't belong here."

"So old Jim goes to fort," he says, like he is mad at me. "Soldier boys say Jim runs away. Put chains on feet. Sends Jim back to boss man plantation. Jim likes Injun camp better."

"What about the girls?" I asks. He grins and says:

"Jim tells Huck secret." He leans forward and whispers, "Miss Peggy don't need no saving. Maybe Huck Finn and Tom Sawyer do, not Miss Peggy."

I don't know what he meaned by that. I don't understand why he wants to stay with them savages who murdered the Mills family, folks who was our friends. A minute before I thinks Jim is wise as Moses, now I thinks he's plumb crazy.

Then I hears something. Footsteps on rocks. Someone coming, likes an Injun. I dives under one of Jim's skins, hoping nobody has seed me. I has one end of the skin lifted up so I can see whose coming.

It's a squaw, the one that was making real Injun moccasins for old Jim. I don't think she sees me because she sits down by Jim and leans her head against his big arm, then closes her eyeballs like she don't have a worry in the whole world. She hain't said a single word. Neither has old Jim.

He put his big arm around her shoulders, then tells me to come out from under the skin. I does it. The squaw sees me and her eyeballs gets real big. She tries to get away, but Jim is holding her with his arm. His other hand is over her mouth so she can't yell to the other Injuns. After a minute she looks up at Jim's face, and sees he's happy, and not scared like she is. Jim stops holding her like a prisoner. She don't try to run away or yell. She just looks at me as she sits real close to old Jim. No more scared.

She don't look real young, or real old, not fat and not real skinny, just a squaw, kind of pretty, them black eyes sparkling like wet coal. Her long hair is tied in two neat braids. Her skin dress is clean except for rows of smashed porcupine quills. She smells like smoke. She leans against Jim and his smile says he likes it. Jim learned me that when two people loves each other, it shows. It did here, in this Injun camp, in the middle of the night .

"Then I go by myself," I says. Jim nods. I sneaks off in the night, gathers up my rifle and food, and hurries off in the same direction them two trappers took Peggy and Flaxy.

Chapter 13

I'd never been out in a wilderness like this before, but I'd growed up in the woods, hunting, trapping and fishing, and knowed something about following trails and tracks. Them trappers with Peggy and Flaxy warn't hard to follow. All them horses and mules left enough tracks that a baby could do it.

I was worrisome that the Injuns might be following me. I looked over my shoulder a lot. At first I just traveled at night, but after a few days, and not seeing anybody, not even any buffaloes, I just hiked along whenever I warn't sleeping. What seemed strange to me was that even though they was riding horses and mules, and I was walking, I seemed to be ketching up to them. The horse apples they left behind was getting wetter and wetter.

After four or five days I followed their trail to a pretty big river for this part of the country. It warn't very deep, but plenty wide. I figured it was the same Platte River we had been camped next to when the Mills family was slaughtered by the Injuns. There was plenty of wagon tracks, and some awful deep ruts. Dust in some places. Lots of horse, mule and ox tracks. The tracks from Peggy's bunch kind of mixed in with the others, so they was hard to follow now. But since all the tracks seemed to be going the same direction, I just followed them all, thinking this was probably the road to Fort Laramie. Some of them tracks probably belonged to Tom and our mules, I guessed.

Three days later I spots what I reckon is Fort Laramie, off in the distance. I guess I am safe from Injuns now so I hurries up, right down the middle of the road, as fast as I can walk. I don't got a plan, just get to the fort and figure things out from there. I cain't figure out why the trappers would pay good mules and whiskey for Peggy and Flaxy, just to take them to a fort and set them free. It just didn't make sense, unless the trappers was preachers or abolitionists who just rode around on their horses helping set folks free. But I never heard of people like that, at least not in this country which is a long way from the United States. So I just hurries towards the fort, hoping Peggy will be there, and maybe Tom too.

I am about two miles off when I sees another person walking along the road in front of me, going the same direction, but at a slower pace. I guess I might ketch up before that person reaches the fort. As I get closer, it looks like the person in front of me is wearing a dress, so I guesses it is a female, a little one at that–a girl or a tiny, tiny woman. As I get ever closer, I can see she has yellow hair, and the dress starts to look like one I has seen earlier, on Flaxy. I starts to run, and finally ketches her just before we gets to the fort.

It's Flaxy, all right, and she's just a crying as she walks along. She is so surprised to see me that she just doesn't know what to do. Finally she sits down on the ground and cries some more. I sits down next to her, and just strokes her on the back, trying to make her feel better. Finally she starts to talk. She says:

"They tell Peggy if she stops making trouble, and promises to ride with them to their trapping camp, they will let me go. She agrees, so here I am, walking by myself to this fort."

"Where's Peggy now?" I asks.

"With the trappers. They went anther way to miss the fort. They thinks the soldiers might be looking for Peggy and me."

"Any idea where they are going?" I asks.

"One of them, a few days ago, when he didn't know I was listening, said something about their trapping camp being near Fort Bridger. They might be going there, but they don't want the soldiers here to see they got Peggy with them."

I give her a drink of water and a chunk of dried meat, which she is happy to get. I want her to feel better so I tells her me and the soldiers are going to save Peggy real soon. She says she and Peggy has decided that when they get free, they wants to go to Iowa where some of their aunts and uncles and cousins live, near Keokuk on the Mississippi River.

I asks her to tell me the names of the trappers. She says they called theirselves Raymond and Zeke. She said they tried digging gold in California, but warn't able to find any, so now they was trapping again, not much money in it, but it was all they knowed how to do.

When I asks her how they hopes to get past Fort Laramie with nobody seeing them, she says they turned south a couple of miles back, before I found her, and was just making a big circle around the fort.

That little Flaxy just held tight to my hand as we walked by a whole village of tepees that were set up on the meadow outside the fort walls. Some of them Injuns stared at us like they would want to come and get Flaxy if I warn't carrying my Hawken rifle, primed and ready to fire.

But pretty soon we is in the fort. We feel pretty safe now because there is lots of soldiers. Some of them is breaking horses in a corral. Others is marching. Lots is just standing around talking. I go up to the closest one and asks where I might find the commanding officer.

He says Colonel Dent is in his office, and points to a log cabin with an American flag on a tree in front of it. We hurries over there and before we know it Colonel Dent is making a fuss over Flaxy. He tells us how he learned all about her and Peggy from Tom Sawyer, and how Tom is out with a bunch of soldiers looking for the girls right now. Tom has told him about me too, and he is glad to meet me. He has a wife and two little girls of his own at the fort, and says Flaxy can stay with them until he figures out a way to get her back to Iowa.

I tells him Peggy is no longer with the Injuns where Tom and the soldiers has gone looking, but she is with some trappers circling south of the fort while we are talking. He don't seem to understand what I am saying, because he says the soldiers with Tom are good trackers and will pick up the trail and save Peggy. When I try to explain that they are going in the wrong direction, he says he doesn't have enough men to send another patrol looking for Peggy.

I tag along while he takes Flaxy over to his cabin so his wife and two girls can start making a fuss over her. When they says they is going to give her a bath and put her in a new dress, that's when I leave. Colonel Dent says I can have anything I want at the cook house, so I goes over to a long log building where they cooks the food for the soldiers, and gets a tin plate heaped with buffalo stew. The cook soldier scoops it out of a big iron pot which he says never gets empty. He just keeps adding new things as the soldier boys eat it down. Sometimes he throws in a couple of antelope, or an elk, even prairie dogs, but mostly just buffalo and potatoes with lots of salt and pepper.

I sits in the shade and eats like a boy who is half starved, and suppose I am, but ain't thought much about it. I don't stop 'til I've cleaned up three plates, and am so full I don't think I can hardly stand up. Pretty soon I am stretched out on the ground like a dead boy, sound asleep.

When I wakes up, the fort is all in shadows because the sun is almost down. I looks across the parade grounds. Not many soldiers to see, so I guesses they is eating more of the wonderful buffalo stew. The big front doors to the fort is open, and pretty soon two Injuns rides in. One of them looks awful familiar. I am sure I have seen him before. Yes. It's Man-afraid-of-his-Mother-in-law. I am mighty sure because he is riding a mule that belonged to Mr. Mills. He and the other Injun with him tie their mules to the hitching post in front of the store the soldiers call the commissary and goes inside. They takes a bundle of stuff with them.

Carefully, I walks closer. I remember Mr. Mills saying this mule was his favorite. I even remember her name, Cleopatra. Then I recognizes the saddle. It belonged to Buck, Peggy's brother. I knows its his, because his name is carved on the skirt.

I first think I better run and find Colonel Dent, and ask him to arrest these Injuns. But I knowed from Tom how the Army did things. First they would put them in jail. Then they would have to find some lawyers. Maybe they'd have to come from another fort. That would take time, while Peggy was getting farther and farther away from here. Then the trial, and I'd be the main witness. The lawyers would want to know if I actually saw Man-afraid-of-his-Mother-in-law kill somebody. It all happened so fast that all I really knowed was that Injuns was doing the killing, and the Mills family was being killed, except for Peggy and Flaxy. And I knowed that Man-Afraid was with them Injuns while it happened. Maybe I knew enough to get him hanged, and maybe I didn't. Meanwhile, Peggy might be in California before the trial was finished. I couldn't wait that long.

I knowed if I was riding that mule, I could ketch up with Peggy real fast, so I might as well just take it. If Man-Afraid ketches me taking it, the soldiers will save me, I thinks. If the soldiers ketches me taking it, with Flaxy as my witness, I can prove I was just taking it back, and that it belonged to Flaxy's family. So I figures I have nothing to lose by taking it, so I just walks over to the mule, gets on, rests my rifle over the saddle horn, and rides out of the fort. I guess Man-Afraid is going to be mighty mad, but I don't think there's nothing he can do. He won't go to the soldiers because he knows the mule and saddle is stole from white folks. He can't track me because the ground around the fort is splattered with millions of horse and mule tracks so he won't know which ones to follow.

As soon as I is around the corner of the fort I heads south at a fast trot. Sooner or later I figure I'll cross the trail left by Peggy and the two trappers, then just follow until I ketches up. Then I'll haveta figure out a way to save Peggy so I can bring her back to the fort to join up with Flaxy. Maybe I will go with them back to Iowa. By now I likes Peggy that much. I would go with her clear to New York, if she would let me.

Chapter 14

There's part of a moon, so I sees where I rides, but I fears it is so dark I might miss Peggy's trail, so I stops on a hilltop and waits for it to get light. The night is warm so it's easy to sleep a little. I wrap the end of Cleopatra's lead rope around my wrist so she can graze, but not pull away while I'm dozing. She is one of those rare mules that can be by herself, or with a person, and not go crazy wanting to get together with other mules and horses. So it was a peaceful night.

At first light I'm riding south again, higher and higher into the hills, looking for tracks and trails, and finally I finds the spur, going strait west on what looks like an old buffalo trail, mostly mule tracks in the bunch, and they looks new, like they was just made. But the tracks aren't as fresh as I first thought because after an hour or two I finds their camp, where they spent the night. The ashes is cold, so I know they didn't build a morning fire. I guess they're hurrying to get around the fort before someone sees them.

By late afternoon I rides to the top of a ridge so I can see a long way ahead. That's when I spot them. They are too far off to tell which one is Peggy, but I can make out three riders among a bunch of mules and horses, so I'm sure it's them. They seem to be moving pretty fast, but I reckon they will make camp soon, and when they do, I will have a chance to get close.

My plan is simple. I will just crawl into their camp in the middle of the night, wake up Peggy, cut her free if she's tied up, then crawl back to Cleopatra. We'll ride double back to the fort, lickety split, as fast as Cleopatra can go.

Somehow plans I make never works out as they is supposed to. The riders was still traveling when it got too dark for me to see them. I knowed they was about to make camp, because their mules were as tired and hungry as mine, but now it was too dark to see where they camped. So I gets off Cleopatra, and just tries to follow their tracks, real slow and careful. But pretty soon I can't see the tracks either, so I just listens and watches as I keep moving along. No moon, only some stars to light my way. I can tell by the outline of a nearby hill that I am going in the right direction. I am hoping they builds a nice fire to show me the way, or that some of their horses and mules wants to fight each other and makes lots of noise. But so far, I can see no fire, and can't hear no mules. I moves real slow now, half a step at a time. Cleopatra is nice and quiet, following right behind me.

Finally I just stops and listens, knowing they got to make some noise, sooner or later, even if they don't make no fire. I sits down and chews on a piece of dried meat while Cleopatra crops at some grass. The night is so quiet I hears her chewing. Pretty soon I rolls over on some grass and sleeps some.

It's starting to get light when I finally hears something, a sharp pounding noise, like a man beating a rock with a hammer. Then I know it's not a hammer that I hear, but a horse's foot, and it has a steel shoe on it. A horse is pawing, maybe the one they kept in camp while letting the others out to graze. I starts sneaking closer.

Then I hears a breaking limb, then another. They didn't make fire when they went to bed, but maybe they are making one now. The night is cool, and maybe they wants to cook some breakfast. I check my Hawken rifle. It's primed and ready to fire. When I know I am awful close, I ties Cleopatra to a tree so she won't get in the way.

The first thing I sees is their horses and mules, scattered across a hill-side, filling up on the dew-damp grass. The pawing sound is closer. Then

I sees the smoke. They is camped behind some rocks. I sneaks higher on the hill, trying to get a look at them.

Then I sees Peggy. She still has that old elk skin covering her up. Her long hair hangs down over the back of the skin. Her hair looks dirty and like she ain't brushed it in a long time. I cain't see her face.

One of the trappers, a tall wire of a man with coal black whiskers, is bent over some smoking sticks, blowing to git a fire a going. The other trapper, a huge hog man, is sitting on a log slicing some meat into a pan. An old brown horse, the one they didn't let out to graze with the others, is still pawing at the rocks. Except for that, the camp is quiet. Nobody's talking. I'm close enough that I can shoot one of them real easy. Both of their rifles is resting against the log where the big man is sitting.

I think of all the trouble it has been for me to find Peggy. I's followed her for many days, in Injun country where I could get scalped. Now I's found her. The chase is over. Now I got to do something to save her. That's why I come this far. She don't wants to be with these trappers no more than she wanted to be with them Injuns. She wants to be with Flaxy, going home to Iowa.

"Lift them hands over yer heads," I says, stepping out from behind some rocks where I was hiding.

Both men looks at me at the same time, and Peggy too, but nobody raises their hands, so I says:

"Hands high or I starts shooting." I cocks the hammer back because I forgot to do it earlier. Still nobody raises their hands. I starts to worry that something is wrong with me. They ain't scared, at least it don't seem that way.

"Huck Finn, following me will get you killed," Peggy says, sounding more mad than glad I come to save her.

"I'm done following," I says. "Now we're goin' back to the fort, and if one of your friends here doan like it, I can put a big hole in his . . ."

"Land sakes," the hog man says, slowly putting the pan of meat on the ground. "We done saved this young lady and her little sister from the Injuns. You ought to be thanking us and giving us presents, not wanting to shoot us."

"Won't be no shooting nobody if Peggy here comes back to the fort with me," I says, pointing my rifle directly at hog man's face.

"We'd a taken her there ourselves, but some of the soldier boys are a little mad about us taking their money in a poker game."

"Give me Peggy and I won't tell the soldiers where they can find you," I says.

"Now that's real nice," hog face answers. Then he says to his friend, "Raymond, roll up her stuff in one of them buffler robes so she can take it with her."

Without getting to his feet, wire man moves from the smoking sticks to a pile of robes and some other stuff. He's not very far from me. My rifle is still pointed at hog face. Even with the trappers being so nice, my finger is on the trigger.

"I don't have any stuff," Peggy says, but I just stands there, so nervous I can't think.

Suddenly a buffalo skin is falling over the barrel of my rifle. Wire slung it there. I try to point it at him as I pulls on the trigger. But I am too late, and the bullet don't hit any flesh as both trappers pile on top of me. They wrassle away my Hawken and bowie, and pretty soon they're holding my hands behind my back. When Peggy tries to grab one of their guns, Hog slaps her to the ground. I feels like I am going to throw up, and don't know if it's from being so scared, or from the stink Hog and Wire has rubbed off on me as they wrassled me. I guess neither one of them even knows what a bath is. They smell like smoke from burning hair, sweaty socks and baby calf manure all mixed up.

"Can I kill him?" Wire asks.

"Later, after I finds out what he knows," Hog replies. Then he asks me:

"Who put you up to coming here?"

I don't see any need to tell the truth because they is just going to kill me anyways, so I says I am a special messenger for Colonel Dent at Fort Laramie, and he'll be coming along in short order. I don't think he believes me because he kicks me so hard in the side I thinks I am going to break in half. Finally, I throws up, all over the buffalo skin that Wire throwed over my rifle. Hog kicks me again, in the other side. I can't throw up no more. I feels like I'm gonna die without them even having to kill me.

"Who knows you followed us?" he asks.

I knows he is just going to kick me again, if I lie, and my mind is so mixed up from the pain in my sides, I just tells the truth.

"I would of told Tom Sawyer I was going to foller you," I explains, "but Tom was going east with the soldiers because he thinked Peggy was still with the Injuns. Only Jim and me knowed you took her, and Jim is still with the Injuns, still cleaning hides as far as I know."

He seemed pleased with my explanation, but then I got to thinking that he and Wire would be more likely to kill me if they thought nobody was looking for me. So I says:

"But soon as Tom and the soldiers find the Injuns, Jim will tell them which ways me and Peggy went, and they'll come a running. Them soldiers feed their ponies grain, you know, so they can travel faster than normal folks. I figure they might be here by nightfall. I leaved them a clear trail. I had a can of red paint from the fort which I poured on rocks and bushes every mile or so." I figured details like this would make my story sound truer. Tom learned me that. He was the best liar of any boy I ever knowed. And I warn't too bad at it myself.

"If the soldiers finds me and Peggy alive they won't have no need to keep chasin', but if we's dead they'll foller you fellers clean to the Pacific Ocean."

"Nobody said nothing about killing Peg Girl," Hog growled.

"She's our squaw now," Wire added.

"Shut up," Hog yelled.

"Just let's kill him," Wire whined.

"Hold up your hands so I can see them," Hog says to me. I obeys.

"No red on his hands," Hog says, more to hisself than to Wire. "A boy pouring red paint on rocks and bushes would get some on his hands. He's lying." Then he says to Wire:

"Cut off his scalp and skin his face. They'll think Injuns done it, and they won't know who he is, if they finds him."

Wire grabs my hair and picks my bowie off the ground. He don't need to be asked twice to hurt me. His face is happy like a boy who just got an ice cream cone on the Fourth of July. He has that old knife against my forehead and is about to start cutting when Peggy says:

"Wait, wait, listen to me. I promised to be your squaw for the winter and not to run away if you let Flaxy go. I will promise more if you don't hurt Huck. I'll be your squaw for two winters, not just one," she says.

"If we don't kill him?" Hog asks.

"Swear on the Bible, cross my heart, hope to die," she says, looking happy like we was playing nigger in the woodpile.

I don't know what to think. This Peggy, the brightest, cleanest, best girl I ever knowed is giving herself to pigs to save me. It ain't right, so I says:

"Don't promise nothing, Peggy."

"Don't promise anything," she says, like she is more interested in correcting my speech than saving her life. Then to Hog she says:

"You better accept before I change my mind."

"All right," he says. "We won't hurt the boy."

"You said I can take his scalp and skin his face," Wire whined.

"No scalp'n and skin'n today," Hog says.

"If'n we let'm go, he'll run to the fort and git the soldiers," Wire protested. He warn't so dumb after all because that's exactly what I was agoing to do.

"Depends how we let him go," Hog sneared.

"You promised not to hurt him," Peggy reminded them.

Pointing his rifle at my face, Hog orders me to take my boots off. When I does it he kicks them over by Peggy. Then he tells me to take off my pants and shirt . When I hesitates, he cocks back the hammer on his rifle, and Wire reaches towards my throat with the point of the bowie.

"You promised not to hurt him," Peggy warns.

"He won't get hurt if he does what we tells him," Hog says. Reluctantly I obeys. The embarrassment of undressing in front of Peggy is almost worse than the fear of the two men hurtin' me. I cain't look at her, although I feel her looking at me. Hog throws my clothes towards Peggy and orders her to put them on, the boots too. She don't hesitate.

When she flips off the elk skin, I am so embarrassed to see the whiteness of her skin that I think I should look away. But I don't. Then I realize it's not her skin I see, but the white pantaloons and night shirt. They are not as white as when she and Flaxy were washing with the squaws in the crick. I guess Hog and Wire had wrassled her around in the dirt and got them dirty. I wanted to kill them real bad, but I was glad Peggy was getting some decent clothes, even if they was mine.

I didn't understand my feelings when she throwed off the elk hide and started slipping into my trousers and shirt. I just tingled all over, up and down my arms and legs and right to the middle between my back and chest. Her clothes was dirty and she had been riding a dusty trail for days without a bath, but she was the most beautiful human being I ever seen, and I thinked if it were possible to worship a human being, I had found the perfect one.

"Why she have to wear the boy's clothes?" Wire asked.

"We'll cut her hair too so folks will think a boy is traveling with us," Hog says. "They won't be near so curious, and won't think nothin' of it."

"Now listen real careful, and you won't die," Hog says. "If you do your walking when the sun is up, it will burn you until you die. If you try to walk at night, when you can't see where you steps, your feet will fill up with cactus needles until you can't walk no more, and you'll die. You got about an hour at sunup and another hour at dusk when you can walk. Oughtta reach the fort in four or five days. By then we'll be so far away the soldiers will never find us. Do as I say and you can live."

What them trappers didn't know was that I had a mule tied up in the bushes not very far away. Riding the mule, I could reach the fort sometime during the coming night. Colonel Dent would send soldiers with me this time, I was sure.

I was sitting on a rock, my bare knees tucked up under my chin when they said good bye. They were all on their horses now, and their mules were packed too.

"Travel at dawn and dusk like he says," Peggy warned as she rode up close. "I don't want you to die, Huck, not for me. It isn't worth it, not any more."

"I'll get them soldiers," I whisper. "I have a mule to take me to the fort. We'll save you, and it won't be very long. Slow them down, if you can." I wink at her, but she don't wink back.

"The soldiers, not them soldiers," she says, correcting my speech again. I don't understand it. She never corrected my speech before her folks was killed. Now it's all she does when I'm around. It don't make sense.

"Huck Finn, don't follow me any more," she says, her voice now loud enough for the trappers to hear. "Get to the fort and make sure Flaxy is on the next wagon to Iowa. Then forget about me. In time I'll come home, but I won't have you getting killed trying to hurry things up."

I guess she is a really fine actor, and that she is saying all that for the trappers to hear, so they don't think I'm going to fetch the soldiers. Then she says:

"My family and Brace are dead. I don't want anybody else to die, not on my account. What I was saving for my husband is gone, and it isn't ever coming back. I will find my way back to Iowa to see Flaxy. Don't follow me any more. Please."

I don't say a thing. Her acting is so good, I am beginning to think she really means for me to stay away, but with them two trappers in ear shot, I cain't ask her to make things clear for me, so I just keep my mouth shut, and my nakedness covered up as much as I can with my arms and legs, looking at Peggy, feeling like an orphan calf looking at a bottle of warm milk. I'd never felt this way about anybody ever before, not even Becky Thatcher, and don't know what to make of it. I'd never been one to risk his skin for anybody, but I am now, for Peggy.

Finally they rides away, and I darts into the bushes running as fast as I can towards my mule, thinking all the while how dumb they is to not think I might have something to ride to the fort. I figure I can be at the fort sometime in the night, and coming back at dawn with a bunch of soldier boys to save Peggy.

When I reaches the last ridge above the place where I tied the mule, I just jumps off the top of the ridge and runs as fast as I can down to her. She is still there, but I guess I surprised her some, maybe a lot, and I guess she never seen a naked boy running at her before. Her eyes gets real big and she snorts all the wet stuff out of her nose, then she decides to go back to the fort without me. I had tied her real good to them bushes, but they ain't big trees, and nothing can pull harder than a scared mule. She pulls them bushes right out of the ground and takes off running as fast as she can go towards the fort, leaving me standing there, wearing nothing but the skin I was born in.

I knowed now I should have stopped at the top of the hill, talked gently to get her attention so there warn't no surprise, then walked up to her nice and slow, giving her plenty of time to see and smell and get used to my naked body, knowing she had never seen nothing like that before. But I can't do it over. She is gone. I made a horrific mistake, and now I will pay for being so dumb. Maybe I will die.

Chapter 15

So I just walk along, following that crazy mule. I reckon if I don't run after her, that she might stop after a while, remember who I was and let me ketch up to her.

The sun is bright and up high in the sky, so I can't use it to decide which way to go, but Cleopatra knows the way back, even though she's only been there once, so all I has to do is follow her until I ketches her or until I reaches the fort, whichever happens first.

Those trappers said the sun would burn me up, but it don't feel very hot and my skin don't feel burned, even with my shoulders and back as white as a slab of hog fat. Most summers I was nice and brown from swimming in the river, but this year, out in the wilderness with so many mean Injuns, we just never had time for swimming and playing, and lazying in the sun. This was the first time I warn't wearing a shirt.

And this was the first time I went walking without no boots, so my feet warn't as tough as they usually was. I hadn't gone very far when I had to stop and pull out some cactus spines. There were cuts too, from sharp sticks and rocks. I could see those trappers was right about me not being able to travel in the dark with bare feet. If I couldn't see where I was stepping, my feet would get slaughtered so bad I wouldn't be able to walk at all. I went slower, trying to be more careful.

The longer I hiked, the warmer the sun felt. Without no clothes, I felt like a strip of buffalo meat, like the Injun squaws hanged on them willow racks in the sun. It'd take about a day, maybe two, for a piece of meat like that to get all dried out. I knowed the same thing would happen to me if I didn't find something to drink. I also knowed that if I dried out I would lose my strength. If I wanted to keep walking I had to drink.

When I starts walking after the mule, my only thought is to get to the fort as fast as I can. But after a couple of hours of walking in the sun, my shoulders are as pink as the skin on the belly of a white pig, and I am so thirsty I knows I might die if I ain't careful enough. Still, with each tender step, I think about Peggy having to ride away with them two filthy men, who bought her from the Injuns like she was a goat or a sack of beans. From what she said I knowed she had been violated, like Tom said. She tole me she warn't worth saving no more, but I knowed she was. She was still the same bright, wonderful, beautiful Peggy. I knowed it because I had seen her with my own eyes. She talked different now, but after all that happened, I could understand why she might change some.

When the sun gets low in the sky, I find a long, narrow valley with a little crick running down the middle, some grass on both sides. I hurries down there, feeling the wet green grass soft under my feet. Then I drops on my belly, and swallers cool water until my insides hurt worse than my feet and back. Then I rolls over on my back and closes my eyes. But I ain't able to sleep or nothing because my back is burned by the sun and is as tender as my feet now. Besides that, the wet grass is full of gnats and mosquitoes who are starting to look for something to eat now the sun is getting low in the sky, and my naked body must look like a Roman feast. Pretty soon I am rolling around in the grass trying to squash the ones that lands in places I can't reach. Pretty soon I make a swatter from some green willows close to the water so I can swoosh them away as I walks along the edge of the water hoping I might see a fish I can ketch with my hands. Ever once in a while I drop to my belly and drink more water. I wishes so bad I had a can or a skin so I could carry water with me, but I don't, so all I can do is keep filling my belly until I can't hold another drop.

The mule tracks had come down to the crick too. I can see where she got herself a drink, and munched some of the tender grass, but since the little crick don't lead to the fort, she soon wandered back up on the prairie to find the trail to the fort. Just before dark I leaves the crick too, hoping the gnats and mosquitos will stay behind. After a while just a few of them were trying to eat me, and soon I scared all of them away with my swatter.

When it was too dark to see where I was putting my feet, I went to the middle of a tall stand of buffalo grass where I rolled up in a ball, on my side, my knees almost touching my chest, and tried to go to sleep. I warn't thirsty no more, but my stomach growled with hunger. I chewed on some grass, but it didn't take the hunger away. If only I was a cow or buffalo, then I could fill right up.

First I would lay on one side, then the other. Sometimes I would sleep a bit, but it ain't easy to sleep when you are outside and naked, even in the summer when it's warm. When I did doze off, I dreamed about Peggy, sitting so pretty by the stream with Flaxy and the squaws, or I would see Blue Fox and Hog Face killing Mister and Misses Mills, or Brace Johnson. Sometimes I see Blue Fox or the trappers coming to Peggy in the night, but I always wake up before they do anything.

As soon as the sky turned gray and the stars started to go away, I started walking again. Not only was I looking for soft places to put my feet, but I was looking for things to eat. I remembered how Tom and I had killed and eaten the rattlesnakes after Peggy had been carried off by the Injuns. But we had had Lucifer sticks so we could build a fire. If I found a snake now, I would have to eat it without cooking. I wondered if I would be able to do that. By the time the sun was high in the sky, I knew I would. I also knew I had to find some shade so I could keep my burning back out of the sun.

Just when I had about decided I would have to shade myself with tall grass, I found another one of them little cricks winding down a narrow valley, and the mule's tracks led right down there, but she wasn't there now. Before running to the water, I picked an arm load of the tall grass to carry with me.

It seemed like a paradise, except there were not coconut trees. There was brush to shade me from the sun, enough cool water to satisfy the thirst of a thousand buffaloes, and lots of green and black frogs that jumped in the water as I walked along the edge of the crick. I was surprised there warn't so many gnats and mosquitoes, maybe because the sun was high enough to make them hide, or maybe because there was an army of frogs to eat them up.

After filling my belly with the cool water, I crawled along the edge of the creek until I ketched me a big fat frog. His back was green and had big black spots, but his belly was white like the ones on cat fishes. I wished I had my bowie to slice him up, but I didn't. He kept trying to wiggle out of my hand, so I slapped the back of his head against a flat rock until he held still enough for me to chop him in half with the sharp edge of a long rock, right where the belly joined the tops of his legs. I throwed away the part with the head and belly, then carefully pulled the skin off the legs. It warn't too hard, just like pulling wet pants off a dead man, I reckon. There warn't very much meat on the legs, but it was firm, and light pink in color like rattle snake, with blue blood vessels running up and down. I bit off the biggest pieces, chewed and swallowed. If I lived through this, and anybody asked how raw frog tasted, I would say it was like chicken that hadn't been left in the pan long enough.

There was only a couple of small bites for me to get off that frog's legs, but I swear I could feel the strength from those frog muscles oozing into my muscles. Now I had more energy to do stuff. I ketched me more frogs, figuring out a better way to do it. Instead of crawling through the grass trying to grab them with my hands, I fetched a stick about as long as my leg and just swatted them like flies. It didn't matter if they was in the water or in the grass. They warn't fast enough to dodge the stick. Pretty soon I had thirty-two frogs spread out in the grass. I cut them in half like I did the first one, then pulled off all their pants. After eating half of them, I spread the rest out in the sun to dry, so I could take them with me when I went back up on the prairie. I didn't think I'd find any more places like this before I reached the fort so I wanted to carry some food with me.

I took a good nap, then began to play with the tall grass that I had brung with me. First I braided and tied a mess of it into a cape to cover my shoulders. There was a hole in the middle that I slipped my head through. Then I tied up a belt to go around my waist, with a clump of braided grass in front, and another in back. Now I wouldn't have to enter the fort totally naked, and I wouldn't be so embarrassed if I ran into some folks on the trail. Then I tried to braid up some grass into shoes. It warn't too hard, but when I tried to put them on and walk around, it didn't take very many steps before they come apart. I tried and tried, but just couldn't make a good slipper. Finally I gave up.

I takes another nap, and when I wakes up I felt even better. But the wind was blowin' now, and big black clouds was coming down from the north. That is, at first I thought they was clouds, but pretty soon I could smell them. They warn't regular clouds, but smoke clouds was coming from the north, on the wind. I runs out of my little valley to the prairie, and looks north. I cain't see nothin' burning, but the smoke looks awful thick off in the distance. I never seen so much smoke in all my years on the river. All I can figure is that the prairie is on fire, but I cain't see no flames. Now the grass up on the prairie is still mostly green, like in the spring, but it's a lot drier than just a few weeks ago because there hain't been no rain in a long time, but lots of wind to dry it out.

With my grass cap and cape and loin cloth I'm ready to march to the fort, but now I ain't sure. That prairie grass is thick and tall, and a fire driven by the wind might probably cook a body, especially one wearing grass clothes. I looked down where I had been taking a nap, where the frogs lived. There was lots of water there, and clover and green soggy grass, not the kind of place that could burn. I wanted to get to the fort awful bad to fetch the soldiers to save Peggy, but I had this sick feeling that if I got ketched by the fire, I might not get to the fort ever. I decided to stay close to the frogs until the fire passed or went out or whatever fires do out in the Injun territories.

I am curious to see what this fire looks like, so I stay up on the prairie, and walk towards the smoke, staying close to the edge of the little valley so I can get down there fast when I see the flames.

Then I think about the buffaloes, and how I'd heard stories how they stampeded in front of fires. I hain't seen very many, but there was sign everywhere; places where the grass had been cropped off, trails in and out of the valleys where the frogs lived, big dusty wallows where the bulls rolled and fought each other, lots of buffalo chips, mostly dry ones. Tom said there was millions of buffaloes in this country along the Platte River. I just hoped they warn't in front of the fire, stampeding in my direction because there warn't no trees in this entire land big enough to climb so a body could get away from stampeding buffaloes.

Tom said you could hear the ground shakin' afore you could see 'em, so I laid down and put my ear on the ground. I couldn't hear nothing, and I couldn't feel nothing, so I guessed if the buffaloes was stampeding, they warn't doing it anywhere close to me, so I kept walking and the smoke got thicker and thicker.

I warn't follerin' the mule tracks no more, but I knowed I warn't lost. The frog crick below me was a little bigger now, and I figured it had to be flowing somewheres, probably to the Platte River, since it was running north. I knew that because the setting sun was on my left side.

Because of the smoke I warn't able to see it clear, but I knowed it was there. If I just followed the little crick north, I would get to the river. Then all I had to do was foller it downstream until I got to Fort Laramie.

When it was almost too dark to see I headed down to the water to find a comfortable place to spend the night. I was happy to find that the gnats and mosquitos were so busy choking on smoke that they didn't want to bother me no more. It was a'gonna be a pleasant night, even though I knowed I wouldn't sleep much because I knowed that sooner or later the fire would come—unless the wind changed, or a big rain storm put it out, but there was so much smoke that I couldn't tell if there were clouds in the sky.

I chews me up a jaw full of frog meat, and tries to get some sleep. I had been dozing a long while, it seemed, when I opens my eyes and sees that the north part of the sky had turned mostly orange. The smoke was thicker than before, making my throat and nose sore, and it was still coming from the north. The fire had finally found me. I hiked to the top of the ridge to get a better look.

In the distance I could see the flames, like the tongues of a thousand monster dragons, racing towards me, licking up every dry thing in their path. It was hard to tell how big the flames were, but I guessed some of them were as high as a man's head, if he were sitting on a tall horse. I knew I couldn't outrun the fire, not in bare feet. And I thought that if I tried to run through it to get on the other side so it would be burning away from me, I would probably burn the skin off my feet, and maybe just burn up altogether. So I runs back down to the little crick. The light from the fire made it easy to see where I was going and what I was doing.

I finds a wide spot on the crick, where it is about a foot deep. There I sit and wait. I don't reckon the fire will burn the soggy grass and clover next to the crick, and I knows if I gets too hot, all I has to do was roll into the crick, and just stick my nose out ever once in a while when I need air. It is a simple enough plan, and it works just fine. When the fire is burning on both banks, right down to the edge of the soggy grass, I crawl into the cool water, and lay right down in it like a hog in a waller on a July afternoon.

Grass burns fast, and the big prairie fire came and went almost before I could make sense of it. And then fresh air was blowing in behind it, not nearly as smokey as before. I found me a soft place on the grass and tried to get some more sleep.

When morning came the fire and smoke had disappeared some-where far to the south. There was little fountains of smoke here and there where thicker bushes and sticks had ketched on fire, and was still burning, but the main fire had left. The rolling hills was black and scorched in every direction, as far as I could see. The land looked dead and black, and awful scary. I decided to stay by my little frog crick as I started north again.

Pretty soon I am distracted from my march, because I am seeing so many frogs jumping into the water as I walk by. I fetch me another stick, and started busting them. Almost before I knows it I has ketched forty more. When I don't reckon I can carry any more, I see a little bush by the edge of the hill that is still smoking. I goes over there and starts breaking off smoking twigs and branches, crowding them into a pile, and huffing and puffing until they starts burning. Now I have me a cook fire and I knows exactly what I wants to do with it. In a few minutes I am roasting frog legs on a stick. Now I have eaten raw legs and cooked ones too. The cooked ones is better. I ketches, cleans and cooks frogs until I am too tired to keep doing it. My belly is full too. I am a new boy, ready to travel. The wet, soggy grass next to the crick is the softest on my feet, so that's where I tries to walk.

Sometime in the afternoon I climbs to the top of the east bank to look over the prairie again, and I sees something there that I hain't seen before, a bunch of big burned bumps out on the ground where the grass had burned away. At first I reckon they is black rocks, but as I gets closer they looks more like a herd of sleeping buffaloes, not a lot, maybe ten or fifteen. I can see some horns, and what looks like feet sticked up in the air. As I walk closer I can see for sure that they are buffaloes, but they ain't sleeping because they is dead.

At first I reckon they has been caught and kilt by the fire, but as I walk among them it seems the skins on their backs has been burned right off, but there is still skin on their legs and faces. Then I sees a broken arrow shaft in one of them. Now I reckon them buffaloes had been kilt by Injuns who had skinned some of them, and taken meat from some, but left before getting all of it. Maybe the fire had chased them off. I look past the buffaloes, in every direction, but can't see no Injuns, or nothing that looks like an Injun camp.

If only I had my bowie, I thinks I could cut off some of that skin and make me some shoes. I could cut out a stomach and make a canteen to carry my water. If only I had a knife. Then I gets an idea. I hurries over to the one that has the broken arrow shaft in his side, and I pulls it out. Bless my good luck. The tip on the arrow ain't made from stone, but good old American iron. Some Injun with a coal chisel had stamped it out of an old barrel hoop, then filed the edges until they was sharp enough to shave a man's face.

I don't travel no more that day. By nightfall I have two new shoes, made from sleeves of shank skin from the hind legs of an old bull, turned inside out so the hair is on the inside. I ties up the fronts and backs with strips of skin. Now I can hike like a soldier, thinking that tough old bull skin hadn't ought to wear out any time soon.

I make me a hide cape to protect my shoulders from the sun, and to help cover me at night. A new skin belt around my waist holds up a piece of soft hide in front and behind, so if Peggy rides up now, I have no reason at all to be embarrassed. I have a loop of skin attached to both ends of a stomach so I can carry near a gallon of water with me. Now I don't have to stay by the crick if I don't wants to.

But best of all, I finds another smoking bush, breaks up the branches and soon have another fire making a happy crackly noise as I cooks a big chunk of buffalo hump meat which Brace Johnson told me was the very best thing a man could hope to eat out on the plains.

Earlier in the day I was thinking that roasted frog legs was probably the best thing a man could ever hope to eat, but after two swallows of hump roast, I didn't care if I never seed another frog as long as I lived. Brace was right. Take me to the queen's palace and set me on a golden chair at the grand buffet and I can't think of anything I'd ruther eat than a buffalo hump roast, medium rare. Only a little salt could make it better.

When I'm full, I lays strips of meat on sticks around the fire like I seen the squaws and Peggy do. Now I would have dried meat as well as water to take with me. I had saved myself. I was gonna live, unless some mean Injuns found me. It was time to start thinking about saving Peggy again. I reckon the fire didn't ketch her because those trappers would be traveling fast, wanting to get far away from them soldiers at Fort Laramie, in case I got there and told them where Peggy has gone.

I was marching a course that I reckon would get me to Fort Laramie the fastest. My canteen was full, strips of drying meat was hanging from my belt, and my new buffalo shoes was strapped on tight. I was thinking again of Peggy and what might happen between us once I got her saved.

I starts wondering how old I am. My pappy never told me. Was I a young boy who had no business thinking of a girl like Peggy? Or was I almost as old as she was, and maybe somebody she might fall in love with? I just didn't know. I wished pappy had told me when I was borned.

It warn't long until my new shoes and my legs below the knees was as black as if they had been smeared with axle grease. The ashes from the fire just made everything that touched it black. I was glad I had lots of water because the day seemed to be hotter than most, maybe it had something to do with sun burning down on the black earth. Everything was black and parched, no cool green meadows, no more.

Then I starts feelin' dizzy, tripping and stumbling a little bit. My head feels like it's on fire, and my stomach is gurgling. I throw up; once, twice, three times. I has to stop and rest more than is usual for a strong boy like me. I keep taking sips of the water in the stomach, but I cain't swallow the meat no more. After a while I ain't sure if I'm going in the right direction. The sun is in the middle of the sky so I cain't tell which way is north, but I just keep walking, sorta stumbling along. I reckon a smart man would stop until the sun was low enough in the sky to tell him which way to go. But I warn't smart no more. My head hurt so bad. My stomach sure had something rotten in it. My legs were shaking. I started falling down until I was black all over. If someone found me now they might think I was a run-away slave. Still, I kept stumbling along. Nothing made sense, not no more. Then I passed out.

Chapter 16

"He ain't no Injun, and he ain't no slave. His name is Huck, Huckleberry Finn. I knows him," were the words that wakes me up. The voice is familiar. It belongs to Tom Sawyer. I opens my eyes. It's Tom's face looking down at me. Other faces too. I ain't dead. I knows it because my head still hurts, something fierce, and my stomach is still gurgling like a hungry alligator, but I ain't hungry.

"He don't look like no white boy," says a man's voice.

I rolls over and starts throwing up again, but my stomach is empty, so nothing comes out.

"He's sick, we gotta doctor him," Tom says.

"We ain't stopping for no sick boy," the man's voice says. "Gots keep moving 'til we get out of the burn, no grass for the mules."

"Cain't just leave him here," Tom says, and I thinks amen to that.

"Chuck him in the possum belly," the man says. "When we gets to grass we can doctor him, maybe clean him up some. Gots to keep moving . . . Huaa," he yells and I can hear the creaking of a wagon starting to move.

Next I feels hands grabbing my hands and feet, but my eyes is bleary and I can't see the faces. I hear swearing and grunting as the hands roll me into the possum belly under a wagon that ain't started moving yet. Soon's I'm in there I feels the wagon move.

Folks who ain't been outside the nice towns of the United States might not know what a possum belly is. When pioneers and freighters travel long distances, sometimes they takes an old hide, punches holes in the four corners so's they can tie it under a wagon. As the folks travels along, and they finds some beautiful pine knots for the night fire, or shoots a varmint that needs skinnin' later on, or just want to pick up buffalo chips to burn, they throws all this stuff into the possum belly because they don't want to get the important truck up in the wagon all dirty. People don't generally ride in the possum belly, even though it might be the shadiest and coolest place around because it is also the dustiest, dirtiest place in the world, and sometimes the bottom of it bumps against rocks and stumps that come along in the middle of the road.

They throwed me in the possum belly, but I didn't much care, being so sick and all. I was just happy I warn't in the sun no more. I was so sick I didn't seem to breathe much anyway so the dust didn't do no harm. I kept thinking I don't want to die because then I wouldn't be around to save Peggy, so I try as hard as a body can to stay alive as the wagon bounces along.

Sometimes Tom crawls alongside, real fast, asking if I am still alive. I just grunts to let him know I am, even if just a little bit. Between those times I didn't know if I am sleeping or knocked out. Anything is better than being awake, feeling sick, swallowing dust and ashes and bumping against humps of dirt and rock in the road.

Then I wakes up and hears men and boys yelling. The wagon is moving fast now, bouncing me up against the bottom of the wagon as the possum belly springs up and down. If this goes on very long I guess I will sure die.

Finally, when the wagon slows down I feels and hears a soft, gentle scratching under the possum belly. We are in grass now--long, tall grass. I smells it. No more ashes. We have left the burned prairie. We stops, and the next thing I knows is Tom pulling me out of the possum belly. I hopes I never has to go in there again.

I am full of thankfulness to know I am still alive. My head don't hurt so bad, neither does my stomach. I'm not hungry, but I feel like I can swallow a river, that if I don't get a drink of water, a big drink of water, soon, I will die anyways.

I see Tom is reading my thoughts. He's standing beside me, a bucket of river water in his hand. He's asking some other boys if they knows were a cup is.

"Gimme the bucket," I says.

I am sitting with my back against a wagon wheel, so Tom, he just sets the whole bucket in my lap, and goes away. Someone is yelling at him to help unhitch some mules. The bucket is nearly full, and some of the water slops over the edge, the coolness spreading over my belly and tops of my legs. It feels good, like rolling off a log into the Mississippi River on a scalding hot day.

After a while I tries to lift the rim of the bucket to my lips, but it is too heavy, like a giant rock. I reckon it ain't really that heavy, I cain't lift it because my arms are so weak. So I starts rocking the bucket back and forth sloshing more cool, delicious water onto my chest. Finally I spills enough where I am able to lift the edge of the bucket to my lips, where I drinks a hundred tiny swallows until I can't get anymore inside me. Then I just closes my eyes and rests, waiting for the water to make me stronger.

When Tom finishes his chores, he comes and sits by me, and we talk. We can see some boys and a big man with a black beard by one of the other wagons. They have themselves a big fire, and are cooking up some supper.

Tom says the man is Mr. Peabody, a sergeant in the United States Army. The Army is going out west to put down a Mormon rebellion and put in a real guvnor over the Utah Territory.

"The Mormons is marrying all the wives they can ketch, and Sergeant Peabody says they kills anybody who disagrees with them," Tom explained. I asked Tom why he had joined up with the Army.

"With the new war out west, the Army don't have enough men to do the freighting," he explained. "Sergeant Peabody has to haul supplies for the rest of the Army, especially grain for the mules. Not enough soldiers to do the work, so he hires boys and slaves. But he says he will die before he hires an Injun or Chinaman. He pays me fifty cents a day, same as the other boys, and feeds us."

"Why you going further from the United States?" I asks. "Didn't reckon you wanted to see more Injuns."

"No I don't, not so long as I lives, unless it's a hanging, with Blue Fox as the guest of honor," Tom says. "But I figures I can't pass up a chance to see a real war. People say the big wars of the world are over, so this might be the only chance a boy like me will ever have to see a real war, even if it is only a little one against the Mormons. Peabody says when they ketches Brigham Young, Lott Smith and Dan Wells he is personally a'going to skin them with a rusty butcher knife. I just hope I gets to see it. Sergeant Peabody says some of the Mormon men grows horns on their heads. If I can get me a set of them I'd hang'm in my cabin some day, and be so proud to have them when the Mormons is gone, and everybody else wishes they had a set of horns too, but there are no more to be got."

"Maybe the Mormons won't fight," I says. "Maybe they will run to California or Mexico."

"They already started fighting," he says.

"You mean fighting and killing and stuff like that," I says.

"Not yet, but they are setting the prairie on fire so the Army mules won't have nothing to eat," he says. "They done burned some Army wagons, and stole some others."

After a while Tom helps me to my feet, and holds on tight as we ambles over to the fire. There's five wagons in a circle. Nice big mules are wandering around filling their mouths with grass like they hadn't eat anything in a week. After we sits down, Tom tells the other boys my name, but Sergeant Peabody don't seem interested. He never looks up from where he's chewing a big wad of tobacco while stirring a pot of boiling buffalo meat with beans and onions. It smells good and I hopes maybe I can have some. Tom tells me if I hurry and gets strong, he thinks Sergeant Peabody will hire me too at fifty cents a day, then I can watch the war between the Mormons and the Army too.

I am surprised that all Tom wants to talk about is the war with the Mormons. I never knowed any Mormons, and neither did he. He don't seem at all curious to know what happened to Peggy and Flaxy, so I says nothing.

Pretty soon Mr. Peabody starts scooping the food onto tin plates that has *U.S. Army* stamped on them. He looks like he's too fat to fit into his blue and yellow uniform. Some of the buttons has popped off his shirt where it cain't fit around his belly. His uniform is dirty from all the ashes, and the parts that ain't stretched tight against his skin are wrinkled. He has a thick, curly, black beard that covers his collar, and his coal lump eyes is too close together. He chews tobacco while he works, once in a while spitting a brown river of juice on the ground. His crooked teeth are yellow-brown from the chewing. The parts of his beard near his mouth are more brown than black.

After Sergeant Peabody fixes a tin plate for all of the other boys, he finally squints at me, a look on his face like he is trying to decide to bury me or feed me, and like he is still not sure that I am a white boy and not an Injun. Finally, he puts some food on a plate which he hands to Tom so he can give it to me.

"Thank you," I says to Sergeant Peabody when Tom hands me the plate. After all the water I feel stronger now, and pretty soon I am swallowing the food, and it tastes real good, and I can feel my arms and legs getting stronger with each bite. Some of the boys try talking to me, asking me to tell them what it's like to live like an Injun.

"Not bad," I says, "if you can eat frogs." I knowed from the looks on their faces that none of them had ever eat any frogs before.

After supper Tom takes me down to the river and helps me slip out of my buffalo skin cape and loin cloth. He orders me to get in the water and scrub off the ashes while he goes back to the wagons to find some real clothes. In a little while I am dressed in cotton pants, a wool shirt and a good pair of cowhide boots, and my wet hair is combed with a nice part in the middle. When we walks back to the wagons, Sergeant Peabody comes over and shakes my hand like he hain't seen me before, like I ain't the same boy they had tossed into the possum belly. After spitting out a puddle of brown juice by my feet, he says in a couple of days, when I don't need to ride anymore, he will give me some chores to do, and start paying me like the other boys. Of course, the cost of my new clothes will come out of my pay.

That night as we lay stretched out on wool blankets looking up at the prairie sky, I tells Tom about Peggy and Flaxy, how the trappers bought them from Blue Fox. Tom gets real fidgety when I tells him how Peggy promised the trappers she would stay with them for a season if they would let Flaxy go to Fort Laramie, and then how she promised to stay a second season if they let me go, after they ketched me.

"Brace was right," Tom says. "She is crazy, being ketched and violated up like that. She shoulda stabbed herself when she had the chance. Now she ain't worth saving."

I told him she didn't seem crazy to me, the last time I seen her, when she talked the trappers into letting me go. I said the honest truth was that I thought she was more worth saving than ever, after what she had done for Flaxy and me.

"When we gets to Fort Bridger I aim to find her and set her free," I says.

"She's been defiled," Tom says like he is the wisest boy in the whole world, like what he says makes what I say about Peggy not worth the air it takes to say it. I wants to beat him up, but knows I ain't strong enough to do it.

"At least I saved Jim," Tom says. He tells that when he went back to Blue Fox's camp with the soldiers, the girls was gone, but Tom argued until the soldiers agreed to free Jim from Injun slavery, and take him back to Fort Laramie.

"Old Jim, he was crazy like Peggy," Tom says.

"How do you mean?" I asks.

"He didn't want no soldiers setting him free. Them black-skinned folks talks all the time about being free, but when the chance finally comes they don't want it. Old Jim, he didn't want to come back to Fort Lamamie with us. He said he'd just like to stay there and scrape hides, if that was all right by us. But it warn't."

I remembered the last time I seen Jim, that night at Blue Fox's camp, and how that squaw had set herself down beside Jim and leaned her head on his big arm, and how Jim seemed so happy about it, like he just wanted to die for that squaw. He didn't much want to come away with me any more than with the soldiers.

"So what'ja do?" I asks.

"The lieutenant ordered him to come with us," Tom explains. "But he don't want to do it, so the soldiers wrassled him to the ground, tied up his hands and feet and throwed him over a mule. He wiggled and yelled halfway back to Laramie. Plumb crazy. I wonder what it is, living with Injuns, that makes folks go crazy, good folks like Peggy and Jim."

I didn't even try to answer his question because I didn't think Peggy was crazy, Jim either, so I asks, "Where is he now?"

"With the soldiers that's ketching up with us. He don't like it, but they made him make an X on a piece of paper so they could make him a cook in the United States Army. You'll get to see him in a day or two."

About this time I hear one of the other boys crying, under one of the wagons where he was supposed to be sleeping. I asks Tom what might be happening. Tom says:

"About every night the sergeant makes one of the boys sleep with him. He must hit them in his sleep, or roll on them by accident, because all of them start crying one time or another, like this one. The sergeant can't get me to sleep with him. I just won't do it."

"Me neither," I says.

We had to stop talking because it was Tom's turn to take the watch. All night the older boys took turns watching for Injuns who might want to steal our mules, or Mormons who might want to burn our wagons.

The next morning I asks Tom if he seen anything while standing watch.

"Just a bunch of stars," he says.

When I asks him if it was hard to stay awake, he said it warn't because he knowed what happened to boys who slept on watch. Sergeant Peabody tied them to wagon wheels, taked their shirts off, and cut lines on their backs with his bull whip. Tom didn't want no part of that. He said he stayed awake by walking around all the time, never sitting or lying down, because that's when old Mr. Sleep ketched a body. When I asked him if he had ever seen Mr. Peabody whip a boy for sleeping, he said he had, lots of times. I thought he might be stretching the truth some, but I said nothing.

The next day Sergeant Peabody put me to work oiling harnesses. The day after that he had me feeding grain to the mules, and oiling harnesses. By the fourth day I was harnessing and unharnessing the mules, giving them grain, and oiling harnesses. He told us boys to enjoy our vacation because one day soon the United States cavalry would ketch up with us and then we'd have a hundred more horses and mules to take care of.

Sometimes after supper old Peabody would put away his plug of tobacco, get out a bottle and start to drinking. After that it warnt long until he started cusin' the things he didn't like. He always started with the Mormons, damning old Brigham Young for making this war necessary and for marrying so many wives. Then he damned the plural wives for marrying Brigham Young, and Daniel Wells for sending men out to burn the prairie, and botherin' the United States Army. Then he'd curse Porter Rockwell, Lott Smith and Bill Hickman for carrying out the orders. Sometimes the sergeant would even curse the Army for sending him boys instead of men to drive his wagons and do his chores. He'd damn the Injuns too, for making him worry so much that he couldn't get a good night's sleep.

Sergeant Peabody sure was unhappy. I never seen him smile, not once. The way I looked at it, he shoulda been happy. He had a good job with the Army, and a bunch of good mules and wagons to be around every day, and he got to see a war where nobody would shoot him because all he did was haul supplies. The Army gave him a good life, and he sounded so miserable, like he just wanted to die. I warn't able to understand it. After awhile I quit trying.

The Army finally caught up with us like Tom and Sergeant Peabody said it would. It brung with it a bunch more wagons, cannons on wheels, a gang of hungry-looking Injun guides, and about seventy soldiers mounted on fine Missouri horses. It was a sight just watching them ketch up to us, but the most wonderful sight of all was at the end of the day when they would put up rows of sparkly white tents. They had a tent office for the officers, a tent for cooking where they cooked in a pot big enough to boil a whole hog, and they even had a tent where the men could drop their trousers and relieve themselves where nobody could see them. Them soldier boys made a beautiful city of white tents wherever we stopped, and they would take it down again the next morning.

The boss of the soldiers was a boy who didn't look much older than me. They called him Captain Price. His first name was Hawk, but nobody called him that. It seemed strange to me that a man so young would be boss of all the others. Tom explained why. Captain Price had gone to a special school for soldiers, called Point West. They made him a lieutenant the day he graduated, and six months later he was a captain. He had curly, blond hair, blue eyes, and there was no stubble on his face, even when he didn't shave. Some of the men didn't like the idea of a boy giving them orders, but there warn't nothing they could do about it. One of the soldiers said Captain Price would start crying for his mamma as soon as the Mormons started shooting at us.

The only soldier younger than Captain Price was the bugle boy who warn't as old as me and Tom. He played beautiful music which told the soldiers what to do. He had a song he called Taps which he played when it was time to go to bed, and another called Revalee which he played when it was time to get up. He had two songs when it was time to eat, one for the men and another for the mules and horses. The boy played a special song when the soldiers was supposed to line up for roll call, another when the wagons was to start rolling, and another when it was time to stop. Tom told me they had a song when they was supposed to charge in and kill Mormons, and another to tell them to run away, but I never heard those songs.

That bugle boy sure had a lot of songs to play, and I loved listening to every one of them, especially the one that told the horses and mules it was time to eat. The tame ones that we let out to graze because we knowed they would not run away, when they would hear that song, they would stampede up to the wagon where I was filling their feed bags, crowding around, snorting and whinnying, pawing the ground, happy as pigs in tubs of sour milk. The horses along the picket line made the same noises, every one of them looking at me with their big, happy eyes. They could hardly wait until I slipped on their bags. They loved me, every last one of them, and I loved feeding them, and listening to the bugle boy play the feeding song. I thought if I told the Army I was eighteen, maybe they would let me join up and do this the rest of my life.

The horses and mules that got tied to the long picket lines got to eat the hay and grain we brung with us, hay at night, oats in the morning. The ones we let graze outside just got oats in the morning. In addition to taking care of the animals, we still had to stand our watches at night. It was our job to watch the mules and horses. Sergeant Peabody insisted Injuns was watching us all the time, just waiting for a chance to steal horses and mules. He said now we were getting closer to the war, there was a greater chance of Mormons trying to steal our horses too. He said any boy who fell asleep now, might get hanged instead of whipped.

When the soldiers joined up with us, we had extra work but it was worth it because we got to eat with the soldiers. Me and the other boys were always last to eat because we had to take care of the horses first, but there was always plenty of food to fill us up—beef, pork, beans, potatoes, carrots, biscuits with real butter and strawberry jam, boxes of apples and buckets of hot coffee with all the sugar and honey you wanted to put in it. I had never eaten so good, not even when I stayed with Tom's Aunt Polly.

While I was loving the food, Tom was always looking for soldiers to talk to. They tells him they hopes to kill lots of Mormons, and how happy they is to get paid to do it. They gets to see the west too. Some talks about going to California to find gold and get free land when they gets out of the Army.

While Tom is talking to the soldiers, I usually takes my food with me to the cook tent were I can talk to Jim. He's not very happy. He says if he didn't think the soldiers would come after him, he's run away and go back to Blue Fox's camp. I just couldn't understand why he would want to be around a killer like Blue Fox. Jim tried to explain.

"Them Injuns nicer to old Jim than any white masser ever war, 'cept Huck Finn," he says. "Them Injuns talks to old Jim like I's a man, not a nigger. Even the squaws, 'specially that one you seed with me. Being with that lady beats cooking for a gang a white boys. Jim go back, after Mormons kill soldier boys."

I don't know what to say back to Jim, so I just listens, and keeps my mouth shut. I think it is interesting that he calls a squaw a lady. I never heard anybody call a squaw a lady before. The only lady I knows out in this wilderness is called Peggy. Jim sees the Injuns different than me and Tom and the Army sees them.

Before long Tom is so excited he cain't think of nothing to do 'cept lie about his age and join the Army so he can get one of them blue shirts, a new rifle with a sword that screws on the end so you can stab folks when you don't have time to put in more powder and lead. Tom says:

"They feeds you like a king, lets you sleep in a new tent, gives you a fancy horse and saddle, and pays you to shoot Mormons, Injuns and maybe some Mexicans too." The way he says it, I wonder if he believes that Mexicans and Mormons is people too, who have mothers who cry theirselves nearly to death when their boys get shot. If Tom knows it, he don't care even a little.

I told Tom that if I wanted to join the Army I wouldn't have to lie about my age because I doan know how old I was. If a boy needed to be eighteen to join, then I would say I was eighteen, and I wouldn't be lying because I don't know how old I really am, might as well be eighteen as any other age. Tom wanted me to join up right now, but I told him it would have to wait until after I found Peggy and set her free.

"And how will you do that?" he asks.

"Don't know," I says. "The trappers said something about going to Fort Bridger. If I go there and sniff around, somebody might have seen'm, then I'll figure out how to save her." I can tell by the twist in his mouth that Tom still thinks I am crazy for thinking Peggy is worth saving.

"Mary warn't married to Joseph when she had Jesus," I says, thinking I had heard something like that one time when I went to church with Aunt Polly. "And nobody's wanting to toss her out with the bath water."

"Mary was a virgin."

"Then so is Peggy," I says.

"You don't even know what it means," Tom says, sounding so high and mighty that I want to punch him. Instead I just tells him how I feels inside:

"When folks says Mary's a virgin, they say it like she's real special. That's how I sees Peggy, so I guess I'll just call her my Virgin Peggy, and if you don't care for that, we can just step outside and see . . ." I rolls my fingers into a fist. Tom kinda backs away. He don't want no fight, but he don't believe what I says, either. We just stops talking about it, and after that we don't talk about Peggy much at all.

But I think about her a lot, being with them trappers and all, thinking she be locked in by promises she made to save Flaxy and me. I figure the time will come when she will have to break them promises, even if it means me killing them trappers. They deserve it, for sending me out naked on the prairie to die. They'll be sorry. I'd see to it.

By this time, my wages had paid for my new clothes, and I was saving every quarter, hoping to buy me a rifle, knife and maybe even a horse or mule when we gets to Fort Bridger. That's when I reckon I'll leave my work with Sergeant Peabody, and go after Peggy. In the meantime we was getting closer to Fort Bridger every day. The Army food and hard work was putting new muscles on my skinny body. I was feeling good, and getting stronger every day.

We is following the Sweetwater River now, 'stead of the North

Platte, and some days we pass wagon trains, mostly families heading for
Oregon or California. Some of their wagons are pulled by ox teams
which walk real slow, so we just go right on around them, waving to the
folks who is driving the teams or walking along on the ground.
Sometimes one of the boys will ride over on a horse and talk for a while.
I thinks of Mr. and Mrs. Mills and their fine strapping boys and how Blue
Fox killed them all, and hope these families will have a safer journey, and
I think they will because there are so many of them, in large bunches,
and there's so many soldiers on the road that I think the Injuns are too
scared now to kill folks, though they might steal a horse or two.

One day we seen a wagon train very different from all the rest. The
wagons were real little, and had only two wheels, one on the right and
one on the left. Instead of being pulled by mules or oxen, they was pulled
by people, mostly men, but sometimes the older boys and big girls was
pulling them too. Tom said they were Mormons, too poor to own mules
and oxen, going to Great Salt Lake City. The little wagons they called
hand carts. Many of the hand cart pioneers had froze to death in winter
storms the year before, near the headwaters of the Sweetwater.

When some of the Mormons saw us staring at them, they waved at
us. Sergeant Peabody yelled back at them, telling them to go straight to
hell, and to stay away from our wagons. He yelled at them that if they
saw us coming back from Salt Lake in a few weeks, they should come
over and he would show them Brigham Young's scalp. Then he laughed
real loud, and squirted a big stream of tobacco juice towards them.

That same evening, finishing my chores early, I wandered over to the
cook tent to see Jim while he helped fix supper. He was sitting on a box,
cleaning potatoes, and throwing them into a big wash tub on the ground.
There was a pile of boxes behind where he was sitting, and some big
barrels the other side of the wash tub where he was throwing the potatoes. I found me a place to sit on one of the barrels. Jim is still not very

happy about the soldiers taking him from the Injun camp.

We are just sitting there, talking about nothing in particular, when Sergeant Peabody comes along, looking mad as ever, his eyes on the ground, chewing on a big wad, mumbling something about the "damn Mormons." It just so happens, with them barrels on his right, and the boxes on his left, old Jim is blocking the way to get through, so Sergeant Peabody orders old Jim to get off his "black ass" and clear a path.

I look at Jim, expecting him to jump up and get out of the way, as all good slaves is supposed to do. But he don't do it. He just keeps cleaning spuds, looking down at his work.

Peabody stops. I see his face turning red, and he is chewing as fast as I ever seen him chew, on a very big wad. He calls Jim a "black turd" and to get the hell out of the way. Jim just keep cleaning spuds, like he don't even hear, but I know he hears every word, and I know there's going to be big trouble real fast. I jumps down from my barrel and starts backing away.

I think Sergeant Peabody is getting ready to kick old Jim right off that box. Instead, I see the sergeant's mouth pucker up as he pushes all the juice he can find to the front of his mouth. Then he squirts a brown stream right at the side of Jim's face. But Jim ain't just looking at spuds, he sees it a coming, so he moves his head at the last minute. The brown stream goes into the wash tub where he has been throwing the potatoes.

Peabody's right boot shoots forward, aimed at Jim's ribs, but the sergeant is too slow. Jim grabs the boot as he explodes out of his crouch, forcing the sergeant to fall over backwards. Jim is on top of him, fists flying, smashing into the sergeant's face and ribs. Peabody starts yelling. Other soldiers yell back. Pretty soon five or six soldiers are jumping on top of Jim and wrassling him away from the sergeant. In a minute they are holding Jim on the ground, and he ain't trying to get up no more. Peabody gets up, holding his jaw with one hand, and brushing dirt off his clothes with the other. His mean eyes are on Jim.

I am so surprised at what Jim has done. It ain't like a peaceful old slave with a tender heart like Jim's to stand up to a mean white man. A slave'd likely get killed for what he just done. He shoulda said, "Yassir," and jumped out of the way, like he always done before when things like this came along. I didn't reckon being free would change a gentle human being like Jim. But it had. If old Miss Watson handed him her chamber pot today, and told him to wash it out, this new Jim might just look her straight in the eye and tell her to do it herself. I wondered if all those abolitionists knowed what they was getting into by wanting to set free all them nice friendly slaves.

I said I was surprised at Jim, but I was also glad he showed some pluck. Peabody was a mean man. A boy had no choice but to let him be mean. But a strong man like Jim didn't have to take it, even if his skin was black and he had been a slave. When he was a slave Jim was a good man, but now he was a strong man, too. Being free had done that, I reckon.

"Tie him to that wagon wheel," Peabody hisses. The soldiers drag Jim over to the wagon and start to tie him up. Peabody orders another soldier to go fetch his bull whip. When Jim is tied up tight, the soldiers move out of the way so Peabody can go to work with his whip. Jim is looking straight into Peabody's eyes like he don't even care if he gets killed.

Just when the sergeant is going to start the whipping, everybody gets real quiet.

"Hold up there," a voice yells from beyond the wagon. It's Captain Price who is hurrying towards us to see what is happening.

"The nigger jumped me and tried to whup me," Peabody explained. The anger was mostly gone. His voice sounded cool and collected.

Captain Price looked at Jim, then says he wants to know who threw the first blow.

"He did," Peabody says, pointing at Jim.

"Is that right?" Captain Price says to Jim, who says:

"Yassir."

"Then proceed with the whipping," the captain says, stepping back to watch. Peabody shakes out his whip.

"Wait a minute," somebody says. It's me. I can't believe I am getting in the way of Army business. I feels as scared as when Blue Fox and his boys were killing the Mills family.

"Speak up," the captain says. So I does:

"Jim didn't jump on him until after Sergeant Peabody spit tobacco juice on your supper."

It takes a minute for the captain to understand what I am saying. Finally, he asks Sergeant Peabody if the boy is speaking the truth.

"It warn't that way," Peabody says, his face getting red. The captain looks back at me to see what I have to say now.

"Look for yourself," I says. "Your supper is right there." I points to the tub where Jim was throwing the spuds. The captain walks over to the tub, bends over and carefully inspects the spuds. Then he grabs the tub with both hands and dumps all the potatoes out on the ground. After he slams down the tub he orders Sergeant Peabody to get out of his sight, that he doesn't want to see him at the mess tent until after we crosses the continental divide, that until then the sergeant can eat oats with his mules. Price then tells two of the soldiers to untie Jim, who goes over to the potatoes by the mess tent and starts picking them up so he can wash them clean. All he says to me is, "Thanks, Huck."

I don't know why they called the place where they fixes the food the mess tent. There warn't no mess there, just lots of food in boxes, bags and buckets, rows of shiny pans that were always washed right after being used. The trash and leftovers was hauled off and dumped in a gully right after supper and breakfast. The mess tent was the cleanest and neatest place one could go and still be outside. There warn't no mess at all, so it just didn't make sense them calling it the mess tent. When I asked Tom to explain it to me, he said I asked too many questions.

That night I waited as long as I could before going back to my wagon to sleep. I hoped I could just roll up in my blankets and not do anything, or see anybody else until sunup.

It doesn't seem like I was rolled up in my blankets very long at all when Sergeant Peabody kicks me in the back, telling me I gotta stand a double watch because some of the boys are sick, and he cain't find Tom. I warn't surprised. I just knowed something like this would happen. I'm wondering what I could have done different so I didn't become Peabody's enemy. He kicks me again. I finally gets up, rubbing my eyes while I's doing it.

To my surprise he hands me a rifle, telling me it's loaded.

"We's in Mormon country now," he says. "They've been burning Army wagons, and stealing others. The captain says they might try to take some horses. You see they don't." He acts like he ain't even mad at me, that this is just normal business, but I know he is mad, and I better be careful because he intends for me to pay a terrible price. I takes the rifle and walks towards the picket line.

The horses and mules are munching quietly on their hay. It's a quiet night, no wind and no clouds. After a long day in the saddle the soldiers has gone to bed. The bugle boy has played Taps, his last song of the day. I cain't stop yawning as I walk back and forth in front of the happy horses and mules. They worked the hardest, carrying their loads and soldiers, but they didn't want to sleep much, just munch happily on their food. I wished I was like a horse and didn't need to sleep either.

The next morning everyone was talking about getting to the Continental Divide. Captain Price says that when we gets there we will stop and have some lunch while we looks at it. I warn't sure what we would be looking at. I didn't know what this Continental Divide really was. I kinda figured it was a line of some sorts, dividing the east part of the country from the west, but I didn't know if it was a line somebody drawed, or a fence, and whether it was red, or green or black. Or maybe is was just a big crack in the earth that went from Canada to Mexico. We hadn't stopped to have lunch at Chimney Rock so I guesses this was something more to see than that. Tom was driving another wagon, so I couldn't ask him to explain it, so I decided to just wait until we got there.

When we finally stopped I looked around and couldn't see nothing worth looking at, just a big gentle sage brush hill with wagon tracks over the top of it. We had crossed a hundred just like it the past week. I looked real close at the ground and couldn't see any kind of line or crack.

Pretty soon Tom wanders over, so I asks him to show me the Continental Divide.

"It's over there," he said, pointing to the flattest part of the hill.

"All I sees is sagebrush," I says.

"It don't mean it ain't there just because Huck Finn cain't see it," he says like he is the smartest boy in the world.

"Then why did we stop to look at it, if we cain't see it?" I asks.

When Tom hesitates, I decides he don't know no more about the Continental Divide than I do. About this time Captain Price rides by, so I says:

"Captain, sir, we don't know what a continental divide is, so we cain't see what we stopped to look at."

He stops his horse, and smiles at me, not the kind of smile that says Huck Finn is stupid, but a smile that says he is amused and pleased that I says what I says. He tells me and Tom to get down from the wagon and follow him. He rides over to the flattest place on top of the sage brush hill. He calls for the rest of the wagon drivers and some of the soldiers to join us.

When everybody is there, he puts his hands on my shoulders and turns me around until I am facing straight west. He tells me not to move. Then he puts his hands on Tom's shoulders and pushes him right up against me, back to back, him facing east, and me still facing west. Then he says to everybody who can hear him:

"I know some of you don't know what the Continental Divide is, and are afraid to ask. But Huck here asked, so Huck and Tom are going to do a demonstration so all of us will remember for the rest of our lives the exact meaning of Continental Divide." Some of the boys are looking at me and Tom like we are smart like the captain, not knowing that we cain't even guess what is about to happen. Then the captain says: "Huck and Tom, undo your trousers and wet the weeds in front of you."

Tom and me had been driving our wagons all morning without a break, so wetting the weeds would be easy to do, but still we hesitated, thinking we might be on the receiving end of some kine of prank, that this nice captain was going to make us fools.

"Undo your trousers," the captain repeated. "This is a serious geography lesson. Unleash the flood gates."

I knowed as men gets older the power of their stream when wetting weeds drops off until it is no more than a trickle between their toes, but me and Tom are healthy boys with strong insides, the power to squirt the weeds five or six feet in front of us, so that's what we did. We warn't embarrassed neither, because there warn't no women around. When we are finished, and has buttoned up our trousers, the captain says:

"The Continental Divide is an imaginary line of ridges and mountains where the east-flowing drainages of the continent meet the west-flowing drainages. Huck's discharge will seep through the ground until it joins the headwaters of the Green River which eventually dumps into the Colorado or Grand River which dumps into the Pacific Ocean. Tom's discharge will join the headwaters of the Sweetwater River on its way to the Platte, then the Missouri, then the Mississippi River before dumping into the Gulf of Mexico which joins the Atlantic Ocean. All water in front of Huck goes to the Pacific, all water in front of Tom goes to the Atlantic. The Continental Divide is theoretically located exactly where their backs touch. Any questions?"

Nobody gots any questions, but as I looks down at where my water has soaked into the ground, I has a hard time believing it is running to the Pacific Ocean to put a yellow stain on a whale's belly. Still, I thinks I understands what the captain has learned us. Still I wishes the Continental Divide was a line you could look at.

After standing two watches the night before, I sure was glad my mules were content to follow the wagon in front of me, allowing me to doze with the reins in my hands. I just wished the wagon seat had a back to it so I could get some serious sleep.

That evening I hurried through my chores, wolfed down a fast supper, then headed for my blankets. I was sleeping so soundly when the bugle boy played Taps that I didn't even hear it. But I did feel the friendly boot against my ribs. It was Sergeant Peabody again, kicking me out of my blankets so I could stand watch. I reminded him that it warn't my turn, that I had done it the night before, but he warn't about to change his mind for the boy who got him in trouble with the captain. Rubbing my eyes, I picked up the rifle and headed over to the picket line.

The only way for me to stay awake was to keep walking. It seemed to help if I talked to the horses and mules, asking if they like their grain, would they want more sugar next time, or should I cook it longer, and pour on a little cream or dried apples. As I walked along, talking to the horses, I believed my watch would be over in a few hours, that some of the other boys would relieve me in the middle of the night, which was our usual way of doing the watch, but the sergeant had different ideas. No relief came. When I realized this, I knowed I had to figure out a way to outsmart the sergeant. I couldn't stay awake two nights in a row.

Each time I reached the far end of the picket line, I looked more closely at some bags of grain that had been placed there for the morning feeding. I reckoned no one would see if I laid down on the bags of grain and went to sleep. I would allow myself to sleep only half an hour. That would be enough, then I would be able to stand watch the rest of the night. There was no other way that I could see to get out of this mess, so I stretched out on those big, soft pillows of grain and went to sleep.

The next thing I remember is the familiar kick of the sergeant's boot against my ribs. My eyes opened. It was light, but the sun warn't up yet. He had caught me sleeping on watch, I knowed I was in big trouble, that there was no way I could talk myself out of a whipping tied to a wagon wheel.

It wasn't until Peabody grabbed me by the collar and jerked me to my feet that I realized I was in much deeper trouble than I had ever been in before. The horses and mules were gone, all of them, even the tame ones we had let out to graze. I could see where their tether ropes had been cut by Mormons or Injuns, probably Mormons. I had slept through it all. There were no mules to pull the wagons, and no horses to carry the soldiers. We were at war, I had slept through my watch. It was my fault the animals were gone. I hoped for a whipping, but feared my punishment might be a bunch worse than that.

Without a word Peabody dragged me back to the wagons, and had me gagged and tied to one of the big wheels. He disappeared for a minute, then returned, not with his whip, but with two soldiers carrying rifles.

He informed the other boys that I was about to be shot. The two soldiers positioned themselves about twenty feet from me, and started checking their loads and primers. I couldn't believe I was about to die, and there was nothing I could do about it. The rest of the boys just stood in a wide half circle, wide-eyed and unbelieving. Except Tom, who yells:

"Wait, wait. This ain't right. It says in the military handbook that only the commanding officer can order executions."

I didn't think Sergeant Peabody had been around Tom enough to know Tom was the best liar and bluffer in the world. I am sure Tom has never even seed any military handbook, but he sounds like he knows more than a general, and maybe Peabody will believe him. I am amazed at what the sergeant says.

"You're right, Tom. But since the captain went out with some scouts last night, looking for Mormon campfires, and hasn't returned, I guess I am the one in charge until he gets back, and since we are at war, I order this execution, and any man who challenges my authority will be put in chains."

The two soldiers starts looking at their rifles again. I figures any second a'going die. But Tom, he ain't about to give up. He says:

"It says on page thirty seven, section c, that a condemned man should be given a last request, if at all possible. Every commanding officer knows that. Sometimes a prisoner wants something special to eat, like a big bowl of bread pudding. Maybe he wants to talk to a priest, or have somebody write to his mother, to tell her he's sorry he ran away to join the Army."

Tom was the best liar I ever knowed, but I wasn't sure where he was headed. The strange thing was that the sergeant was hesitating because of Tom's words. Seeing his words are hitting a mark, Tom walks over to me and removes the gag from my mouth. Then he says loud enough for everyone to hear:

"What is your last request?"

I sure ain't hungry, and I don't know what else to request 'til Tom whispers to me:

"Think of something that takes a lot of time. We gotta stall until the captain gets back. He won't kill a boy who ain't enlisted up yet."

I try to think of something that takes up time. I cain't think of something good, so I says:

"I want to hear the bugle boy play all his songs." Tom repeats what I say so everybody can hear. Someone runs to get the bugle boy. Sergeant Peabody is scratching his chin like maybe he is figuring out that Tom's been lying. When the bugle boy comes the sergeant says I gets to hear only one song, not all of them. The bugle boy comes over and asks which one I wants him to play. He is crying, knowing I am about to die.

I takes a long time deciding, hoping all the time that the captain will ride up and save me. Someone said he had gone off to the north, so I looks that way, hoping to see him riding back, but I cain't see nobody. My time is running out and I don't know what to do about it. Finally, the sergeant says I must pick a song now, or he will pick one for me, and he will pick Taps because that is the shortest one. So I asks the boy to play the song he plays for the mules when it's time to get their oats. I don't know how long it is, only that I like it the best, because it makes the horses and mules so happy.

The bugle boy wipes away his tears and plays the song, nice and loud and slow, but he ain't slow enough, because when he is finished, I still cain't see no sign of the captain. Tom tells him to play it again, but as soon as he starts, the sergeant makes him stop. It's time for me to die. The two soldiers with the guns checks their balls and powder again. Tom is jumping up and down like he just can't stand what is about to happen, like he is trying to talk, but don't know what to say.

Then somebody says they sees some dust. Maybe the captain is hurrying back. But the dust is in the road to the west, and the captain went north. Someone says that maybe the Mormons is coming to get us, now we don't have any horses to get away on. Everybody keeps watching the dust, not knowing what else to do until they knows who was coming.

Well, it warn't the captain, making all that dust, and it warn't the Mormons either. It's our horses and mules. They heard the bugle boy's song and got away from the men who stole them, and are running home for breakfast. But there's more horses than got away. Some of the new horses have saddles on them.

I learned later that when the Mormons who stole our animals stopped to wet the weeds, that's when the bugle boy blew his horn. Them Army mules warn't about to miss breakfast, so they starts the stampede back to camp. The Mormons' horses, hoping there might be enough oats for them too, pulls away from where they has been tied and joins the Army stock. The boys who were watching me a minute ago are now running down the picket line to the big bags of oats which they starts pouring on the ground so the horses and mules will have a snack while they are being ketched. Even Sergeant Peabody runs to help.

By the time all the animals are tied up and fed, the captain comes riding into camp. He hasn't seen all the business with the animals, so the first thing he does is ask Peabody why I am tied to a wagon wheel. The sergeant says all the animals was stolen while I was on watch, and he had ordered me shot.

"How many animals are missing?" the captain asks.

Peabody don't know the answer, so he sends some boys to count. When they returns, they says all the animals is here, plus twelve new ones.

"Don't know if I want to shoot a boy who increased the size of our herd," the captain says. It was clear now he don't want them to shoot me. He tells one of the boys to cut me loose. The sergeant says he don't want no boy working for him who sleeps on his watch. The captain tells him he can fire me, but he can't shoot me. So he fires me, right there.

The captain then asks if I want to enlist and become a solder now he has new horses to increase the size of his cavalry. I tell him I would like to ride with him, but I have personal business at Fort Bridger. He tells Tom to rustle me up a sack of food, but not to give me a horse. He says I can hitch a ride with any of the wagon trains we'd passed in the last week, and they'll take me where I want to go.

An hour later the Army is moving west, leaving me alone in the middle of the road. I'm happy they didn't shoot me, but it worries me to be alone again. I finds me a hiding place in some bushes where I can ketch some sleep while waiting for a wagon train to come along.

Chapter 17

I don't know how long I sleeps, but it seems to be late in the day when I hears voices of people talking, English, so I knows they ain't Injuns. But I don't hear the creaking of big wagons, and the noises made by horses in harness. Then I see a hundred or so of those little two-wheeled wagons coming down the road, being pulled and pushed by men, women and children. Some of them are singing. I watch them from my hiding place until they start to make camp for the night, not very far away. I know they are Mormons, and that the Mormons are at war with the United States, but these Mormons don't look very dangerous. In fact they look very tired from pushing those wagons all day long. I gets up and walks among them until I find a boy about my own age. I find out he is named Heber, and starts asking him questions:

"You folks headed to Fort Bridger?" I asks.

"Great Salt Lake City," Heber says. "If Fort Bridger is along the way, I suppose we'll stop there, but we don't have any money to buy anything."

I explained that I had been driving wagons for the Army that had passed them a few days earlier, but had quit my job. I asked him what had happened to the wagon train we had passed, the one I thought was between the Army and the handcarts.

Heber said they had passed the wagon train that morning. He said the handcart companies were faster than most wagon trains because they didn't have to spend so much time taking care of animals. He said their little carts were light and fast, and when the people had good weather, food and shoes it warn't nothing to cover fifteen or twenty miles in a day.

He said two of the ten handcart companies the previous year had started too late, been caught in winter storms, and many people had died. The company the boy was with had started plenty early to avoid a similar disaster. I asked him if he thought it would be all right for me to travel with them as far as Fort Bridger. I told him I was not a Mormon. Heber told some men about what I wanted to do. They asked me a lot of questions, then held a meeting to decide what to do.

Finally, they told me I could travel with the handcart company if I would help push the cart of a woman whose husband had died. But they would not be able to take me to Fort Bridger because Jim Bridger had turned against the Mormons to help the Army. They would take me to Brigham Young's new trading post, Fort Supply. From there I could find my way to Fort Bridger, which they didn't reckon to be very far from there. The arrangement seemed fine with me. They told Heber to introduce me to Sister Alice Jensen, and her daughter Kristina, maybe a little bigger than Flaxy.

We found them huddled over an open fire, trying to cook their supper. They was too tired and hungry to give me a warm welcome. In fact Sister Jensen, that's what the other Mormons called her, didn't even shake my hand. The daughter, Kristina, smiled kindly, and welcomed me to their camp. It wasn't until Heber left that I noticed what they was cooking for supper. Ash cakes, the kind I had seen the Injuns make–dough made from flour and water squeezed by hand into pancakes and placed on the hot coals of a fire. Upon my arrival the mother had placed a third cake on the fire so I could eat with them. The ash cakes was mostly without flavor, no salt or sugar. They was hard to chew, and had grit in them from being cooked on the ground. We washed them down with water from the Green River.

I was wondering if there might be some frogs around, when I remembered the gunny sack of supplies the captain had given me. Heber had thrown it in the Jensen's hand cart about the time he introduced me to them. I retrieved the bag and looked over the contents, then asked Sister Jensen what she had planned for dessert. She just looked at me, deciding my question was not worthy of an answer. When I tossed a can of peaches into her lap, she stared in amazement, then began to cry as Kristina began to clap her hands and squeal.

They didn't have any kind of tool to open the can, so I did it with my knife, sipped off some of the juice, then watched with pleasure as the mother and daughter slurped up the peaches and juice like two hogs at a trough. I left them alone to clean up every last drop because I knew what it meant to be hungry like that. After all I was the boy who had chewed on raw frogs to stay alive.

The next morning I fried up some bacon, and was surprised when Sister Jensen said she wanted to cook the ashcakes in the bacon drippings instead of on the fire. When I told her the cakes would get soggy in the grease, she said bacon drippings was too precious to waste. We ate every last drop, all soaked up in the ash cakes.

By the time the sun came up we were on the trail, moving our hand-carts along as fast as a body walks down the road. I was in front, pushing against the front bar. Sister Jensen and her daughter took turns pushing from behind. If we had to go up a hill, both of them pushed. If we were going down a hill, they just let me guide the cart all by myself. Pushing the hand cart was easier than I thought it would be. We began passing slower carts, some being pulled by big strong-looking men. By mid afternoon we were in front. Slowly I realized the reason for our advantage. Thanks to the rations the captain had given me, we had more energy because we done had a better supper and breakfast. The rest of the people had had little more than ashcakes. I began to feel ashamed of myself for showing off how strong I was, passing everybody on the trail.

That evening as Sister Jensen was cooking our ashcakes, I noticed that half a dozen children gathered around to watch. They had heard about the peaches the night before, and smelled the bacon at breakfast. They didn't come to beg because they had been taught that was wrong. They just wanted to watch someone eat something better than ashcakes.

I fished around in my sack until I found a large can of black olives. As I began to open the can Sister Jensen cautioned me not to pour off the juice. Everybody knowed you was supposed to pour off the juice when you opened olives, but not if you are in a Mormon handcart company. Every drop of juice was to be swallered too. Sister Jensen poured it in a cup and gave each of the children two sips before we had any. I then gave each of the children three olives and sent them away. We ate the rest with our ashcakes.

After supper, Sister Jensen asked if I would join them for their evening prayer. I remember how Aunt Polly had told me that if I prayed for the things I wanted, God would give them to me. That night I had knelt by my bed and asked God for a new knife, some fishhooks, a Hawken rifle, a fast horse with a new saddle, and a spy glass. The next morning when I looked around the room, none of the stuff was there. When I looked outside there was no horse either. I didn't pray much after that, figuring that if I couldn't get what I wanted by myself, God warn't about to get it for me. Maybe he might get stuff for other folks, but not for Huck Finn. I told Sister Jensen that I would join them in prayer if I didn't have to do the praying. She agreed.

All three of us kneeled down on the blankets next to the handcart. I figured it would be a real short prayer because these poor folk didn't have much to thank God for. Their husband and father had died about five hundred miles ago, they was nearly out of food in the middle of a wilderness full of mean Injuns, winter was coming, and they wanted to go to a city where they didn't know nobody.

Sister Jensen starts right out thanking God for good old Huck Finn who brung them peaches, olives and bacon, and who pulls their hand-cart for them. Then she thanks God for our warm fire, the beautiful river we got to walk beside all day, the blue sky, the majestic mountains we get to see, the fresh air, the clean water in the river, and that we have ashcakes to keep us alive. Just listening to her one might reckon this Sister Jensen was so smothered in blessings she might just be crushed from the burden of it all.

Then she asks God to bless Huck Finn for his goodness, to give him wisdom and strength to protect him from evil men, to give him the righteous desires of his heart. Now she had my attention. There was only one righteous desire in my heart, and that was to save Peggy. A good woman with more faith than food was asking God to help me do it. Her words touched my heart, just a little.

The next morning I cooked the last of the bacon, and an extra ash cake in the bacon grease because I could see more children gathering around. When I gave them each a little piece, all soaked up in pig fat, you'd think from the happy looks on their faces I was giving them gizzards soaked in butter.

As we was getting ready to begin the day's march, a thin, mostly bald man asked if he could speak to me for a minute. He said the unborn baby in his wife's belly was using up so much of her energy that he didn't think she could continue with the group another day. He guessed the hopeless feeling of being left behind, might cause her to stop fighting and die. He said he boiled up some dandelions and wild onions every few days to go along with the ash cakes, but it warn't enough. He bowed his head and said he knew it was wrong to beg, but he wanted to know if there was anything in my bag I might spare to save a woman's life, and probably the life of her baby too. I felt so bad I wanted to give him the whole bag. Instead I reached inside and handed him a can of beans and pork. He said he would pray to God to help me achieve the righteous desires of my heart. Two people were now praying for God to help me save Peggy. Even though I had never much believed in prayer, I reckon I could feel a growing confidence, deep inside, that somehow things would work out for Peggy.

As we pushed the handcarts down the road that day, I no longer wanted to pass people who were going too slow. We just stayed in our place in the line, resting when the carts in front were going too slow. I watched the people more, and decided there was nowhere else in the United States where you could put together a group of this many people, old and young, male and female, where all of them, especially the women, would be so skinny. Nobody had any fat on them, not a good thing with winter coming. There just warn't enough food to go around. These were poor people who couldn't afford teams and wagons, and hadn't spent enough on food either.

The captain had put enough food in my sack to get me to Fort Bridger, but now I was sharing it with hungry Mormons, the food would be gone long before reaching the fort. I reckoned maybe I ought to set out on my own, and not cast my lot with the Mormons no more. After all, I didn't share their faith, even though they prayed for me to achieve the righteous desires of my heart.

By the next afternoon I had about decided to set out by myself. I hadn't seen any Injuns in a long time, so I figured I would be safe enough. That's when we caught up with the Army company under Captain Price. They should have been getting further and further ahead of us, instead we had caught up with them. It seems some Mormons stole some of their horses again, and this time the bugle call hadn't brung them back. They could travel only about half as many miles in a day now, and that's how it would be until more horses arrived. We passed the Army tents, then camped about a mile down stream.

That night after everyone was bedded down, I dumped the

remaining contents of my gunny sack into the handcart, then, with the empty sack tucked under my arm, I sneaked back to the Army camp. I knew the night guards would be watching the picketed animals and supply wagons, so I snuck into the camp from the other side, and headed straight for the mess tent. The bugle boy had already played Taps and, except for the lookouts, everyone was in their blankets. The cook wagon that carried all the pots and pans and cook stuff was parked next to the mess tent, and I knowed they had Jim sleep under the cook wagon so he could keep an eye on things.

"Jim," I says, poking his blanket, "wake up. It's me, Huck."

"Land-o-goodness," he says, rolling out of his blankets. He wrapped those big powerful arms around me and squeezed like I was his lost child finally come home.

"You done freed Miss Peggy yet?" he asks.

"No," I says, "got to get to Fort Bridger first 'cause that's where them trappers took her."

"After that, you comes to free ol' Jim," he says.

"But you's already free."

"I was, but ain't no mo," he says. "Me put X on paper, now property of Army. If I runs away they shoots me."

I told him I would find a way to get him out of the Army after I had saved Peggy. I said I was traveling with the Mormon handcarts, but some of the people were near starving, and my supplies were about gone.

"You waits here," Jim says, as he rolls out from under the wagon and disappears into the mess tent. A minute later he returns and gives me a side of bacon and a 20-pound bag of rice. I tucks it all in my sack and sneaks out of the Army camp. I runs all the way back to the handcart camp. The next morning everybody fills up on bacon and rice soup. Everybody is feeling so good they thinks we might have a twenty-mile day, but I tells them that if we don't get too far in front of the Army, there's a good chance I might find some more food like we had for breakfast.

The next time I sneaks in to see Jim he gives me a bag of rice and a bucket of dried apple slices. By the time the handcart folks eats all that up, around every campfire they is praying that Huck Finn will have the righteous desires of his heart. I figure if prayer does any good at all, Peggy is as good as saved. I try not to think much how I am a thief.

The Mormons now are always thanking me for the food, patting me on the back like I am the best feller ever. The children follow me around, like I am a great warrior or the best ball player in the world. I reckon I am starting to feel real important, and I like having so many people loving me more than my pap ever did.

One night after supper, Sister Jensen, a big smile on her face, starts in again on how wonderful I am, and suddenly I have heard enough, because I knows that deep inside I am not the wonderful boy she thinks I am. I lie. I am lazy. I don't like going to church or reading the Bible. And it don't bother me to steal. So I says:

"Stop it."

"Stop what?" she asks.

"Stop telling me what a wonderful feller I am when I am nothing more than a thief."

"You are not," she says softly, still smiling.

"Where do you think I gets all the stuff you folks eats?" I asks. "I steals it from the Army. If they ketches me they will put me in jail, or maybe shoot me. Stealing from the United States government is serious crime. You think I just finds this food under a tree somewhere? No, I steals it. Stop telling me I'm a Jesus-Moses saint because I ain't. I'm a thief."

"You're a saint to me, and other people too," she argues in a very gentle way.

Then book saints and real saints ain't the same, I reckon. Neither are book thiefs and real thiefs, anyway not all the time.

"God will not hold it against you," she says. "He is using you to answer prayers. To me you will never be a thief, and I don't think God considers you a thief either."

I suppose Tom Sawyer would be very disappointed if he could see me now. I can't even win an argument with a woman. I takes my blankets off in the sage brush so I can sleep by myself.

A few days later I brings back to camp a heavy box of canned sardines. You'd think it was Christmas the way folks is fussing over a bunch of smelly fishes in cans. They do their best to eat most of them up before we starts out for the day. The problem is nobody thinks to hide or bury the empty cans. Later in the day some soldiers finds the cans, and tells Sergeant Peabody about it.

The next morning, real early, while some of the folks is getting their fires a going, and others is finishing off the last of the sardines, Sergeant Peabody and seven or eight soldiers rides into camp. Now there's more than a hundred of the handcart folks, and about thirty men, so you'd reckon them soldiers'd be a might careful, but it warn't so. Most of the handcart folks talk kind of funny because they are from far-away places like Denmark and England, and don't have many guns. There warn't three or four guns that you could shoot something with in the whole outfit, and not a single man who could go out and shoot an elk or buffalo and bring in the meat, and Sergeant Peabody knowed it.

Sergeant Peabody, dad fetch him, orders two of his men to git off their horses. Another soldier hands each of them an axe, then Peabody tells them to start chopping spokes. He means the spokes in the handcart wheels. The handcarts is stretched out in a straight line ready to start the day. The two soldiers go to the last handcart, one on each side, and chop out three or four spokes. Then they moves to the next cart and chops out more spokes, on both sides again. Peabody is santering in front of them, telling folks to git out of the way, to stand back. Everybody obeys. Some have a hand over the mouth, looking stunned, like an ox that is hit in the head with a hammer. Others look away. Some are crying. One woman is saying a prayer.

"You folks look a little short on firewood, so we reckon we'd chop a little fer ya," Peabody says. Then he laughs. I never seen him so happy, except when he thought them boys was going to shoot me. I feel like I would ruther be somewheres else. I don't have a gun, and I am just a boy, so I feels as helpless as the Mormons around me as Peabody's men are moving from cart to cart, chopping more spokes as they go. I am ashamed, and I thinks the Mormons are too, that we ain't men enough to stop Peabody and his boys. I'm thinking that when they leave we can run into the mountains where there are lots of trees, and chop more spokes. Shouldn't lose more than a few days. But what if Peabody comes back and chops the spokes again? Every day we can't travel brings us closer to the winter storms that make handcart travel impossible.

Then when I think about half of the wheels have been ruined by the soldiers, the chopping of a sudden stops. I don't hear nobody crying neither. But I can hear soldiers mumbling words like Danites and Brigham's destroying angels. I looks up. The two soldiers who have been chopping the wheels have dropped their axes, and are now holding their hands high in the air. Peabody's hands are up too. All the soldiers have their hands up, like they been ketched by an enemy army or a whole herd of Injuns.

Then I sees what has frightened the soldiers. It ain't an army, or Injuns, only two riders approaching on horseback. The morning sun is just coming over the Continental Divide behind us, shining right into the faces of the splendidest riders mounted on the keenest horses I have ever seed. Now, I growed up in Missouri and thought I knowed what a fine horse was, but never had I seen animals like these—a black and a bay, taller than most horses, the muscles in their shoulders and hips bulging like they was about to break through the skins, and you could see the muscles bulging and stretching under the skin like there was no skin at all. Their nostrils flared, and the sweat on they's arched necks glistened in the morning sun. They looked like they could run forever, and that no other horse in the world could ketch them.

The men is as powerful splendid as the horses, wearing white hats as wide as a desert sunrise, heavy broadcloth shirts, and cotton trousers tight on legs bulging with muscles from lots of riding. Mexican spurs is on their sturdy cowhide boots. The biggest bowie knives I ever seed is strapped to the tops of their legs. They wear holsters carrying Navy Colt revolvers, the kind I had seen a sheriff or two carry. I can tell from the bulges in the pockets of their elk-skin coats that they have extra cylinders to quickly replace the ones in the pistols. Each man holds a double-barreled shotgun balanced across the front of his saddle. The two riders got enough fire power to kill fifty soldiers, and they are powerful handsome, at least in my boy eyes they are. No wonder Sergeant Peabody and his men are scared enough to hold their hands high in the air.

Both riders have steel-gray eyes that don't blink, and the skin on their sharp jaws looks like it hasn't been shaved in weeks, but the beards are not long and thick like men who never shave. They is strong men, mounted on splendid horses that can take them through hell and around the world. I feel the same fear the soldiers feel, and don't know why because I knows these terrible beautiful riders ain't mad at me.

After looking over the damage on the handcart wheels, one of the riders approaches Sergeant Peabody, asking him how he wants to pay for the damage. Peabody says he don't have no money with him. The rider orders him and the rest of the soldiers to take off their boots.

"Eleven pairs of boots for eleven pairs of handcart wheels," the rider says, his voice quiet and calm, but everyone can hear what he says.

"Sounds fair to me," the other rider says.

After the soldiers has their boots off, the two riders send them scampering back to the army camp, without their horses. What is interesting to me is that neither one of the riders ever takes his pistol out of the holster, or never points one of the shotguns at the soldiers who is quick to do everything the riders asks them to do.

The riders gathers up the Army horses, and meet with some of the Mormon men as Peabody and his men disappear over the closest hill. This is when I learns the names of the two riders, Porter Rockwell and Bill Hickman, Mormon gunfighters who report directly to Brigham Young.

When the soldiers are out of sight, Rockwell and Hickman slip the bridles from the Army mounts and drives them in front of them as they disappear into the foothills to the south. I think the handcart men will be going into the hills to gather new spokes, but I am told to get my belongings ready to throw into wagons which will be coming shortly to take all of us to Fort Supply.

It is late afternoon when the wagons show up. I don't know the men who drive them, only that they are Mormons, and I don't know where the wagons come from, only that axle grease is smeared over the side boards to cover the US initials. The sacks of flour, beans and rice in the wagons looks like the ones Jim and me borrowed from the Army camp. The wagons are pulled by fine big mules. Axle grease was smeared on their shoulders to cover up the US brands.

I began to think that it might be time for me to find some other fish to fry, that maybe I should strike out on my own. I don't want to be an enemy of the United States government. All I want is to save Peggy.

I learn that the new Fort Supply is only ten or fifteen miles from Fort Bridger. Since I don't got a gun or a horse, I decide to stay with the

Mormons a little longer, at least until we gets to Fort Supply. That's when I will leave them and go to Fort Bridger and find Peggy.

On the way to Fort Supply, we don't pass any more wagon or hand-cart companies, or any more Army camps. Nobody bothers us, and we travel fast. We have lots of oats for the mules, so they pull the wagons all the day long. In a couple of days we are in Fort Supply, a busy place with lots of horses, mules, fighting men with guns, stacks of hay, and barrels of food stacked higher than a man's head, when the man is on a horse. There is a blacksmith shop, a store, corrals for animals, and cabins where some of the visitors can sleep.

I don't spend a lot of time saying goodbye to every body in the handcart company because I am in an awful hurry to get to Fort Bridger. I still don't have a gun or a horse, but I am not sure I want a horse because it is easier to hide and sneak around when you don't have a mount to watch out for. But I wishes I had a gun. I reckon I will need one to take Peggy away from the trappers. I reckon it might take all winter to earn enough money to buy a gun, if I can find work, so I reckon I might as well be earning gun money in Fort Bridger while I am trying to find out where them trappers is hiding with Peggy.

Chapter 18

The Mormons give me some flour, bacon and dried apples to feed me on my journey. They don't think it is wise for me to go to Fort Bridger because the Army might be trying to ketch me for stealing. Plus the wind is starting to blow real hard, out of the north, maybe bringing in the first winter storm. Everybody at the fort is wearing coats and hats. But I have already made up my mind. Just when I am ready to leave, the wind gets real cold and I start to see a few snow flakes, but I rolls up my stuff in a blanket, picks up the sack of vittles they gave me, and starts up the trail to Fort Bridger.

After a mile or so the snow begins to stay on the ground, but I ain't cold because I am walking real fast. After another mile there's a couple of inches of new snow on the ground. When I have to go up a hill, my feet slip some. My toes is getting cold. The snow is falling powerful hard now. I wish I had stayed at Fort Supply and waited out the storm.

Pretty soon I am running some, especially when the trail is downhill. I am determined to make Fort Bridger by nightfall. I have plenty of vittles, and some Lucifer sticks to light a fire,

But I'd ruther not spend the night out in a storm, so I hurries along just as fast as I can go.

It ain't even dark yet when I sees the fort off in the distance, some cabins and a barn, lots of stock in pole corrals, and three or four stacks of hay. At first I am real happy that I won't have to sleep in the woods, but then I sees that the track I am following passes through the river before it reaches the fort. I am cold and wet from being snowed on all day, so the idea of wading waist deep through an ice cold river, don't set too well. So I stops at the edge of the river and looks right and left, hoping there might be an easier place to cross, maybe where a tree has fallen across it. The river looks more narrow upstream, so I heads that way.

I hasn't gone far when I hears something grunt under some snow covered bushes. I stops, thinking maybe I have stumbled on a bear, or a wild pig. I pulls out my knife, and looks for a club. I hears the grunting noise again, but there's so much snow on them bushes that I can't see what it is that's grunting. All I know is that it ain't no happy grunt. Finally I finds a nice club which I picks up. Now I can protect myself, I ain't nearly so scared, so I reaches out and taps some of the branches on the bush to make the snow fall to the ground. Now I can see that there's something on the ground under all the snow. It's moving a little, but it ain't no bear or pig. It's a man, and he's grunting and wiggling like he don't know how to get up. Maybe he's sick, or wounded. Then I smells the whiskey and knows he's powerful drunk. I also knows he will die if I just leaves him to wrassle and grunt in the snow like this. It's late in the day, and when it gets dark, it will be even colder.

I puts down my stuff and kneels down. I rolls him onto his back, and brushes off the snow and looks at his face. I reckon I have seen him before, but I don't know where. His hair is dark because it is wet and matted against his head. His beard don't look more than a week or two old. His eyes is gray and fierce, but he don't seem to see me, though he knows he's been rolled over. I pulls him over to a tree and props him up, but he is so relaxed he falls over again.

"My hat, find my hat," he grunts, his words all slurry.

"Don't see no hat," I says. "The ground is covered with snow."

"Please, my hat," he moans, so I goes over to the bush where I first found him, and starts kicking around in the snow. Pretty soon I finds a hat. It's almost as white as the snow, except the wetness makes it look darker. It has a wide brim. I remember where I have seen a hat like this before. The two riders who chased off Sergeant Peabody and his men. Now I know who this is, the one the Mormons calls Bill Hickman or Brother Hickman. The soldiers calls him the Danite or Destroying Angel, but he sure don't look like no angel, and dad fetch him, he's near freezing to death and all he wants is his hat. So I gives him the hat, but he can't put it on because his head is sideways against the ground. So I props him up against the tree again, and somehow he manages to stay in a sitting-up position, but he still can't put his hat on because his head is leaning back against the tree.

"My horse, my horse," he says, "Git my horse."

Now this seems like a good idea, fetching his horse, that is. He can't walk, so maybe I can get him back to the fort if I finds his horse and puts him on it. So I starts looking around, and pretty soon I sees some horse tracks, about half filled with snow. I follows them a bit, just santering along quiet and easy so as not to scare it off if it sees me first. Pretty soon I sees the big bay gelding he was riding when he and Brother Rockwell chased off Sergeant Peabody. He still looks awful splendid, the horse that is, even with the top of his back wet with snow and his tail tucked tight between his hind legs against the cold. The saddle and bridle are still on him, and a coiled-up rope is hanging on the side of the saddle. He is chewing up big mouthfuls of snow-covered grass.

He is so big and powerful that I feel a little scared about just getting on him and riding him back, so I leads him through the snow, back to his master. I ties the horse to a tree, then helps Brother Hickman to his feet. He leans on me real heavy, but he is finally able to put on his hat.

I pushes him up against the horse where he grabs onto some saddle strings. Next, I lifts up his leg and puts his toe into the stirrup, but when he tries to push up, even with me helping, the toe slips out and he falls back down. We try the same thing three or four times, but it ain't no use.

The horse is too tall, and Brother Hickman has swallered too much whiskey.

It's almost dark now, and I just can't think of any way to get him across the river, so I decides to get on the horse myself and go to the fort for help. I ain't afraid of the horse no more because when I was trying to push Brother Hickman onto his back, he just stands there like any good horse is supposed to do, not acting wild and spirited at all. So I gets on and rides back down the river to where the road crosses over to go to the fort.

Now I had never rode such a horse before. It feels like he is strong enough to carry ten men as he takes big powerful steps through the snow. But he ain't rough like other big horses, but smooth as glass, like he is just gliding along.

When I reaches the place where the road goes through the river, I turns the horse towards the water, which looks like swirling black danger now the sun is no longer shining on it, but the horse don't hesitate to just wade right in like he can just splash the whole river empty if he wants to. When we comes out the other side I leans forward and clicks my tongue, letting him reach out into a powerful gallop so strong and fast that I feels like I couldn't be ketched by the entire United States Army, and that if I turned and charged into them, my horse was powerful enough to knock them all down. He feels like he can run forever, and I reckon if I had a horse like this I could find Peggy in a day or two.

One of the cabins in front of me has light shining out from the window so I rides to it, leaning back in the saddle and pulling the reins a little to let the horse know I want to stop. He does it so fast I has to grab the saddle horn to keep from falling off. I like this horse a lot and wish I owned him. If Brother Hickman freezes to death, I reckon I might take his horse.

Three men are looking at me as I enter the big cabin. They are sitting at a table, playing cards. All three have beards, and they are wearing dear and elk skin clothing. I wonder if one of them might be the famous Jim Bridger.

"There's a drunk man in the snow on the other side of the river," I says. "I needs help bringing him over."

I reckon saying that a man needs help, they will all just jump up and run to help, but none of them moves.

"He needs to be brung inside or he will freeze," I says. "By myself I cain't get him on his horse."

"Is his horse a tall bay, and is he wearing a big white hat?" one of the men asks.

"Yes," I says. "His name is Bill Hickman."

"The world could use one less Mormon Danite. Let him freeze." They starts playing poker again, acting like I am not even there.

I reckon these men ain't going to help. They don't even care if Hickman dies, so I says:

"When Porter Rockwell finds out you just let him die there'll be hell to pay."

They puts down their cards, and all three looks at me again. I reckon from the looks in their eyes that the name Porter Rockwell makes them scared, but not so much they jumps up to help.

"Let the Mormons at Fort Supply save him," one says.

"That's too far away," I says.

"We ain't going to cross no river to save Bill Hickman," one of them says in a voice so loud and firm that I know he means what he says. I think maybe this one is Jim Bridger. The other two are looking down at their cards.

"The little cabin, over there," he says, pointing out the window, "is empty. If you gets him across the river you can put him in there. There's a good stove, and wood by the door. You can pay me a dollar in the morning."

All three men are looking at their cards now, and don't want nothing more to do with me, so I goes back outside and unties the horse. I leads him over to the little cabin. The door ain't locked so I ties up the horse and goes inside, and starts a fire in the wood stove. Then I gets back on the horse and rides across the river. I still don't know how I will save Brother Hickman.

I ties up the horse to the same tree where I tied him before, and tries again to push Bill into the saddle, but he is still so loose and relaxed that I just can't do it. His face and hands are blue from the cold, but he ain't sober enough to shiver. Whenever I lets go of him, he just falls back to the ground. He ain't all the way unconscious because he keeps saying stuff that I can't understand.

Finally, I reckon it just ain't no use trying to get him on the horse, and I thinks that if I did get him up there, he'd just fall off, probably in the river, and that wouldn't do him no good at all. I think there must be a better way to do this. He will die if I don't think of something. Then I notices the rope tied to his saddle, and gets an idea. I remembers how I started the fire in the cabin, and knowed it must be awful warm in there by now. So I takes the rope off the saddle, and puts the noose around Bill's chest, below his arms. Then I puts his white hat on me so it won't get lost, then with the other end of the rope in my hand, I gets on the horse. I dallies up tight on the saddle horn, going around three or four times, so the rope won't slip, then I starts for the river, old Bill sliding along in the snow behind me.

The problem is the river, and I am wondering how I can drag him through it without drowning him to death. And all that cold, black water is bound to suck away the last of the warmth keeping him alive. If I wanted to kill him, the best way would be to just throw him in the river, and now I am doing it on purpose, but I thinks the only way I can save him is to get him to the cabin so fast that he don't have time to die on me.

So I turns the horse straight at the river and kicks him as hard as I can with both feet, and then just hangs on as hard as I can as the horse plows through the deep water with old Bill scooting along behind, yelling like he is being murdered until his head goes under the water. Then he comes up, his face in and out of the water as he spins on the end of the rope. In few seconds I am pulling him up the far bank, but I don't take time to check if he is still breathing. He ain't yelling no more. I kick the horse again and we gallop across the meadow to the cabin, old Bill sliding along on the grass and snow like a dead body.

When I reaches the cabin, I hop down, tie up the horse, remove the noose from Bill, and drags him inside where my fire has made it as hot as the attic in Widow Douglas's house on a July afternoon, maybe a hundred degrees. Bill don't look like he is alive at all as I stretches him out on the floor, as close as I can get him to the rattling stove, and starts pulling off his clothes, which are soaking wet and half frozen, and don't want to come off, but I pulls them off anyway.

His skin is all blue and I am surprised that he don't look nearly so big and strong, all naked like that on the floor. I opens up the front door of the stove, so the fire can shine right out against his blue skin. I still ain't sure if I am going to save him or just cook him, but one way or the other he ain't going to be cold much longer.

Then I see his chest move like he is trying to breathe. One eye opens about half way, then his mouth. I am real happy because I think I have saved him, then he says:

"My hat."

I guess he saw it on my head, and thinks I am stealing it, so I takes it off and drops it on his chest. His head can't wear a hat because it's on the floor. Then I pulls him around so I don't cook the side that's closest to the fire. He moans like I am hurting him real bad. I am pretty sure now that he ain't going to die.

I looks around the cabin and sees over in the corner two copper pails, and a pretty big wash tub. I fills up the buckets from a ditch behind the cabin and puts them on the stove. Then I drags the wash tub to the middle of the room. I cain't lift Bill up to put him in it, so I tips the tub on its side, rolls Bill over the edge, then tips it back on its bottom, with Bill inside. I knows he is getting stronger because he starts yelling that I am trying to kill him.

In ten or fifteen minutes I pours the hot water from the buckets over the top of him, then I fetches more water from the ditch. Bill is making so much noise now, that I go outside and shut the doors. I unsaddles the horse then leads him over to one of the haystacks where I ties him close enough so he can eat.

Pretty soon I pours two more buckets of water over Bill. He is thawed out enough by now that he is cursing me for hurting him, and demanding more whiskey. I don't get him none. In an hour I help him out of the tub, roll him up in wool blankets, and put him to bed on a pile of clean straw. Pretty soon he is snoring like a baby. I rustle up something to eat, then tries to get some sleep too.

The next morning while old Bill is still sleeping, after I builds a nice fire in the stove, I steals some money out of his pocket and takes it over to the big cabin. I says I don't know if we will stay a second night, but gives the man enough money for it. He seems happy about it because he gives me a slab of meat and some coffee beans for our dinner. After that I takes Bill's fine big horse over to the ditch for a drink, then ties him so he can eat more hay. When I return to the cabin, Bill is awake but bedded down on the straw. He is yelling that if he don't get a drink of whiskey real soon, he is agoing to die for sure. But I been around my pappy enough to know that ain't true. Men don't die from not getting any whiskey. So I just ignores him while I smashes up the coffee beans and puts them in a pot I finds hanging on the wall. I then adds water from the ditch and gets the coffee to cooking. Then I fries the meat on top of the stove, putting plenty of salt on it. I don't know if its from a cow, or buffalo or elk, but it sure smells good when it starts to fry.

Pretty soon I cuts off a chunk for Bill and gets him to chewing while I cuts off a chunk for me. The meat is real tough, but it tastes good. I keep cutting off chunks for me and Bill, and don't want to stop until it's all gone. I get more hungry with each bite. But I stops in the middle and pours the coffee in a big cup, the only one I can find, and Bill and me starts sipping that too.

Bill is feeling a lot better now, and asks me to tell him how he got in the cabin, so I tells him everything, how I found him in the snow by the river, how I couldn't get him on his horse, so I got on it myself and went for help, but nobody would come, so I had to drag him across the river to the cabin, then how I poured hot water all over him to warm him up.

"You saved my life," he says when I am finished telling what happened. "I'd a died out there if you hadn't come along. What's your name?"

I tells him I am Huck Finn, and that I am trying to save a girl named Peggy who was carried off into the mountains by two trappers. He asks where my horse is because he had already looked out the window and saw his over by the haystack. I tells him I don't gots a horse.

Then he asks what kind of gun I have to help me steal Peggy back from the trappers. I tells him I don't gots a gun neither. He asks where Peggy and the trappers is hiding out. I tells him I don't know exactly, only that they are trapping in the mountains, that sometime I think they will come to Fort Bridger for supplies, and when they do I will be able to follow them and save Peggy.

He scratches his chin and looks at me real careful. Then he says, real slow:

"Just a boy, no horse, no gun, and trying to steal a woman away from two mean trappers in mountains where you never been before. How old are you, Huck Finn?"

"I don't know."

"What do you mean you don't know. Everybody knows how old they are."

"My ma's dead, and my pappy never told me when I was borned. I don't know."

He thinks about what I says for a minute, then he says:

"That's good, real good. By not knowing your age, you can be any age you want. If the Army wants you to join up to help kill Mormons you can tell them you are too young, only fifteen. If that girl Peggy is seventeen and wants to fall in love with a boy nineteen, you can be nineteen. Hell, you can go into any post office in the United States, tell them you are thirty-five and run for president, and you can be twenty-one anytime you want to go into a saloon or visit a cock fight. All you have to do is pick a number. Which one do you like best?"

"Nineteen," I says, thinking of Peggy.

"Nineteen," he says, thoughtfully, "not a good age to die."

"I hope I don't die."

"Them trappers might have a different idea. No gun, no horse, no one to back you up. You will likely die, unless . . . ." He takes a big swaller of coffee.

"Unless what?" I asks.

"Unless I teach you some things that will save your life."

"Like what?"

"Where's my saddle bags?" he asks, looking around.

"Still on the saddle," I says, "over by your horse."

"Fetch them for me, please," he says, drinking more coffee, slowly getting to his feet for the first time.

When I returns with the saddle bags, he opens them up and takes out two Navy Colt pistols, and I can tell by looking at the cylinders that they is loaded. He removes the cylinders, then hands me one of the pistols.

We's facing each other now, each holding one of the pistols. He slips the barrel of his pistol into his belt, moving his hand a few inches away. Then he tells me to point my pistol at the center of his chest and cock back the hammer. When I done that, he tells me to pretend I am one of the trappers who has stolen Peggy, and that I just found Huck Finn sneaking into my camp. He is Huck Finn, caught by surprise, his gun still in his belt. He tells me to pull the trigger if Huck does anything I don't want him to do, then he tells me to start bossing him around, pretending he is Huck Finn, and I am the trapper.

I tells him to get down on the floor and put his hands behind his back.

Then I sees his hand reaching for his gun, I decides to kill him and pulls the trigger. Click. Click. Both guns has fired against the empty cylinders, but his hammer clicked first. I think he was lucky. Then he explains what has happened:

"I can pull a gun out of my belt or holster and fire a shot in less than half a second," he says. "It takes over half a second for a man pointing a cocked gun at me to see me make the first move, decide to kill me, and then pull the trigger." I gets him to try it again. Click, click. He is first again. We did it lots of times, and he always gets away the first shot. Then he says:

"You saved my life, Huck. Maybe I can save yours by teaching you how to do this."

"I don't got no gun," I says.

"You do now," he says, handing me one of the Navy Colts.

I tries to give it back, but he won't take it. I say nobody has ever given me anything that important before. I knows a new gun like that can cost around twenty-five dollars. He said he thought his life was worth a lot more than twenty-five dollars, and said I must keep it. He says he will get me a holster for it too, and a horse, at Fort Supply.

After a while we goes outside and shoots real powder and lead at cans and rocks. Pretty soon we has to go to the big cabin and buy more powder and lead. We shoot and shoot and shoot, and I starts hitting the things I am aiming at. I had shot a rifle before, plenty of times, hunting squirrels and coons and such, and was a pretty good shot, but shooting a pistol was like having to learn it all over again. Late in the afternoon, it started to rain, so we went back in the cabin and practiced fast draw until it was dark. It was early fall, and the snow which had covered most of the ground the day before had pretty much melted. Bill said in a week I would be one of the most dangerous men in the mountains.

"Most dangerous boy," I corrected.

"If you are nineteen, you're a man, at least in these parts," he argued.

I thought about what he said. A nineteen-year-old with a gun would have a better chance against the trappers than a boy with a stick. I decided to be nineteen and start acting like a man. I might even start shaving, though I still didn't have any whiskers.

The next morning when Bill tells me we is going to Fort Supply, I tells him I don't want to do it, that I needs to stay in Fort Bridger in case one or both trappers come in for supplies. Bill then explained that in two days there wouldn't be a Fort Bridger no more. President Young had ordered his men to destroy it. Bill had come over to scout the target and see how many men were on hand to offer a possible defense. He said it would be best if I warn't around. Someone might see me, and then the U.S. Army would be after me too. I agreed to go to Fort Supply. After Fort Bridger was destroyed, the trappers would have go to Fort Supply for supplies, anyway, and I could follow them back to Peggy from there.

We got on his big horse, him in front, me in back. The snow was all gone now and it was a wonderful sunny day. We each has one of the Navy Colts in our belts, and shoots at rocks and rabbits as we rides along. He tells me about guns and fighting, and says he ain't proud of it, but that he has shot seven or eight men in gun fights, and killed two or three more with knives. I ain't afraid he will kill me because he knows I saved his life.

Finally, I asks him what he thinks of coming with me to save Peggy from the trappers. I figures they would just wet their pants and run away if they sees Bill Hickman coming. Saving Peggy wouldn't be any work at all, just a matter of picking her up.

He says if I knowed where Peggy was right now he would help me do it, but he can't make any promises about next week or next month. The Mormons is at war with the United States and he has to follow orders. In a week or two he might be in St. George helping fight an army from California. He just can't make any promises that don't have anything to do with the war. But he wants me to know I am like a son to him, he will do what he can for me, but most important of all, he is learning me things so's I can take care of myself. That's why he gived me the gun, is teaching me how to use it, and is going to get me a horse in Fort Supply.

When we reached Fort Supply, the Mormons from the handcart company had moved on, but there is still plenty of men with guns, and a bunch of them have orders to help Bill destroy Fort Bridger. He tells them to be ready to leave the next morning.

The men has butchered a beef, and are roasting two of the quarters over fires as they sit around waiting to go with Bill or other leaders to do war with the Army. Bill lets me unsaddle his horse and turn it in a corral with a bunch of hay, while he goes to meetings with some of the Mormon officers. While I am waiting for him, I practice drawing and clicking my pistol about two hundred times. I am getting better at it, and want to practice all the time.

When Bill returns, he brings me the prettiest little chestnut gelding I has ever seen. It even has a saddle on it, and brand new saddle bags to carry my stuff. He just hands me the reins, and says it is mine. He says it don't have a name, that I would have to pick one out. I climb on and ride around a bit. It turns, and lopes in circles, real easy. It ain't tall and powerful like Bill's horse, but it is as nice as any horse I ever rode. I name him Tom after my old friend Tom Sawyer. I don't know if I will ever see Tom again, so now I have a horse that will remind me of my old friend.

Before it gets dark Bill gives me a holster for my Navy pistol, and we practice drawing on each other again. I still cain't draw and click faster than he can pull the trigger when he already has his gun pointed at me, but still I'm a lot faster than before, and Bill promises that if I keep practicing, I will be faster than he is. When it gets dark we carve off big chunks of meat from the roasting quarters and have ourselves a feast.

I feel real proud hanging around with Bill Hickman. He is the big dog at Fort Supply. I never saw him get rough or mean with any of the men, but they always talk to him real nice, and never get in his way, like they fear and respect him. They admire him a lot too, and know he can kill any one of them in a fight if he wants to, but he is too noble of a man to want to do it.

When I wakes up the next morning, Bill and his men are gone. I practices drawing and clicking my pistol until my arm is so tired I can hardly lift it. There is plenty beef left over from the night before, so I eats and rides my Tom, while I waits for Bill to come back. When my arm is rested up, I practice drawing and clicking some more. When it gets dark, Bill has not returned. Nor does he return the next day, or the next. Nobody knows what's happened, and some are starting to think he and his men might be ketched or killed by the Army.

Finally, on the third day, old Bill comes riding in, and all the men who left with him are still with him, so none was killed. But Bill don't look so good. He's not quite straight in the saddle. His eyes are all red. There ain't no smile on his face, he don't seem happy to see me at all. In fact, if I didn't know him better, I would think he was getting ready to kill somebody. I didn't think he was drunk because his speech wasn't slurred when he tells me to put his horse away while he goes to bed in our tent. When I comes back to the tent he is sound asleep. I hears from some of the other men that they destroyed Fort Bridger, without even a fight.

The next morning he looks a lot better, gets hisself a paper and pencil and starts writing a report to Brigham Young. He is real careful, and real serious as he scratches out the words. I waits and watches, thinking what a wonderful man this is. One day he is teaching me how to shoot, even gives me a gun and horse. He is brave enough to fight the U.S. Army and destroy forts. Then he can sit down and write a long letter to the most powerful man in the west. He told me when we was riding to Fort Supply that he is studying the law so he can be a lawyer when the war is over. I thinks a wonderful man like this can do anything, and wonders if there is a chance a boy like Huck Finn could ever be like Bill Hickman.

Bill, he writes a couple of pages. Finally he is finished. He looks at me, smiles, and asks if I wants to hear what he wrote. I says I does so he starts reading the letter.

He reads how the traders and soldiers, when they found out the Mormons was coming, they gave up the fort without a fight. Even Jim Bridger was not around when the Mormons arrived. Bill described how they burned the cabins and haystacks, and busted up the corrals, after they took out the stuff they wanted. They found flour, powder, lead, traps, lots of grain, harnesses, saddles and other stuff which they brung back to Fort Supply. Then he tells how they found about a hundred bottles of whiskey which the Mormon officers decided to destroy all by theirselves, one dose at a time. He said they worked so hard at it that by the time they was finished there warn't a single officer able to stand up. Now I know why Bill looked so bad when he came back to Fort Supply. He was hanged over from swallering all that whiskey. I wondered why such a strong, splendid man would want to drink like that. I guessed there were things in his life I didn't know about.

After he folds the letter and pushes it into an envelope, he turns towards me as he pulls his Navy Colt out of his holster, kicks out the cylinder, and points it at my chest.

"Huck Finn," he growls, "If you make one move I'm going to pull the trigger on this here dog leg and blow you in half."

I knows the game. We's played it before.

"Please don't, Mr. Hickman," I cries. "I will do . . ."

Without finishing what I was saying I draws and pulls my trigger. My hammer clicks before his.

"I knew you could do it," he says, jumping out of the chair and throwing his arms around me. I am smiling so hard my face hurts. He is proud of me. I am proud of myself. I am so happy. Then real serious, he says:

"Someday what I have taught you will save your life, maybe the lives of others too. You keep practicing."

My smile is gone now. I can feel goose bumps on my arms, and ice against my back. I believe he is telling the truth, and I am scared. We practice our game a few more times. He beats me once, but I beats him the other times. He says he is amazed that I had gotten so fast in such a short time, but he says I gotta be even faster if I want to stay alive. He says it'd be harder to draw and shoot when I was doing it with real bullets, and knowed someone was going to die, maybe me. I knows he is right. I practice every chance I git, and spend lotsa time shooting at targets with the powder and lead Bill bought me.

A few days later Bill says he's gotta go. He's arranged for me to stay at the trading post, helping with the wagons and teams, so I would be close by if Peggy's trappers show up to buy supplies. The days was getting shorter, and the nights colder. Soon the heavy snows would come. The Army would have to wait until spring to continue its war with the Mormons. I hoped the trappers would want to buy some last minute supplies before the deep snow came. Things were not very busy at the fort now as most of the Mormons was returning to the valleys and their families to wait out the winter. I had plenty of time to practice the draw and click, and started to build myself a grubstake, betting men that I could draw and click faster they could pull the trigger.

And then one day I sees a horse I recognize tied to the hitching rail in front of the store. It's the one Hog rode off on when he took Peggy away and left me naked on the prairie. There was a pack horse tied next to it, but I didn't remember it. I hurries around to the back of the store, sneaks inside, and takes a peek from behind some flour barrels. It's Hog alright. He gathers up some lead and powder, then some bacon and flour. He asks the clerk to give him some peppermint candy for his woman. He tells the clerk he's got a woman to take care of him and the trapping's going to be good. Then he tells the clerk to get him four bottles of whiskey.

Chapter 19

I hurries out to the corral, saddles my horse, fills my saddle bags with food, Lucifer sticks, powder and lead, puts on the heavy coat Bill gave me, ties the saddle bags and a wool blanket on my saddle, then buckles on the holster with my Navy Colt, making sure all the cylinders is ready to fire. By the time I gets everything ready, Hog has already headed out, going south towards the big mountains where Bill says the Spanish used to have their gold mines.

There's a few inches of new snow on the ground, so I knows he will be easy to follow. I take my time getting started. I don't want to follow too close and risk him seeing me. My hands is shaking as I gets on my horse. I wishes Bill was around and coming with me, but he ain't. I am scared, but knowing that Peggy is up in some camp with Wire, and that Hog is going there too, there is nothing else in the world I want to do but go after her. Being scared don't matter none. I knows what I has to do.

Sometimes at the top of a hill, I can see Hog riding ahead of me, but most of the time I am just following his tracks. Every time where I see where he has stopped to get off his horse for something, I stop too, and wait a while, not wanting to get too close. My horse is a gelding, so I don't think he will start whinnying, but I stay back plenty far just in case.

When it gets dark I climb up on a hill and look around until I see the fire where Hog has made camp. Then I get myself behind a hill a couple of miles away where he cain't see me or my fire, and make my own camp. I stays dressed and ready while I eats something and rolls up in my blanket. My horse is staked out on a short rope in some thick, heavy grass.

Hog gets an early start the next morning, and I am following him real careful. The weather is good, the sun is shining, and the snow is starting to melt in the open places where the sun is bright. We travel all day, and camp again.

The next day about noon, I see a cabin in some aspen trees in a draw, about a mile away. Hog's tracks is leading right to it. Smoke is coming from a stove pipe in the roof. My heart is pounding. I reckon this is where Peggy is. I tried to save her once before and failed. Now I will do it right, or maybe die.

My hands are shaking as I look around trying to figure out what to do. I know I cain't just walk up to the door and ask for Peggy. They won't give her to me just cuz I ask. I must take her at gun point, against their wishes, or I must sneak her away when they are sleeping or out trapping. I don't know which plan is best. I decides to tie up my horse, sneak up close to the cabin, and see what I can figure out.

I am in the trees about fifty feet from the front door when I hears a bunch of yelling inside. I can't make out many of the words, I only know that Hog is real mad. I think he is probably mad at Peggy, and I can't think why anybody might ever be mad at her.

Then the front door swings open, and Hog marches over to the horse he unsaddled a little while ago, and starts putting the saddle back on the horse. Then I sees somebody else step into the open doorway. My heart is pounding because in the shadows behind the door I think Peggy is coming out where I can see her. But it ain't Peggy, it's Wire, and he is mad too, kind of crying and mad at the same time. He says:

"Had to sleep some time, couldn't stay awake a whole week. Didn't reckon she'd run off."

Suddenly I realizes that Peggy is not there, that she has run away. Now all I has to do is find her before the trappers does. I listens carefully, hoping Wire might say something about which way she went. I knowed she didn't take the trail to Fort Supply, or Hog and me would have seen her already. With winter coming I don't think she'd go higher in the mountains. I reckon she took one of the horses from their corral instead of trying to get away on foot.

"I'll come with you?" Wire whines, pacing back and forth in front of the cabin door.

"No. Stay here in case she comes back," Hog says.

"Why would she come back?" Wire asks.

"Cougars, bears, storms, Injuns–anything might scare her enough to come back. If she shows up, tie her up."

"Don't think she'd be scared by Injuns," Wire said.

"Why's that?" Hog asks as he slips on the horse's bridle.

"She run off right after some Injuns come a beggin' for flour."

"What Injuns?"

"Three bucks, maybe Utes."

"Did you give them flour?"

"I tells them no, but Peggy, she brung out the sack and poured some into each of their pouches. Wouldn't stop when I tells her to get back in the cabin. It was right after that when I goes to sleep and she runs away."

"Which way was the Injuns going?" Hog asks.

"West. One said something about the Bear River. They knowed a lot of English, probably been around Mormons, that's why I thinks they was Utes."

Hog hurries back in the cabin and brings back two bottles of forty rod whiskey which he pushes into a parfleche tied to the back of his saddle. I thinks the whiskey is for trading, to get Peggy back. He gets on his horse and goes west, following a nice trail with lots of horse tracks on it. I think it's the one the Injuns rode out on, Peggy too. I sneaks back to my horse, and follows him.

As I rides along I wonders what Peggy is thinking, wanting to surrender herself to Injuns again. After getting away from Blue Fox who killed her family and made her a slave, I didn't think she would want much to do with Injuns ever again, but now it looks like she has run off to join some Utes. I don't know nothing about Utes. Maybe one of them smiled kindly at her when she poured flour in his pouch. Maybe she reckoned these Injuns was different, that they might be nice to her. Maybe she gave them the flour, hoping to make friends who would help her when she runned away. Women does things like that.

I follows old Hog for a couple days. The sun melts away most of the snow, and traveling is easy. Finally he stops at the top of a hill, in some aspen trees, and sneaks around careful like he has seen something real important. I cain't see it yet because I am behind him, so I sneaks around to a hill north of him so I can see what he sees. There's a big valley with a beautiful river running to the north.

Lots of Injuns is camped in a big meadow, maybe a dozen tepees made out of skins, and two or three made of wagon canvas. Dozens of horses is eating the grass. Fifteen or twenty children with long sticks in their hands is running around in a patch of tall grass, stabbing and slapping around their feet, almost like they is ketching frogs. Lots of buffalo skins is stretched out on the grass where squaws is busy scraping them. Other women is in the bushes beyond the camp, picking some kind of berries. I don't see very many men, maybe they's out hunting. These Injuns looks different than any I have seen because most of them is dressed partly like white folks. Some of the men is wearing wide-brimmed hats. Some have cotton shirts, mostly red and blue ones. Some squaws is wearing regular pioneer dresses that hang almost to the ground, and their hair is tied up in colored pieces of cloth. A couple of the women is wearing white bonnets. I figure these Injuns have been around white folks a lot, maybe the Mormons by the Great Salt Lake. The Mormons has been in this country maybe ten years, and it makes sense that they would give a lot of stuff to the Injuns they see every day. So I reckon Wire is right when he says these people be Ute Injuns.

I is too far away to know if Peggy is with the women, but I thinks she is, and Hog thinks she is too. As I look over at the hill where Hog is hiding behind a tree, I see he has pulled a brass spy glass out of his pocket and is looking through it.

Finally, he puts the spy glass away, unties his horse, and rides straight for the Injun camp, no longer trying to hide himself. He must not be afraid of these Injuns, and I don't know why that is. I unties my horse and rides closer, trying to stay hidden in the trees.

Hog rides right through the middle of the camp to the women in the bushes who is picking berries. He gets off his horse and ties the reins to a bush. All the Injuns is watching, but they is too surprised and curious to do anything but stare at him as he marches over to one of the women in the bushes and grabs her by the hair. When she tries to pull away, he kicks her feet out from under her, kicks her in the belly when she is down, then grabs her hair again and starts pulling her towards his waiting horse.

I reckon Peggy is the one he has kicked, and is dragging back to his horse. The Injuns would fight him if he just rode up and done that to one of their squaws. They must think the woman is his. So it has to be Peggy. My hands is sweating. Bill told me it is hard to kill a man, the first time you do it, but I think it is going to be easy. I want to kill Hog right now. I rides out of the trees, galloping towards the camp. I don't care if the Injuns sees me now, and some does as soon as I leaves the trees. But Hog, he don't see me because he is starting to kick Peggy again. The Injuns is gathering around to watch him do it. I can hear Peggy screaming, not like a frightened child, but like a wildcat wanting to scratch out a man's eyes, but she can't seem to get past Hog's boot as he keeps kicking her.

By the time I rides up Peggy is a sobbing heap on the ground. Hog is huffing and puffing like he has done some fine work. The Injuns, women and children and a few old men, gathers around to watch but don't dare to interfere with the business between a man and his woman. They don't pay much attention to me, though many have already seen me.

Hog steps over to his horse and gets the two bottles of forty rod whiskey out of the parfleche. I reckon I knows what he is thinking. He don't want to take any chances with some Injuns wanting to save Peggy. Let them fight over the forty rod instead. He holds up the two bottles so everybody can see them. Some of the people gathers around him like they hopes to get a drink. A big yaller dog is with them, like he wants some whiskey too

I am real close now, and see a chance to use what Bill Hickman learned me. I draws my Navy Colt out of the holster. Some of the Injuns sees me do it, but old Hog is too busy showing his whiskey to the Injuns, a bottle in each hand, high above his head. He is turning so everybody can see what he has. The big yaller dog is wagging his tail like he thinks he is going to get some too. I take careful aim, waiting until Hog is turned just right. Then I shoots, smashing both bottles with one shot. The whiskey and glass splashes all over Hog. He sees me now. I cock back the hammer for a second shot.

Hog is coming to me now, and Injuns is scrambling out of the way. With one hand he grabs his rifle that is hanging on the side of his saddle. With the other hand he pulls a long skinning knife out of his belt. I wonder why he ain't scared of me. I hit both bottles of forty rod with one ball. That was a pretty good shot, so he knows I can use my Navy Colt, but he is still coming at me real fast. It is time to shoot him dead. I take aim, and tell him to stop, but he don't do it. Now I am real scared, thinking maybe I cain't kill a man. Bill was right when he telled me it is a hard thing to do. In a second or two that skinning knife will be slicing me open, if he don't shoot me first, and I cain't pull the trigger. My mouth feels like it is full of cotton, and I feel sick. I see Peggy sitting up and looking at me. Time is passing real slow, like all the clocks has stopped.

Then I thinks if I can't kill a man, maybe I can shoot him in the foot, so I tries that. As soon as my gun fires, Hog goes down, his long rifle going off at the same time, but his ball don't hit me, or none of the Injuns either, only the big yaller dog who starts yelping as he runs off, a smear of blood on his side. Hog has a big hole in his right foot, and he is cussing and yelling that he is going to kill me, but that ain't something he can do now that his gun has fired, and he has a big hole in his foot. All the Injuns is looking at me, but they looks nice and respectful, like they wishes to stay out of this fight, but they ain't backing away because they wants to see every little thing that happens.

I cocks back the hammer on my pistol again, and tells Hog that he won't be able to get on his horse if I shoots his other foot. He stops cussing. He knows now that I means business. I takes careful aim at his other foot. He gets on his hands and knees, leaving his rifle and knife on the ground, and crawls towards his horse. Nobody tries to help. Without taking his eyes off me, he unties his reins as he stands up on one foot. He asks one of the boys to fetch his rifle, but before the boy can do it, I gets off my horse and picks it up myself. I don't want him riding off a hundred yards or so, then putting a ball in me. I tells him the rifle belongs to me now. When Hog says it don't, I points my Navy Colt at his good foot and squints down the barrel like I am going to shoot. He shuts up and crawls onto his horse. Blood is dripping from his shot-up foot. It needs doctoring real bad, but when I thinks what he done to Peggy I know he won't get no doctoring from me. He pulls his horse's head around and starts riding back the way he came. I puts my Navy Colt back in the holster. I looks real careful at the Injuns' faces. Some smiles at me, liking what I done for Peggy, but I don't think they are happy about me shooting away their forty rod. I don't reckon they wants to hurt me.

Peggy gets up now, and runs to me. She ain't worried about the Injuns neither. So I gets off my horse, hands Hog's rifle to a boy, and throws my arms around Peggy. Her hair smells like cottonwood smoke, smashed berries and buffalo meat, but that don't bother me none. My heart is about pounding out of my chest.

I think I feels happier than when I escaped from Pap's cabin, even happier than when I ketched the giant catfish. Peggy is saved. Now she can find Flaxy and go back to Iowa, or she can go to California and have a new life. She can do what she wants, and maybe I can do it with her.

For a short minute I think I am so happy I can just die and never worry about anything else ever again, but I have learned that happiness is like a blowfly on a piece of meat. It just don't stay in one place very long.

I starts to worry about these Injuns, and what they might do to Peggy and me. She is comfortable with them, but she ain't been with them only a few days. I knows how these Utes make good business selling children and slaves to the Mexicans. I reckon Peggy will bring a top price, and they knows that.

Something else begins to gnaw at me too. I reckon I should of killed Hog. He is my keenest enemy now, and will kill me first chance he gets. I had a chance to kill him, and let it pass, now I will have to sleep with one eye open the rest of my life. I shot a hole in his foot, shamed him in front of all these Injuns, and I takes his woman. I knows he ain't going to forget, and he will never stop hating me as long as he lives. He might not find me if I goes back to the Mississippi River, but if I stays out west, he could find me about anytime he wants, and next time I might be the one with a hole in my foot, or my gut or my head. The thought occurs to me that he might not be agoing very fast, a hole in his foot and all, so I might could catch him and kill him right now, and not have to worry about him no more, but I still ain't sure I can kill a man, so best to let him be, at least for now.

"What's wrong?" Peggy asks. She sees that I am deep in my thinking, and guesses from the frown on my face that I ain't too happy, so I says:

"Just a wondering what old Hog will do next, and thinking maybe we ain't out of the woods yet with these Utes. They trade slaves."

"They don't trade white folks," she says. "Just other Indians–Goshutes, Paiutes and digger types. I think we are safe. They are friends with the Mormons, do a lot of trading with whites. They are going to their wintering grounds on the south side of these mountains, and will take us with them. They tell me some Mormons live there. Maybe they can take us to Great Salt Lake City."

Chapter 20

I'm thinking, this Peggy, she sure is smart. Already, she has a plan all figured out, and I can't see nothing wrong with it. We just santer along with these Utes until we find some Mormons who will take us to Great Salt Lake City. I hope she is right, thinking these Injuns don't trade white slaves.

"What do you want to do when we gets to Great Salt Lake City?" I asks.

"Find Flaxy. I hope that lady at Fort Laramie has taken good care of her, and I can get her back."

"Will you take her back to Iowa?" I asks.

"At first I thought that was the thing to do," she says, placing her hand gently across her stomach, looking down. "But now I don't know. People in Iowa don't look kindly on someone like me. Perhaps my baby and me will have a better life in a new place, like California."

It hit me like a snowball someone throws at you when you ain't looking. Not only had she been defiled by Blue Fox and them trappers, but she was going to have a baby. I knows like she does that the good Christian folks in Iowa don't think kindly of unmarried women having babies, even if they can't help it. I looks down where her hand is across her stomach. She don't look no bigger than any other woman, so I guess the baby ain't very big. I feels my face turning red, but I have to ask her something. I says:

"Who is the father?" I think she is going to tell me it's Blue Fox or Hog.

"Don't know for sure," she says, real serious, "And I don't much care.

I don't like any of them, the way they forced me, and all."

"I reckon the baby will want to know, some day," I says.

"Maybe I'll say it's Huck Finn," she says, cocking her pretty face sideways, grinning at me like she is teasing me. And I just stands here looking at her like she is the most wonderful person that God ever made. Even better than perfect, with a new baby a coming. I think how Hog was beating on her. If' I'd known about the baby, I'd a done a lot more than shoot his foot. I remembers all them Christmas stories, and thinks I understands how Joseph felt when he was taking Mary to Bethlehem. Now I had my Mary, splendid as a human being can be, taking her to Great Salt Lake City where them Mormon midwives will know just what to do for Peggy and her baby, and I bet she don't have to have it in no manger either. But if she tells folks Huck Finn is the father, the ones like Tom Sawyer will still call her defiled, and they will think I am the keenest scoundrel that ever did live, but I don't care none about that.

I don't feel like no scoundrel. Her saying that makes me feel proud, like I am a president or governor, or a general. Dad fetch her, anyway. I am feeling so proud, so embarrassed that I can't think of nothing to say, but it is like she is reading my mind , because she says:

"Of course, if folks thought you were my husband, it wouldn't be awkward at all, and we wouldn't have to explain anything."

Now I am stunned like an ox that just got hit on the head with a three-pound hammer. I raises my hands and rubs both my ears at the same time, thinking maybe they ain't working right. The most wonderful woman alive on the planet wouldn't ask a worthless boy like Huck Finn to be her husband. Then I understands. She is teasing me again. I knows she is. I thinks I can play this game too, so I says:

"You don't even know how old I am?"

"You rode alone into a camp of a hundred Indians, saved me from a beating, and shot the meanest man alive right in the foot," she says. "That's old enough for me."

"Maybe I am only fourteen, and not old enough to get married," I says.

She is tired of playing games, because she says:

"How old are you really? I want to know."

I remembers what Bill Hickman told me, that since I didn't know my age, I could be any age I wanted, so I says:

"Nineteen."

"Just right," she squeals, throwing her arms around me again. I reckon someday I will tell her the truth about why I don't know my age, but not now. Nineteen makes her happy, so I'll be nineteen, at least for a while. She talks like she ain't teasing, but I know she is. I don't like this game, because I am not sure how to play it, so I looks around, hoping we can do something else.

I notices for the first time that all the Injuns have left. I cain't see a single one of them. Hog's rifle, the one I handed to the boy, is laying on the ground. Peggy notices the Injuns is gone too, and starts looking with me.

Beyond the farthest tepee we sees some smoke. As we walks closer we see squaws and children gathered around a fire. There's a tripod made of green lodgepole trees over the fire and a copper bucket hanging in the flames. They are cooking something. We goes closer to take a look. I am powerful hungry, thinking they might be boiling up a mess of buffalo tongues or beaver tails.

We see older children coming from the meadow where earlier I saw them hitting sticks against the ground. Some of them are carrying bags of whatever it is they ketched.

When we gets real close we see that it is not water that is boiling in the kettle, but golden sweet honey. I guess some of the boys has found a bee tree, maybe two. The hot honey is bubbling, sending white steam into the cool air. Some of the smaller children are poking fingers in the hot honey, pulling them away real fast, and licking them clean. I wishes for a bowl of oatmeal to put the honey on.

At first I reckon maybe the children are bringing back frogs they ketched in the tall grass, but when they starts opening the bags, I see they has gathered up a mess of mice, the kind white folks call field mice. I understands why a boy wants to ketch and kill mice, but I has never seen a boy bringing a bag of dead mice home to his mother, and these Injun children are bringing home hundreds of dead or wounded mice.

All my questions is answered when one of the old squaws picks up a dead mouse by the tip of its tail and dips it in the boiling honey, and lets it stay there for a long time. I reckon she is cooking the mouse so she can eat it. I thinks this is not a civilized way to eat a mouse. If I were doing it, I reckon I would cut off the head and feet, skin it, then remove the insides. Then, after it was cooked, I would eat real careful, sure not to swallow any bones. But this ain't how the squaw done it. She dipped it in the honey without doing anything to it. She waits a minute or two until it is nice and brown, then pulls it out, holding it up for everyone to see, like a tiny piece of golden fried chicken hanging from a wire. Then she pops it in her mouth, biting hard to cut off the tail with her front teeth. She throws the tail away and chews on the rest. I can hear the bones crunching between her teeth. The other squaws and children squeal and clap their hands and start doing it too.

I want no part of the mouse feast, and decides I don't want no honey either, not after a hundred mice have boiled in it. But Peggy, she has a different way to look at it. She says:

"Someday, if my child says I don't love him, or her, I will say I loved him so much when he was in my womb I ate wild mice so he would be smart. If it's a girl I will tell her how the mice were boiled in honey to make her sweet." Not waiting for me to respond, Peggy picks up a mouse by the tail and dips it in the bubbling honey. I shrug my shoulders and grab a mouse too. As it turns golden brown it begins to look and smell pretty good, but I knows little gray hairs help hold the beautiful crust together, and inside little strings of entrails, hearts, livers, lungs, brains, ears, eyeballs and little black droppings are cooking along with the meat and bones. But when I see Peggy toss hers in her mouth and bite off the tail, I reckon I can do it too, so I does it, forcing myself to chew a long time so I don't choke on a bone. When a squaw offers me a second mouse, I pats my stomach like I am already full. So does Peggy. I don't reckon she likes boiled mouse any more than I do, but she is a good sport about it. I think the squaws and children are pleased that we shared their feast with them. Peggy don't want to leave. She enjoys being with the squaws and children who are all very happy.

Like I thought at first, most of the Ute braves are out hunting. Every day or two some of them comes home, usually leading pack horses heavy with meat from buffalo, elk and deer, sometimes wild sheep or antelope. These men are splendid hunters, and most of them use bows and arrows. The women keep busy making jerky and pemmican and preparing the hides. With all this work to do we don't travel very fast to the wintering grounds. We'd break camp once every two or three days, traveling only five or six miles, then camp again.

Peggy and me are invited to sleep in a tepee belonging to a brave named Pan-a-carry-kinker. I don't know what that means, if he is Yellow Wolf, Gray Eagle or Spotted Horse, and he don't know enough English to translate his name for us, so we just calls him Pan-a-carry. He has two squaws and five little children, so it is real crowded and noisy in the tepee, and nobody has any privacy. Pan-a-carry gives each of us a buffalo robe, and we just roll up and go to sleep wherever we can find a place. If either one of us wants to bathe or wash our clothes, we'd do it during the day when we can hide away in the willows by the river. About the only times we go in the tepee is to sleep, or to get out of the rain or snow.

Peggy warn't about to live with the Injuns for free. Every chance she got, she was helping make jerky and pemican or cleaning skins. I didn't care much for that kind of work, not so much because it was hard or messy, but because I seed that none of the men and boys did it either. It was women's work along with cooking, gathering firewood, making clothes, and tending the children. The men made weapons, trained and cared for their horses, hunted, and went to lots of meetings or pow wows with each other where they drank watered down whiskey, smoked tobacco, and talked about hunting, scalping and stealing horses. They let me come to the meetings, where the ones that understood English tried to explain to me their business.

Finally, we crosses the pass that divided the north side of the mountains from the south side, and pretty soon we is following a stream of clear water running south. More snow than rain is falling, most every day now. I reckon its November, but I don't know for sure. Tom and me didn't keep up on dates when we left the United States, and I was so busy at Fort Laramie and when I was with Bill Hickman that I never did ask about the date, so I didn't know now. I only knowed that it was getting colder every day now, and winter was acoming fast.

Because I didn't want to work with the sqaws, I started going hunting with Pan-a-carry. He was real happy about this because I had a rifle and a pistol, and all he had was a bow and lots of arrows. He would find an elk or deer and I would shoot it. If we got real close I would use my Navy Colt. Sometimes it would seem like there warn't any game at all, but Pan-a-carry knew all the right places to look. We never had to go very far from camp, just a few miles, before he would find an animal for me to shoot.

We brings in more meat than Pan-a-carry's two squaws and Peggy can take care of, so every second or third animal we gives to a family that don't have enough meat. The hunting is hard work, and there is lots of nights when we cain't go home, and have to huddle around a little fire until it gets light again. I wonder why Pan-a-carry wants to hunt so hard, when he is bringing home more meat than his family needs. I wonder why he works so hard to give food to other families who ought to be getting their own meat. When I asks him about it his only words is that life is better when everyone has enough to eat. I reckon he is pretty wise for a savage. He ain't like Blue Fox at all. But he ain't like Tom Sawyer's book Injuns either, because one day he tells me the best way to get horses is to ketch little Goshute children and trade them to the Navajos.

When he says this I gets up my courage and asks him if he ever trades white women like Peggy to the Navajos. He hardly has to think before he answers. He says Mormons won't stand for it. His people have to get along with the Mormons because the Mormons gives them lots of food and have a sacred book about the ancient ones.

"But its alright by the Mormons for you to sell Injun children to the Navajos?" I asks.

He says they don't like that either, and the Utes aren't selling children as much as they used to. But sometimes they have to do it, when they need more horses. After this conversation I mostly stops worrying that these Utes will want to sell Peggy to the Navajos. Because I am helping Pan-a-carry bring in so much meat, all the other Injuns seems to like me. I thinks they respect me for what I done to Hog. They likes Peggy all along. How can anyone not like a splendid woman like that?

All the time when I am not out hunting with Pan-a-carry or sitting in on the pow wows, I am with Peggy, but she don't bring up the subject of me marrying her no more. She talks about her baby a lot, and wonders all the time if it will be a boy or girl. She seems happy to be having it, but never talks about any of them who might be the father. If I say something about Blue Fox or Hog or Wire, she changes the subject or just leaves to go do something else, anything except to keep talking to me.

Sometimes when we walks, I takes her hand in mine. She don't seem to mind, and chills go up and down my arm, but still I reckon something is wrong, and I don't know what it is. One time she puts my hand on her stomach to feel the baby kick. When I feels the bump, I am so happy, and all I wants to do is care for Peggy, to bring her good things to eat, to make sure she is warm and safe, to do all her work for her, even squaw's work.

I am afraid she was just making fun that time when she talked about us being married, because she don't talk about it no more. I am scared to ask her about it, and I don't know why, unless I am afraid she will tell me she was just teasing. But even if she was teasing, I know I will go anywhere and do anything for her as long as I can breathe and walk. I wish I could tell her that, but I cain't.

Then one day as we are traveling along a new river, dragging our stuff through about six inches of snow, we come upon a cabin with a smoking chimney, pole corrals full of mooing cows, and the most splendid barn I have seen since leaving the United States. White people must live here, maybe Mormons. Maybe they know how I can get Peggy safely to Great Salt Lake City.

A white woman in a blue dress opens the door as all the Injuns stops in front of the cabin. A little boy with yellow hair is standing behind the woman's skirts, peeking at the Utes. Pretty soon the squaws starts going through their packs to find little pouches and tin cups. Then they starts lining up in front of the cabin so the white woman can give each of them a cup of flour. There's not a lot of talk about it so I guess they have done this before. I guess the woman must be a Mormon to be giving out so much food. Bill Hickman told me Brigham Young said it was better to feed the Indians that to fight them, a lot cheaper too.

After all the squaws have fetched their cup of flour, Peggy and me go up to meet the woman. When she sees us she throws her hands over her mouth and squeals like a puppy that's just been stepped on. She is so glad to see us, like we are her lost relatives. She hugs Peggy, and shakes my hand like she is pumping water from the well. She drags us into the cabin and pushes us into chairs in front of a plank table. Almost before we knows it she shoves a big plate of sugar cookies in front of us, and is pouring each of us a big cup of milk. The cookies is crunchy and full of sugar crystals, and just melts in your mouth. The milk is fresh and cold and washes the chewed up cookies down just right. I kept thinking how I'd ruther eat sugar cookies and milk over mouses boiled in honey, any day.

After we been fed, the woman's got to know what we is doing in this unsettled, wild, basin country. She asks if Brigham Young sent us here to help her husband. I look over at Peggy, and reckon she can do the answering better than me. She don't disappoint me, because she says:

"We aren't Mormons, just Christians on our way to California. We got mixed up in the war out on the plains, so when we lost our stuff, and figured the main roads weren't safe, we joined up with these Utes. My husband, he is trying to get me to Great Salt Lake City where we hope some Mormon midwives can help me have my baby."

I just about chokes on my cookie. Peggy called me her husband. I feels so proud I can almost bust open. But I knows it ain't real. She is pretending we are married so she won't have to be ashamed and have to tell about being violated by the Injuns and trappers. I don't blame her and reckon I am glad I can help. But it surprises me how good she can lie. Back before the Injuns killed her folks, I didn't reckon she could have told a lie even if she wanted to. But things was different now. Peggy was different. The things that had happened to her had changed her. Tom Sawyer would argue that being violated had ruined her, but I reckon it made her stronger and wiser, even if she did learn to tell lies.

On finding out Peggy has a baby in her, the woman pulls her up from the chair and pushes her real gentle over to a bed next to the cabin wall, and makes her lay down, then sits down on the edge of the bed next to Peggy. The woman says her name is Mary Chandler, and her husband's name is Forest. She says her husband and the hired hand, an Indian named Buck, are gathering up their cattle so they can go to Great Salt Lake. President Young has asked all the saints in the far out wilderness places to come home because of the war with the United States. She says the men should be all done with the gathering in a day or so, and we could come with them to Great Salt Lake City. Looking at me, she says they can sure use an extra hand with the cattle.

Peggy tells her our names are Huck and Peggy Finn, and we would be grateful if we can to go with them to Great Salt Lake City. About this time I notice the Injuns is still outside, so I goes out and finds Pan-a-carry. I gives him a cookie, then tells him that Peggy and me has decided to stay with the Chandlers and help drive their cattle back to Great Salt Lake City. He shakes my hand, the way white men do it, says goodby the way white men say it, then gets back on his horse.

All the Injuns get back on their horses, and pretty soon they are gone. I reckon they is real close now to their wintering grounds. I finds an empty corral for my horse, and gives him some hay. I practices my fast draw a couple of times before going back in the cabin.

When I opens the door, I gets hit with a wave of hot air, so hot I take a step back. Mary has built up a roaring fire in the stove. She has decided Peggy needs a bath, and Peggy she ain't arguing against it, saying she hasn't had a real bath since leaving Iowa, if you don't count splashing around in icy streams with squaws and children. Mary has covered the top of the stove with buckets and pans full of water that is warming up, and she has dragged a big wash tub into the middle of the floor. The little boy, his name is Jed, and me gathers up a bunch of wood so they can have lots of hot water, then wanders over to the barn to look at the animals.

Jeb says the dogs has gone out with his father and the Injun Buck. He shows me where some skunks lives, and where their garden was before the weather got cold. As I look around I wonders if there might be a chance for Peggy and me to have a place like this someday—a warm cabin, a nice big barn, lots of country for my cattle to graze in, friendly Injuns so you don't have to worry about being scalped, maybe some neighbors down the road a piece in case you need some help with something, and so Peggy can have another woman to talk to every week or so, and to help her have a new baby every year or two. Pretty soon I would have sons to help with the work, and daughters to go riding with me to check the cattle. It seemed like paradise, but I knowed I was just dreaming.

Jed and me are at the woodpile chopping more wood for the stove, when Mary opens the door and tells us to come to the cabin. She says Peggy is all done with her bath, and that I should do it now. She says it'd be a crying shame to waste all that hot water. I ain't about to take a bath in front of two women, so I starts to back up, but she grabs me by the hand and drags me inside. She tells me she and Jed will take a walk while I do the bathing, but Peggy can stay behind and scrub my back. As I looks over at Peggy, who is dressed now, I feels my face turning red. She can see it, and makes me feel better by saying she is going for a walk with Mary and Jed.

Bathing in a tub warn't something I took much stock in even before leaving the United States. Swimming in the big river, once a day in the summer and every week or two in the winter, had always been enough bath taking for the likes of me. Aunt Polly and Widow Douglas made me do it a time or two in an iron tub, and I didn't like it none, but I figure if I aim to be a family man with a wife, cabin, barn and a herd of cows, I ought to be more civilized, even take a bath once in a while, so I locks the cabin door, slips out of my clothes, and walks over to the big tub. The water is all gray now, some soap bubbles floating around on top. I wonders what was on Peggy to make the water gray. She never looked gray. Finally I decides its just good old mountain dirt. Not much for drinking, I figure, but it looks mighty splendid anyway, not just because its warm and steamy, but because it has been washing all over Peggy just a few minutes ago. Now it can wash over me. Once more, I feels myself blushing.

Now if Mr. Peabody or Blue Fox had washed off in that water, I knowed I just wouldn't want to do anything except dump it out in the corral, but as I sits down and leans back, feeling the warmness flood over me, knowing Peggy was there a minute ago, I feels splendid. I reckon if this is part of being civilized, I can stand some more of it.

About the time darkness arrives Forest and Buck come riding in, pushing about 15 cows in front of them. Two dogs is trailing behind Forest's horse. Forest is tall and skinny, and probably ain't no heavier than me. He has a lantern jaw and a long beard, it's as black as coal. I help them push the cows into a corral with some others. At first Forest acts real careful around me, like he don't trust me, like he might be wondering if I be an outlaw or rustler. But when he sees Peggy and thinks we are a married couple, he don't seem to worry about me no more. But he ain't friendly, and he don't smile. In fact the whole time we knowed him, I never seen him smile.

The Injun named Buck, he don't say much to me or to anybody, but just goes about his chores. Forest says he thinks we won't have any more snow for a couple of days, and that we will leave for Great Salt Lake in the morning. I think maybe Peggy and me will get to sleep in the barn, but Mary ain't about to let Peggy sleep anywhere but in the warm cabin, considering her condition and all. But the cabin has only one room, and a little loft where Jed sleeps. Mary says Peggy must sleep on a little bed against the wall, the one she was resting on earlier. Forest and Mary has their big bed on the other side of the room. But I must sleep out in the barn with Buck. I was glad to hear that, because it would be mighty crowded and uncomfortable with me in the cabin too.

The next morning after a big breakfast of eggs, salt pork and hot cakes I helped Forest load the last of their things into the wagon. He had gone out to the barn before light, ketched the chickens off their roosts and put them in basket cages which we put in the back of the wagon. Little Jed rode in the back of the wagon while the women drove it. Forest, Buck and me rode our horses so we could push the cattle and a couple extra horses along.

We could have moved a lot faster but we didn't have much of a road to follow. Sometimes we had to get off our saddle horses to move logs or big rocks out of the way. Sometimes when the road sloped down to the right or to the left on the side of a hill, we would tie ropes to the wagon which we would dally up on our saddle horns so we could keep the wagon from tipping over. Once we was too late with the ropes, and the wagon just rolled on its side, throwing the two women into the brush. Jeb was under the canvas screaming, and chickens was flying everywhere because two of the cages busted open.

I don't worry none about the wagon, but hurry right to Peggy because she is squirming around on the ground like her back is hurt. Mary is sitting up, rubbing the side of her head. Jed stops screaming when Forest pulls him out of the wagon. I makes Peggy lay out flat on the ground, and starts asking her questions. She says it ain't her back that hurts, but her side, just below the ribs. As I tries to loosen her dress some, so it won't hurt so much, she rolls over and throws up. I just don't know what to do with her, but Mary is along side now, and sends me to help Forest with the wagon.

We makes camp right where the wagon fell over. There is plenty of grass for the cows and horses, and water in some beaver ponds down the hill. Soon we have a big fire going, and chickens roasting in the Dutch ovens. Forest said he couldn't catch the ones that got out of the cages because they flew too high in the trees, so he shot them for our supper.

Peggy is feeling better after we eat, but during the night she starts bleeding. Mary sends me away, saying she will take care of it. I wishes there was something for me to do, but there ain't. When morning comes, Mary tells me that Peggy will be fine, but she has lost the baby. We stay there one more day so Peggy can rest up. I tries to talk to her about the baby, but she won't do it. She won't talk about Blue Fox and the trappers that violated her either. But she will talk about what we got to do next. She says she has to find out what happened to Flaxy, but she don't want to go back to Iowa, not after all that's happened. She thinks maybe California would be a splendid place to start a new life, after she finds out about Flaxy and knows she is safe. I asks her if she still wants me to pretend to be her husband, now the baby is gone.

"We started down that road, so I guess we better follow it to the end," she says, and I ain't sure what that means, only that we will keep the Mormons thinking that she is Mrs. Finn. That night I sleeps by her. A couple of times when I hears her crying, real soft and quiet, I takes her hand and squeezes and pets it, like she is a little girl who has fallen off her pony. I reckon Peggy ain't as wise and strong as I thought she was. I wishes I could do more for her.

When we gets to Heber, we learn that many of the Mormons has moved out of Great Salt Lake City, so they won't be there when the Army comes in. So instead of going there, we follows a trail down the Provo River to Utah Valley. Forest says he has a brother in a place called Lehi, and we can stay there. Peggy is feeling better every day now. Sometimes she changes places with Forest so he can sit by his wife and drive the wagon, and she can help me push the cattle. Forest is always real nice to Peggy, adjusting the stirrups on the saddle, and helping her mount up. Sometimes at supper he brings her food instead of letting her fetch it herself. I reckon maybe he is too nice. If he were any regular American I wouldn't think a thing about it, but he is a Mormon, and Mormon men take extra wives, and their church blesses them to do it. I wishes I had a ring to give to Peggy to wear on her finger, so every time Forest sees it he will remember that she belongs to me. But she really don't, and maybe he knows it, or maybe he just thinks I am a gentile heathen and don't matter no how. I wish we weren't going to Lehi, but that's where we ends up, and I finds out right away that Bill Hickman's best friend, Porter Rockwell lives there too. I remembers Rockwell and what he looked like when he and Bill rode into the handcart camp on those splendid horses.

Chapter 21

The first day in Lehi, I finds out where Rockwell lives and rides over. I am real lucky to find him home. At first he don't want to talk to me, but when I tells him I am the boy who saved Bill Hickman at Fort Bridger, and shows him the Navy Colt that Bill gived me, he knows all about me, and offers me a drink of whiskey like I am one of his best friends.

He tells me him and Bill are getting ready to do a special errand for President Young, to take some mail to Fort Laramie. The Army has closed down the regular mail routes, but they think if they can get the mail to Laramie, the Army will take it to the United States from there. I tell him how I dropped off Peggy's sister, Flaxy in Laramie, and how I have to find out what's happened to her. I asks him if he will try to find her for me and Peggy.

I feels real disappointed when he says he thinks him and Bill will be too busy to look for a little girl, but if I wants to come with them, I can look for her myself when we gets there. I tell him that's what I wants to do. He says the trip won't be easy, it being winter and all, and not knowing what the soldiers might do to us. I tells him I don't care about none of that, so he says to be at his house before daylight the next morning, and to bring a warm bedroll and my gun.

Peggy gets real excited when I tells her I am going to Laramie to find Flaxy. In fact she says she wants to go with me. I tells her it is winter and she has just lost a baby. She has to stay home and get better. Still, she says she is going, so I tells her she is not invited. Rockwell and Hickman don't want a woman along. This she accepts, but she ain't happy about it. I ain't real happy about the way Forest says he will take good care of Peggy while I am gone.

When I gets to Rockwell's house the next morning, I am surprised that he is hitching up a four-wheel buggy with spring axles to a team that looks like race horses. He tells me we can travel faster in a buggy, will be warmer, and won't get near so tired. I unsaddle my horse, and turn it out in his pasture, and we are on our way. I notice Rockwell is wearing two Navy Colts. Plus he has a double-barreled shotgun in a boot by his seat. He tells me Bill is going to meet us at Fort Supply.

We picks up the mail at the church office, and changes teams at the Colorado Stables, owned by Rockwell. We changes teams a lot: at Farmington, South Weber, Morgan, and Echo. I didn't know it was possible to travel so fast. There ain't much snow to slow us down. In four days we arrive at Fort Supply.

Bill throws his arms around me like I was his lost boy. I swear he is so happy to see me that his eyes gets all wet. We goes inside one of the cabins while Rockwell puts up the horses. Bill gives me a drink of whiskey, then we plays the fast draw game so he can see what he learned me. He is happy that I am now almost as fast as he is. When Rockwell comes in, we tries to get him to play with us, but he don't want to.

The next day we don't travel near as fast. Rockwell says we can't change horses near so often, so he don't want to work them near as hard. Plus we are leading three saddle horses behind the carriage, so we can make a get-away if the Army tries to ketch us.

At night we camps in deep draws, or thick groves of trees, to get out of the wind, and so Army scouts won't see our fire. When we left Fort Supply Bill throwed in three big buffalo robes, for sleeping, and to throw over us in the carriage when the Wyoming wind gets to blowing real hard. It being winter, the Army don't seem to be out looking for anybody, so we makes really good time. In a week we arrive at Fort Laramie.

I hurries to the cabin where the commanding officer, Colonel Dent lives, where I had left Flaxy. I am so happy when Mrs. Dent comes to the door. I feared earlier that the commander might have moved, and nobody there now would know about Flaxy So I asks Mrs. Dent what has happened. She says:

"You asked us to send her to her relatives near Keokuk, Iowa, so that's what we did," she explained. "A couple of months ago."

"Do you know if she arrived safely?" I asks.

"Yes, I received a letter from her Aunt Flora. She said Flaxy is going to school, but she says they are all worried sick about Peggy, and want to know if she is all right. I wrote back saying Peggy was no longer with the Indians, but some trappers. The Army was trying to find her so they can send her back to Iowa too."

I asked Mrs. Dent if she would write back to Aunt Flora and tell her that Peggy got away from the trappers and was in Great Salt Lake City, safe and sound. She promised her letter would go out with the next batch of mail. I thanked Mrs. Dent for her help then went looking for Hickman and Rockwell. My business in Laramie was finished. I knowed Peggy would be happy to know Flaxy was in Iowa and going to school.

I found them at the commissary, sorting through a big batch of letters addressed to various Mormons in Utah Territory. They tells me they will be ready to head back in the morning, so I watches and waits. I don't go outside anymore because a north wind is blowing so hard I cain't keep my hat on without holding onto it. Soldiers come in and go out. None of them seems to care that Mormon outlaws are busy sorting mail for their Mormon friends in Great Salt Lake City.

I don't want to get Hickman and Rockwell arrested, but I am real curious to know why the soldiers here at Fort Laramie act like there ain't no war to worry about, so I goes up to a young lieutenant who is sitting on a flour barrel like he don't have a thing to do, and I says:

"I just come from Utah Territory."

He looks up at like he is wondering why I might brag about a thing like that.

"The Mormons has gathered up their guns, is marching in the streets and getting ready for war. They is moving their families out of Great Salt Lake City. But when I get out here, there ain't very many soldiers, and they don't seem like there's anything for them to do, like there ain't a war going on."

"There ain't no war," he says, then spits some tobacco juice on the floor.

"The Mormons don't know that," I says.

"Ain't nobody been killed, on either side," he says. "In wars folks get killed."

"Then what's going on, the soldiers trying to get to Utah and all?" I asks.

He explains, as he chews on his tobacco, that congress appointed a governor to go to Great Salt Lake City and run the Utah Territory, that congress didn't think the Mormons would be too happy about Brigham Young having no more say in things, so an army was sent to stand by the governor. The new governor's name was E. E. Cummings.

The lieutenant said the Mormons was mad and was stirring up the eastern newspapers with talk about war because they didn't want no appointed governor instead of the one they elected. Congress was determined to get Cummings in power so there would be a separation of church and government in Utah like the constitution required. He said Mormon bishops was holding court on civil matters, things like stealing horses or beating women. He said the bishops were ordering executions for things like apostasy and adultery. He said federal judges was being sent with the new governor so a regular government could be set up. Brigham Young and his bishops would no longer be allowed to run the government, only their church. The Army was coming to Utah to make sure all this happened. The Army was going to Utah so the Mormons wouldn't think very long about not letting the new governor and the judges take over the government. He said the Mormons had burned a few wagons and a bunch of grass to slow down the Army, but he didn't think the Mormons wanted a real war.

I was surprised when I tried to explain all this to Hickman and Rockwell. They said it warn't right in the United States for a people not being allowed to elect its own governor. Rockwell said there might be fifteen people in the whole territory who wouldn't vote for Brigham Young, and about ten thousand who would, so President Young ought to be the governor, if this is the United States. Now congress was sending in a governor who couldn't get a hundred votes if he campaigned for two years. What happened to the constitutional right for people to elect the leaders who governed them?

Life was a lot simpler when Jim and me was floating down the Mississippi River on our raft. But when it came right down to it, I really didn't care if Utah Territory had an elected or an appointed governor. I warn't no Mormon, and didn't live there. My only interest in the whole dad fetching place was a certain young woman named Peggy who was staying there. Everybody out there thought she was my wife, and I hoped that would become a real thing. I knowed I would follow her to California, back to Iowa, or anywhere else she took a notion to go, and never look back.

We had been gone from Utah only a few weeks but I missed Peggy something awful. I was ready to return, but when I looked out the window, not only was the wind blowing harder, but the sky was now black with clouds, and some snowflakes was shooting sideways past the window. By morning the road was covered with snow drifts about three feet deep. Rockwell said we would wait a day or two before starting back. By afternoon the drifts on the road were six feet deep. Hickman said it might be a month or more before we could go home now.

That lieutenant was right about this not being a real war with the Mormons. By the time the storm had blowed itself out and some of the snow was starting to melt, which was more than a week, Hickman and Rockwell had cut a deal with the United States Army to help get supplies to a bunch of soldiers who were camped at what used to be Fort Bridger. When the soldiers went there, they didn't take enough supplies because they thought they could buy stuff at the fort. They didn't know it was destroyed. Of course Hickman knew all about that because he was the one who done it.

Hickman and Rockwell agreed to break trail through the snow drifts with their mail buggy so they could lead an Army wagon full of food, clothes and oats to the stranded soldiers and their horses. The Army gave Rockwell fifty dollars to do this. I reckon the Army had just turned two foxes loose in the hen house. When we was alone practicing our fast draws I asked Bill if he and Rockwell were going to steal the wagon before we got to Fort Bridger.

"Might help myself to the whiskey," he said with a happy wink, "and take any powder and lead that might be used against us, but not the food."

"You told me the Mormons was at war with the United States," I says. "All summer and fall you been stealing wagons and supplies."

"Nobody was in danger of starving or freezing to death, until now," he said. "The Army ain't killed a single Mormon, and we ain't killed a single soldier, and don't aim to start now."

I wonders if this might be the first war in the history of the world where killing was not allowed. If so, it is a fine new way to make war. But I wonders how they will decide who the winners is, if fighting's not a part of it. Guess I'd just have to wait and see.

In the meantime, while waiting for the storm to pass, I snoops around the Army headquarters cabin to see if I could find out what has happened to Tom and Jim. I learns that a Tom Sawyer had been driving one of the wagons accompanying the soldiers going to Fort Bridger, and that one of the cooks was a former slave named Jim. Now we were being paid by the Army to go there too.

Before we leave I ask Rockwell if he is going to give me any of the fifty dollars the Army had given him to lead the supply wagon to Fort Bridger. He gives me a funny look, then says he has been wondering how much to charge me for bringing me to Fort Laramie and back home again. It is clear he don't want to give me any portion of the money, and I has about decided he is a cheap dad-fetching-son-of-a-gun when he tells me the Army wants to hire me to be one of the drivers on the supply wagon. If I go over to the headquarters office and sign a paper, they will give me fifteen dollars. I hurries right over there and before I knows it the paymaster has handed me some gold coins. I couldn't have made that much money working all winter at Fort Supply. I feel rich and happy.

Nothing happens on the road to Fort Bridger. There is less snow at South Pass than at Laramie, so we hurries right on through. When we finally gets to Fort Bridger, a bunch of happy men crowds around us. They'd been eating oatmeal three times a day. We starts throwing down cases of peaches, sides of bacon, shanks of ham, bags of beans and flour and sugar, coffee beans, boxes of hard candy, even some boxes of eggs. A very serious captain is making marks on a list as we throws the stuff down. When we are all done he don't seem very happy as he stares at his list.

"Where's the salt?" he asks, looking up at us men who was unloading the wagon.

I tells him I helped load the wagon in Laramie, and had helped unload it here, and there warn't no salt.

"Men can't eat meat without salt," he said, like he expects me to go all the way back to Laramie for a bag of salt. I ain't about to do that.

About this time I sees Jim and Tom hurrying up to the wagon. I jumps down and runs over to them.

Now Jim, he just starts right in hugging and kissing me, big horse tears running down his cheeks. I feels embarrassed that he is making such a fuss, but it makes me feel awful glad too. Now Tom, he just shakes my hand like he knowed I was coming, and like I hasn't been gone more than a day or two. But that's the way Tom is, and I don't feel bad at all. But as soon as he gets done shaking my hand, he cain't do nothing but talk about the Navy Colt on my hip. It's like he never seen such a splendid gun before.

"Just like what the officers wear," he says, reaching out and touching the pearl handle.

"Now don't get to playing," I says. "She's loaded and ready to go."

He pulls his hand back, looking admiringly at the gun and at me, like he thinks with a gun I am all growed up now, and no longer the river boy Huck Finn. Tom is only seventeen, but I decided to be nineteen so Peggy wouldn't think I was too young for her to marry me, so I guess I was all growed up even though I still didn't have no whiskers. I tells Tom I have a fast draw game I will show him in a little while.

About this time somebody starts yelling at Jim to get his sorry butt over to the mess tent. He lets go of me and runs away to do his duty. But Tom, he just wants to keep playing with my pistol. He asks where I got it. I points to Bill and tells Tom that the Mormon gun fighter gave it to me for saving his life. Now Tom cain't hardly believe this. The soldiers has told him all about the two famous gunfighters, Rockwell and Hickman. He cain't believe I knows such men. He keeps looking at them, over by their buggy talking to the officers.

I borrow Bill's Colt and show Tom the fast draw game. He don't believe I can draw and shoot faster than he can pull the trigger, so I do it five times in a row. He still can't believe it. He thinks I am somehow tricking him. I just shrug my shoulders and offer to do it again.

I am surprised that while we are doing all this that Tom still hasn't asked about Peggy. I knowed if I had been in his boots, the first thing I would want to know was what happened to Peggy. But Tom don't even ask, so I decides to tell him anyway.

I tells him how Peggy got away from the trappers and how I followed Hog to the Ute camp, then had to shoot him in the foot when he was beating up on her, and how Peggy and me ended up in Lehi. I didn't tell him that Peggy was going to have a child but lost it, but I did tell him how we pretended to be man and wife so the Injuns would leave her alone, and so the Mormons wouldn't ask too many questions. He thought that was pretty smart. He didn't have any questions about how Peggy was getting along, after the Injuns and trappers had kept her a slave and defiled her. He didn't want to talk about her anymore, or any of the things that happened to her, and that was fine with me, because I didn't want to talk about those things either. I just thought Tom would care more because Peggy had been a friend to both of us before the Injuns killed her folks and took her away.

Before we could leave Fort Bridger another storm sets in real bad. The soldiers gots plenty of tents and lots of food so we stays around and helps them eat it. After a couple of days Tom up and decides he wants to come with us to Great Salt Lake City. When I asks him if he can get out of the Army, he says he was never in it, that the Army just had him sign a paper to drive a wagon, and he can just up and quit any time, unless there is a battle going on, and that ain't happening now. I asks Rockwell and Hickman if Tom can go with us to Utah, and they says he can.

The next thing I knows is Jim wants to come too. Now this ain't so simple because Jim done made his mark on a piece of paper to join the

Army. It don't make no difference that he didn't know what was happening when he made his mark. They just told him to do it, so he did, not knowing what he was getting on with. I explains all this to Bill, who says:

"Why does an ex-slave want to go to Utah?" he asks.

"It ain't so much that he wants to go to Utah," I explains. "He just don't want to be in the Army no more. Too much like being a slave again, he thinks. He didn't want to be here in the Army, but they made him make his mark. He thinks if he goes to Utah with us he can be free again. He says the Mormons don't keep no slaves."

Bill says Jim is welcome to go with us, but he ain't about to help a man run away from the Army and make the United States more mad at the Mormons than it already is. Bill says if I can get the captain to let Jim go with us, so he ain't no deserter, then he can come.

So I asks Bill how I can do that. And he says a smart boy like me ought to figure out a way. I starts thinking about it, and comes up with an idea. I goes and finds the captain, the one who was checking off the list when we unloaded the supplies, and just up and asks the captain if he is getting used to not having salt in his food. That captain he don't even answer, but just stares at me like he is wondering why anybody would ask such a dumb question.

Now I says that the biggest salt deposit in the whole world is only a hundred miles away, and I am going there with Hickman and Rockwell as soon as the weather gets a little better, and it's just too bad I'm so busy helping Hickman and Rockwell with this war, because if I warn't, I'd dig up a bag or two of clean white salt and bring it back to the captain.

The captain is real happy now, and telling me how much he will pay for three or four bags of salt. Then I tells him that I will get to the salt real easy because I have Hickman and Rockwell as my guards, but I don't know how I will get back to Fort Bridger. It is too dangerous for a boy like me to travel alone with so many Injuns, outlaws and trappers on the roads. Real careful, I asks if he might be able to send a guard with me, so I won't have to come alone when I brings back the salt. The way he rubs his chin I can see he is thinking about my request, and he wants that salt real bad. He tells me how he don't have enough soldiers to fight the Mormons if the war starts again, so he is afraid to send one with me.

Now I sees my chance, so I says that instead of sending a soldier to guard me, why not one of the cooks. I told him in Missouri I knowed the cook Jim when he was a slave, and that I'd like him to come with me to help dig the salt and bring it back. The captain hems and haws and keeps rubbing his chin as he thinks about this. Finally, he says that will be fine with him. I tries real hard not to seem too happy, and when I tells Jim, I says he has to act just like this is another job he has to do.

Tom ain't very happy when I tells him how Jim is going to come with us. I tell him I helped Jim run away from being a slave in Missouri, and now I am helping him run away from the Army.

"When they ketches a run-away slave," Tom says, "they whip him and send him home. When they ketches a run-away soldier, they calls him a deserter, stands him up against the wall and shoots him."

Tom says I have to leave Jim here, where the Army takes good care of him. He has a warm place to sleep, and gets to eat three times a day. An ex-slave like Jim ought to be real happy to be in the Army.

So I tells Tom if he can convince Jim when we gets to Great Salt Lake City that staying in the Army is good for him, he can come right back with a sack of salt, and he won't be in no trouble at all. Tom sees no harm in this, so he stops arguing for Jim not to come with us.

Pretty soon this storm passes too, and the bunch of us goes over to Fort Supply where the few men who are there are hunkered down to wait out the winter. When I'm in the store I notices that they have four or five bags of salt. I buys one of them, and gives one of the men a dollar to take it over to Bridger and give it to the captain. "Tell him it's from Huck Finn," I says. The man says he will do it tomorrow. I feels better now knowing that if Jim don't want to come back, at least the captain will get his salt which is what he wanted in the first place.

The next morning when I goes outside to feed the horses, I hear a voice behind me.

"Huck Finn, turn around so's I can shoot you in the foot."

I knows who has a voice like that. It's Hog. Slowly I turns around. Hog and Wire are sitting on their skinny horses, and Hog is pointing his rifle at me. One of his feet is wrapped up in a dirty shirt and is so big it cain't fit in the stirrup. I am standing behind a watering trough, too far from the store door to jump back inside. Nobody else who can help me has come outside. I am alone, and after what I did, I knows Hog will shoot my foot off.

"Git out from behind that trough so's I can see your feet," he says.

I don't move, knowing he is going to shoot me. I starts thinking about the Navy Colt on my hip. It's loaded. I have been practicing drawing and shooting for months now, and knows I am as fast as Bill. I can draw and shoot in less than half a second, and knows it will take longer than that for Hog to pull the trigger after he knows I am making a move. He don't know how fast I am, so that gives me some more edge.

"Git," he says, waving his rifle for me to go to my right. It is time for me to draw and shoot. I knows how to do it, and knows if I don't my foot will be shot to pieces, but my hand won't move. The air is freezing cold, but I can feel hot sweat on my hands and face. My heart is pounding a hole in the front of my chest. My hand is shaking, but it won't do what I tells it to do.

I cain't move so I starts talking, glad at least my tongue will move. I tells them I am working for the Army now, and am supposed to get salt for the soldiers. The United States Army will come after him if he shoots one of their men.

Now Hog raises the barrel of his rifle so it ain't pointing towards my feet anymore but right at the middle of my chest. I reckon he has decided to kill me instead of wounding my foot. Then I can't tell the Army who done it. I tells my hand if it won't go for the gun now it is going to die. It just keeps shaking. Now I can hear my heart pounding like it is inside my ears. Then I hears something else. Voices.

"Huck, introduce us to your friends," says the voice of Bill Hickman. I can see out the side of my eye that Bill and Port have stepped around the side of the store. Both of them has their arms folded like they are in church, but their coats is open so Hog can see their guns. Both of them is smiling like all of us is brothers having a splendid family reunion.

"Bill Hickman and Porter Rockwell," I croaks, knowing Hog and Wire knows the names if they don't know the faces.

Now Hog is smiling too. Slowly, he lowers his rifle.

"Came in for food and medicine," Hog says, wiggling his foot, the one wrapped in the dirty shirt. "Outlaw shot me in the foot, aim to kill him first chance I gets."

Hog and Wire gets down from their horses, goes in the store and buys some food and whiskey, then leaves without another word. I cain't wait to get out of this Wyoming country and put as many miles as possible between me and them.

Chapter 22

In a day or two we is headed down Echo Canyon to the valley of the Great Salt Lake. Bill and Port leading the way in their light carriage, and I am following behind driving one of the big wagons they stole from the Army. Tom and Jim are on the wagon seat with me. Just like old times. Me and my friends, and we is going to see Peggy. I feels real happy, safe too. With Port and Bill in front, I feel protected, like the whole United States Army is coming with us.

The only thing that surprises me is the way Tom is starting to act. When we first came out west, he wanted to live with the savages, like the ones he was reading about in books. But pretty soon he learnt that book Injuns and real Injuns ain't the same. Then Tom takes up with the Army, where he learns that book soldiers and real soldiers ain't the same either, at least not with men like Sergeant Peabody who makes them little boys cry at night.

Now Tom is all fired up about the Mormons and their religion. I been around Mormons longer than he has, but I still ain't sure what the difference is between book Mormons and real Mormons, except that most folks don't think of Mormons as splendid gunfighters and horsemen like Porter Rockwell and Bill Hickman. Tom has only been around these men a few weeks, and now wants to be like them.

First thing he starts saying *Brother* Hickman and *Brother* Rockwell when talking to the gunfighters. Then before I knows it, Rockwell gives Tom one of them Mormon bibles, but Tom, he don't just politely take it, saying thanks. He starts reading it, and asking lots of questions about them people who were the first Mormons in America thousands of years ago. If I didn't know better, I'd say Tom liked that old book the same as if James Fennimore Cooper had wrote it hisself.

Now Tom, he just seems to want to swaller every little thing Port tells him about that Mormon book. Why Port tells him those ancient folks just wrote that book on plates, I suppose when they got done eating, and the plates was made of pure solid gold like men finds in California.

And the mules in the Mormon book fly kites. Now, I don't know how a smart boy like Tom can believe that. I knowed some boys who tied a kite to a dog's tail once, and that kite flyed just fine as long as the dog run in a straight line, but if you tied a kite to a mule's tail he'd just as likely kick your head off, and I never seen a mule yet that would run in a straight line with something tied to his tail. I ain't about to believe in no book that says there was Mule kites.

When I asked Tom how the first Mormon, Joe Smith, was able to take funny markings on gold plates and make a story on paper that white men could read, he said Smith just looked at a big old thumb, from a man named Erman I think he said, and it told him what to write. "Who cut Erman's thumb off?" I asked, but Tom he don't know the answer.

Tom said there is lots of real nice fights and wars in the book, and that almost gets me interested to read it too, but as I hear Tom and Port talk about the wars, I gather it must be some kind of funny fighting they did. I knows all about fist fights and rock fights and sword fights. But I never heard of knee fights before, and Tom and Port are talking about knee fights all the time. Tom can believe all that if he wants, but not me.

When Tom and Port gets a going on the Book of Mormon, that's when Bill pulls a big brown law book from under the seat of the buggy and starts reading it so he can be a lawyer when he is all done with gunfighting.

While the bunch of them is reading, I borrow Bill's Colt so's me and

Jim can practice fast draw. But I am doing it different now. When Jim stands there pointing his gun at me, I half close my eyes, pretending he ain't old Jim, but Hog or Wire, or Blue Fox, or Sergeant Peabody trying to get me to come to bed. Then I draws and shoots. My hand works good now, and when Bill looks up from his book he tells me I am the fastest he has seen. Sometimes Tom wants to practice with us, but he don't work very hard at it. Maybe if it had been him instead of me standing in front of Hog's rifle, knowing he was about to die, he would try harder.

When I tells Tom how Hog was going to kill me, Tom wants to know why I didn't draw and shoot like I had been practicing to do. When I told him my hand wouldn't do it, he didn't believe me. He thought I was pulling his leg, but he didn't know why I would do that. At first I couldn't understand why he didn't believe me, but as I thought about it the reason became clear as a dew drop on a leaf on a spring morning. Tom didn't know that book fights and real fights ain't the same. And I reckoned it warn't no use trying to explain something like that to someone who hadn't been in a real fight where someone wanted to kill him.

And just when I thinks all the scripture reading is making Tom about as religious as a boy can be, he starts saying prayers over the food whenever we eats. Port teaches him how to do it. Aunt Polly and the Widow Douglas had tried to get Tom to pray, but it didn't take. But it is different now, and I just cain't understand the need to do it. Now if we was eating polecat jerky made by an Injun who never washed his hands, I can see a need to pray over it. Or if we was chewing up raw frog legs because there ain't no fire, somebody might want to say a prayer. Once I saw a slave wipe maggots off a piece of meat before he cooked it, and I think a meal like that might need a powerful blessing. But we is eating good, clean Army food: canned peaches, beef boiled in salt water, beans with onions and bacon, white flour biscuits with butter and honey, and boiling hot coffee—clean food, nothing that could poison a body. No need to pray over these kinds of fixings that I can see. But Tom don't see it that way. If Porter Rockwell and Bill Hickman say it's the right thing to do, then dad fetch him, Tom is bound to do it. But I don't see Port and Bill praying over the food. They just smiles, bows their heads, and lets Tom do it all the time. I reckon I has seen a miracle when a couple of tough and splendid gunfighters are better than Aunt Polly at putting religion into Tom. I figure before I know it he'll be wanting to go to Sunday School. But I ain't going with him.

One of the first nights in Echo Canyon we camp at a place with nice wide meadows and good water where horse bones is scattered all over the ground. I asks Port if Injuns has massacred a wagon train here. He tells me to look at the dried up horses feet and see if I can answer my own question. I walks around among the bones looking for feet. I finds lots of them, and for the life of me can't reckon how looking at feet will tell me about a massacre. I am about to go back to Port and ask my question all over again, when I realizes that none of the feet has horseshoes nailed on them. The bones is not white men's horses, so I knows there warn't no massacre of white men here. So I asks Port if a bunch of Injuns was killed here since none of the hoofs have shoes on them. He asks me to explain why I see only horse bones, and no man bones. I says that after the fight is over and the white men are gone, other Injuns carried off the dead ones and buried them. Port seems pleased that I thinks like this, but he says there was no Injun massacre here either, just a horse massacre. I asks why anyone would want to kill a bunch of horses. I never knowed anyone who would rather shoot a horse than ride it, except my pappy who was always wanting to beat his mule half to death.

Port said one time two Ute chiefs, Walkara and Arapeen, who was brothers, stole a bunch of horses from the Shoshones up Wyoming way and were bringing them home down Echo Canyon. Port said Walkara was probably the greatest horse thief in the history of the world because one winter before the Mormons came he and his friends stole five thousand horses from the Spanish settlers in California.

Anyhows, when Walkara and Arapeen was camped at this same place, they decides it's time to divide up the horses they stole. There was a really fine buckskin among the new horses, and Walkara said he would take that one. Arapeen objects, saying that's the one he wants more than all the rest. They argue a while, but in the end both still wants the buckskin, so Arapeen just goes over and puts his rope on the buckskin, saying he is taking it. Walkara gets mad, so he picks up his rifle and shoots the buckskin dead. Arapeen don't say a word other than asking Walkara which horse he wants now he can't have the buckskin. Walkara gets up to put his rope on a nice black, but before he can ketch it Arapeen shoots it. Port said they just kept doing this until they had shot all the horses, even the ones they was riding when they went to Wyoming, so they had to walk back to Utah because they had killed all the horses.

I cain't see me and Tom shooting a bunch of horses because we can't figure out how to divide them up, so I asks Port if he is sure that is how the bones got to be here. He said he warn't here to see it himself, but Walkara told him about it, then a year or so later he finds this place with all the bones, so he believes what Walkara said. Port said he used to think there was a lesson to be learned here about human pride, greed and vanity, but after camping here a bunch of times he has decided it was just a pissing match between two big chiefs.

One time after supper I asks Bill how many men he has killed. He is sitting on a rock, a tin cup of boiling hot coffee between his palms, staring into the fire. When he don't answer, I point to his Navy Colt where I seen some lines scratched on the bone handle, and asks if he scratched a line for each man he killed. He says the lines got scratched there when he fell off his horse and slid on his side across some rocks.

He keeps staring into the fire. It seems like a long time. I waits. Finally, he says:

"Say a man kills a clerk while robbing a store and is galloping out of town with a sack of money in his hand. And all the people are yelling *holdup, robbery, he killed Brother Smith*, and things like that—I raise my rifle to the shoulder, take careful aim, pull the trigger, shoot him out of the saddle, he's dead before he hits the ground. That's what I call a clean kill. People slaps me on the back, buys me a bottle of Valley Tan, and maybe President Young sends me a twenty dollar gold piece for the fine work. Maybe I make a mark on the stalk of my rifle. I eat a big steak for supper, and sleep like a baby."

Bill stops talking as he tosses two more sticks on the fire. I wait, hoping he will say more. He does.

"Say a man rapes a woman, or steals some horses. They catch him. The brothern hold court. They pray, listen to witnesses, consider the evidence, then decide the man is guilty and must die. Any place else in the country they slip a rope around his neck and hang him in a tree, or stand him up against a wall and shoot him. And sometimes they do that here, but not all the time because President Young believes a man who sins can pay for it by shedding his own blood. So if he's a Mormon they call in good old Bill Hickman to do it. If the man don't go along peacefully, it takes five or six men to hold him down for me. If he keeps fighting, blood squirts all over the men who hold him. If he goes peacefully, he just bends over a basin while I do it. Then I hold him like a baby while the life runs out of him."

Bill looks up from the fire, his eyes lock on mine.

"Old Bill will never do that again, not as long as he lives. Suing instead of killing, that's what I aim to do."

As he continues to look at me, he makes a grim smile through his wet eyes. I wonder if Tom knows his book gunfighters and this real one ain't the same.

"Going to be a lawyer, and help folks win what is rightfully theirs, in court. I'm all finished settling differences with a gun and a knife."

It had never occurred to me that lawyers helped people. So I asks: "Can you help Jim?"

"How?"

"You knows I ain't bringing him to Great Salt Lake to get salt. I am helping him run away from the Army. Tom says if they ketches him they will call him a deserter and hang him."

I explains how Jim didn't know he was joining the Army when they made him make his mark on a piece of paper.

"We could sue the United States government for unlawful enlistment and entrapment," Bill says. "Jim could be his own witness, tell the judge how they forced him to make his mark. Should be easy to win."

"Let's do it," I says.

"Don't know. It's still risky."

"How's that?"

"Might get a judge who thinks men with black skins ought to be guilty."

"So what do we do?"

"Nothing. When the new governor is sitting on his throne maybe the Army will go back to St. Louis and forget all about Jim. He wasn't a soldier anyway, just a cook."

"But if they don't go back to St. Louis, and ketches him, what then?" I asks.

"Then come see me, and we'll sue the government for unlawful enlistment."

"How much would you charge to do that for Jim?"

"We'd demand two thousand for damages and mental cruelty. I'd take a third and give the rest to Jim."

I found Jim who had been cleaning up some pans from supper, and told him he didn't have to worry about the Army hanging him no more, that Bill was going to be his lawyer if they ever ketched him.

Bill and Port didn't seem to be in any great hurry to reach the valley of the Great Salt Lake. It was winter. If it snowed sometimes we'd just keep agoing, but if the wind blowed very hard we'd stop in some trees, or up against the mountain, turn the horses out to graze, and build a big fire. Sometimes we'd put up an Army tent that was in my wagon. Jim would get to cookin', Tom and Port would get to studying their Book of Mormon, and I would pester Bill with fast draw practice while he was a studying his law book.

Sometimes I goes for a walk, so I can be alone. And when I does all I can think about is Peggy, how splendid she makes me feel when I am around her, how my heart about busted out of my chest when she told them Mormons I was her husband, how beautiful and perfect she is. I wished we were traveling faster so I could see her sooner.

Chapter 23

When we finally reaches the valley of the Great Salt Lake there ain't no more snow on the ground, but the green grass of spring still ain't growing either. As we travel south to Great Salt Lake City we see that many of the houses are empty, and some of the businesses has the front doors locked. Bill says many of the Mormons has moved south so they won't be around when the United States Army marches in. President Young thinks there might be fighting, so families is supposed to leave the valleys along the shore of the big lake.

When we reaches Great Salt Lake City we stay two nights at Port's Colorado Stables. Port and Bill have a meeting with President Young to tell him what they saw on the plains, and what the Army is doing. I think about Peggy and practice fast draw with Jim.

Jim ain't sure what he wants to do now he is gone from the Army. He likes that woman in Blue Fox's camp, but he don't think he can find her now the Injuns has moved.

Finally, we moves on to Lehi, but when we gets to the place where Peggy is staying, she ain't there no more. Forest is the only one home. His brother and sister-in-law went to Provo to get some seed. Forest is frowning like a big mouth bass with his jaws locked up tight, a look that has his lantern-jawed face looking even more that way than before--and he is dancing around on his spider legs, and chopping wood like a wild man, all sweaty, a wild look in his eyes. He says Mary and Peggy done run away together, and he don't know where, and they took little Jed with them, and they been gone near a month. He don't know what to do. Then he starts to crying, wringing his hands.

I couldn't draw a gun when Hog had his rifle pointed at me, but I sure can if I needs it to see Peggy again. I slaps Forest across the face, real hard with my left hand, then before he can hit me back, I draws my Navy Colt and points it right at his nose. I does it so quick, it gets his attention real fast.

"Where'd they go?" I demand.

"If I knowed that," he whines, "I'd be after them myself."

"Why did they leave?"

"I don't know."

I cocks back the hammer on my pistol, and pushes it close to the end of his nose.

"Why did they leave?" I asks a second time. He can see I ain't foolin', so he says:

"Mary told me Peggy really ain't your wife. She'd been talking about the Church and all, about ready to be baptized I figured, so I decides to invite her into my family, a second wife, you know. All the brethren does it. So I starts courtin', primin' her up so I can get her to do it." He stops talking. There's a far away look in his eyes, like he sees what he's telling me.

"So what happened?" I asks, as I waves my gun to get his attention back where it belongs.

"Mary seed what was happening. Got so mad I thought she was going to chop me open with an axe. Said she didn't want to be married to me no more. Then she gets all quiet and won't talk to me no more, only to Peggy. One day I go to town. When I come back, both of them is gone, and Jed too. Some folks said they went to the city to hide. Others say they headed west, to California. I don't know." He looks down at his spider legs, turns around and santers back to the wood pile.

I reckon I am looking at a rare species of human being, if Mary don't come back. Forest might be the world's first bachelor polygamist. I finds out later that men like Forest ain't so rare, not in Utah Territory anyway. Mary warn't the first woman, or the last, to leave her man when he tells her he is agoing to get a new wife. And when the new wife-to-be sees the first wife don't want the man no more, then maybe she don't either, so another bachelor polygamist is made. I don't understand none of it because I am just a boy from the big river who ain't been to school and don't read books. Polygamy don't make no sense. I reckon if Peggy would let me be her husband, that would be all the happiness I could stand for the rest of my life. I don't know why I would want another woman to have with Peggy, even if the Mormons said I could do it.

As I looks at that lantern-jawed Forest, back to chopping wood and crying, stopping now and then to wring his hands, I knows exactly where to find out where Peggy and Mary had gone. Porter Rockwell was home. We had just left him at his house. If anybody in Utah Territory could find out where two women would run away to, it was Rockwell. Tom, Jim and me jumps on our horses and gallops over to Porter Rockwell's house.

He is surprised to see us again so quick. I don't make no small talk, just tells him what has happened and that I needs to know where the women went. He just laughs and points west. I can see this ain't the first time a woman run away in Utah because of polygamy. Port says if they go north or south all they finds is more Mormons who will send them home. The roads to the east are closed because the Army's a coming, so the only way for them to go is west, to California. He explains how to get on the road to California, how it first goes to Simpson Springs, past Government Creek and Fish Springs, then Caleo and Ibapah where Howard Egan has a big ranch. He says Egan makes regular trips to Sacramento, carrying mail back and forth for President Young and the rest of the Mormons. He said the Shoshones along the Humboldt River west of Ibapah are some of the meanest in the world, and pale faces like us would get scalped for sure if we tried to go by ourselves. The only safe way to Sacramento is with one of Egan's mail parties. That's how the women would a done it. He says they is likely in Sacramento already, but he don't know for sure.

Porter fixes us up with a pack horse, and sells us some supplies from his store. The next morning we is on our way west. Winter is mostly gone, so the road is dry. We make good time. We ride right on past Simpson Spring which ain't nothing but a cabin and some corrals. We stop long enough to give the horses a drink, but don't see nobody. As we rides along I am always looking at the tracks in the road, wondering which ones might belong to Peggy and Mary. The way Forest talked, I guesses they traveled this way about a month ago, so their tracks probably ain't here no more, but I still studies the ones I sees, wondering if some might belong to Peggy's horse.

The next morning we is pushing hard, when I sees the biggest track I ever did see. Tom says he went to a circus once in St. Louis where they had elephants, so he knowed what an elephant's foot looks like, and only elephants can make tracks this big. He says there gots to be an elephant wandering down the road in the middle of the Utah desert. I says there ain't no railroad to carry an elephant to Utah, so it don't make no sense for an elephant to be out here.

"If it ain't an elephant track, then what kind of track is it?" Tom wants to know. I don't know the answer, but Jim says we ought to turn back, that anything that could make a track that big might want to eat us up. The tracks they goes right down the middle of the road, on top of all the horse tracks, so we knows they is fresh as tracks can be.

After we follows them a while, I sees where some of them is caved in on the sides, and don't look as fresh as the first ones we saw. I tells Tom and Jim that we is going the wrong way, that the elephant, or whatever thing it is, is going the other way. Since the tracks is freshest where we first seen them, the thing has to be back there somewhere. Jim wants to keep moving and put as many miles as possible between us and the track maker, and since I wants to ketch Peggy, that's what I want to do too, but Tom insists we have to go back and find his elephant. He says if we ketches an elephant we can sell it for a hundred dollars. Jim says we'd get killed for sure if we tries to ketch a wild elephant. Tom argues it ain't likely wild, that it has run away from a circus in California or Chicago or someplace like that. We can feed it peanuts, and teach it to do tricks, and we'll be rich. We can start our own circus, and own it ourselves.

When I tells Tom we don't gots no peanuts, he just says that after we ketches it, we can send Jim back to Great Salt Lake to get some. It don't do no good to argue with Tom. He can wiggle out of any corner when you thinks you got him trapped. So we turns around. I don't like putting more miles between me and Peggy, but I want to see Tom's face when he sees the track maker ain't no elephant. I just wishes I knowed what else it might be, but I don't. Jim, he don't like going back at all, but he don't want to be alone either, so he comes with us.

A little bit farther than the place where we first seen the tracks, they goes off the road and into the sage brush. We stops and looks around for a minute. Jim sees it first, a black thing sticking out of the top of the sage brush, and it's moving. The black thing is too close to the ground and too little to be an elephant, but it be right in line with where the tracks is headed. We gets closer. The black thing moves some more. Jim is holding back now, not wanting to get too close, but Tom and me just a keeps a riding. I put my hand on the butt of my Navy Colt, just in case.

Pretty soon we see the black thing is a head, maybe the head of an Injun. Tom says maybe he is getting ready to ambush us, but I don't reckon he'd be a showing his head if he was in the middle of an ambush. I rides a little closer. I can see the Injun's face now, and it looks like he is just squatting there in the sage brush, doing some personal business, or waiting for us to come. It don't make no sense at all. I keeps waiting for him to stand up, but he don't do it.

When we gets up real close, he says *good morning*, his English pretty good for an Injun. Then I sees why he don't stand up. He don't have no legs. He is wearing a leather pouch over his lower parts, and their ain't no leg holes in it.

"White boys no hurt Injun No Legs," he says. I suppose he means me and Tom when he says white boys. Then he sees Jim, and says: "Ike, big Goshute chief. Friend No Legs."

Other than a stick in his hand and a knife in his belt, I don't see no weapons, so I reckon we don't need to be afraid. I gets off my horse. Pretty soon Tom and Jim gets off their horses too, and we all meets Injun No Legs. Tom keeps looking around like there might be an elephant somewheres, or thinks we will be ambushed, but nothing happens. I tells No Legs we is about to have some dinner, and would he like to join us. He nods that he does. I can't see where he has any food himself. He has a jug of water, made of willow branches wound in circles, and sealed tight with pine pitch. In one hand he holds a stick about four feet long. When he wants to go somewheres, he pushes up and forward, his left hand using the stick, his right palm on the ground. He can go over a foot with each hop. His bottom hitting the ground between hops is what made the elephant tracks in the road.

Tom spreads out a Army blanket on the ground, and throws apples, carrots and boiled beef sandwiches on it. No Legs don't waste no time before he starts pushing stuff into his mouth. He is powerful hungry. I asks him what he eats when white boys like us ain't around to share dinner with him. He says he ketches his dinner with his stick, mostly lizards, but once in a while he gets lucky and gets a mouse, or a rabbit or a rattle snake. Once he ketched a badger. When he can't find any meat he has to eat bugs. Now I understands why he likes our boiled beef sandwiches so much. We tries to keep him talking while he eats. He says he wintered with some Injuns at Fish Springs and is now going to Deseret to spend the summer with some other Injuns. He says he has to travel alone because he cain't ride a horse like other Injuns. Tom asks him why he has no legs.

He says one winter his legs got froze real bad in a storm. Some whites found him and took him to a white doctor who said No Legs would die real soon if his legs warn't cut off. So the doctor cut them off. No Legs spent the rest of that winter with the doctor. That's where he learned some English. White women sewed up the leather pouch that covered his bottom. When spring came he returned to his people, the Goshutes. His squaw went with another man, and with no legs, he couldn't get her back, so he is alone now. Different groups of Injuns feed him if he can get to their summer and winter camps. He learned to travel on the ground because Injuns don't have wagons like white men does.

As he was telling us about his life with no legs, he didn't seem very sad about it. In fact, he seems a lot happier than Forest. I asks him how he could be so happy. He didn't have to think how to answer my question. He says he dreams about his squaw every night, and that was enough to keep him happy. As I listens to him I reckon a woman can be a big thing in a man's life if just memories of a woman can make a man with no legs happy. I think Peggy can do that for me, if I can just find her.

Tom asks why he called Jim Ike. He says one of the Goshute boss men was big like Jim, and had black skin too. His name was Ike and he used to be a slave to the white man, and No Legs thought Jim was Ike. Jim asks how a black slave became a Goshute chief, but No Legs says he don't know how that happened, only that it had. He says Ike was a good man, and very strong, and loved by all the people, except the men who lost their wives to him. Ike had five wives, but he warn't no Mormon.

When the lunch was finished, we rolls up the blanket, leaving the left-over food with No Legs. I tells him we was going to Ibapah, then to California, but would try to find him and give him more food when we returned. We got back on our horses and was soon traveling at a fast trot to Ibapah.

Bill Hickman had been my first new friend in the Utah Territory. Howard Egan was the second. One day we just shows up at Ibapah, riding down from the desert hills like a band of wandering Injuns, but Howard Egan treats us like we was princes or presidents from New York. He is happy to see us, like we was his sons or brothers.

Injun boys takes our horses, women in long dresses brings us cookies and cold buttermilk, and big slabs of fried beef that they called steaks. Egan shows us to a new cabin where we could stay until it is time to go to California. He says we don't gotta do no work to get to stay there. He makes it clear that Jim can stay in the cabin too and not have to sleep outside. He treats Jim the same as me and Tom, not like he was a runaway slave or Army deserter.

Egan had a cookhouse where women and children is always fixing things to eat, not just for Egan and his family and workers and guests like us, but for any Injun who might wander in off the desert. He gots fields full of new grain and hay starting to grow, a vegetable garden as big as a city block, and orchards full of trees covered with spring blossoms. He gots a library with more than a hundred books in it, and says we can read what we want while waiting to go to California. Out on the desert he gots herds of cattle, horses and sheep watched over by Injuns and white boys. I don't know how many wives he gots, but I never saw a woman there who looked like she wanted to run off to California with Mary and Peggy.

We had come to paradise. The king here is Howard Egan, a man in his prime, not old and not young. He has fierce eyes that look right through you, but he's quick to smile if he thought you's scared. He has broad shoulders and powerful arms, a man not afraid to roll up his sleeves and work side by side with the Injuns. Children follows him around, and warn't afraid to talk to him.

Tom fetches hisself a couple of books from the library while Jim and me visits the places in the fields and orchards where men was working, helping when they would let us. On the morning of the second day Egan comes to our cabin. He says he is taking some supplies out to Ike's camp because early spring is a hard time for desert Injuns to gather food. He wants Jim to come with him so he could meet Ike. Jim hurries out to the corral to saddle his horse. Egan said I could come too, so I joins Jim at the corral. Tom wants to stay behind and finish his book.

We rides most of the day, through a mountain pass then south along some foothills. Egan is leading a pack horse loaded heavy with bags of flour and dried apples and smoked meat. Though the land looked like a barren desert, twice Egan leads us into draws or side canyons where there's good water to drink.

When we finally reaches the Injun camp there is no tepees like I had seen before in Pan-a-carry's camp, only brush huts. At first we don't see any people. Egan assures us there is plenty of Injuns around, that they would come out of hiding as soon as they knowed we were not Utes coming to steal their children. Pretty soon faces begin to appear in the thick sage brush that surrounds the camp. In a few minutes we is greeted by several dozen women and children, wearing rabbit and antelope skins. These people is darker and shorter than the people in Blue Fox's and Pan-a-Carry's camps. Egan guesses the men was off hunting. Some of the women point south, indicating that's where the men had gone.

We unloads the food which the women eagerly divides among themselves, then we heads south. A boy comes with us, riding one of the pack horses, to make sure we find the men. He leads us along sage brush flats next to the steep snow-topped mountains. There's lots of juniper trees and an occasional pinion pine. Bands of antelope watches us ride by, and some glide effortlessly along our flanks. Twice we sees small bands of wild horses.

It's late afternoon when we reaches the Goshute hunting camp where six Goshute braves and the former slave, Ike, was roasting rabbits over an open fire. All of them knows Egan and welcomes us into their camp. Egan makes happy introductions, all around, before giving them some flour and bacon. Immediately, the men begins wrapping strips of raw bacon around the roasting rabbits. They kneads water into the flour which they fashions into round cakes which they roasts on the hot coals beneath the rabbits so the fat dripping from the bacon would fall on the cakes.

Ike cain't leave Jim alone. Jim is probably the first black man Ike had seed since coming west. Egan says Ike has been with the Goshutes about twenty years, after escaping slavery and coming up the Missouri River with a white boy, Dan Storm, in 1838. Ike keeps patting Jim on the back, and talking to him in the broken English common among slaves.

As dinner is being prepared and eaten, I watches Ike closely. He looks more like a king than a slave. Even though he must be nearly fifty years told, his tall frame gots as many big strong muscles as a man half his age. He stands tall and erect. He don't cow to his white visitors like all the other slaves I had known. He is the boss here, and we is his guests. He is as graceful as a cat when he moves, and the only thing that gives away his age is the silver streaks in his long, wavy hair which sticks straight out in every direction, hair too big for a big bushel basket to be able to fit over it. His only clothes is antelope skin moccasins and loin cloth and a huge rabbit skin cloak. I keeps thinking this is what Moses must have looked like when he opened up the Red Sea, and I don't know why I thinks that except that this Ike is the splendidest looking man I ever did see, after Bill Hickman and Porter Rockwell, and I figures Moses must have looked this way too. It's hard to believe that a man like this had once been a slave. Jim keeps staring at Ike the way I do.

The next morning, before the sun comes up, Ike leads us down through the juniper trees to a flat near a spring. There is piles of rocks across the flat forming straight lines that gets closer together the farther you get from the spring. Where the piles of rocks ends, there are two rows of dead juniper tress making fences which get closer and closer together until they reaches a big corral made of dead trees.

Ike and Howard and a couple of other men with horses go out to round up a herd of antelope they think might be coming to the spring to drink. When they sees the antelopes they will run them towards the drift fences. Ike tells me to hide behind one of the rock piles and peek around it at the antelopes when they starts running, but not to let them see me unless they come right at me trying to get through the line of rock piles. If they tries to do that, I am to stand up and wave at them trying to get them to stay inside the line of rock piles, and eventually the tree fence. My horse is tied in the trees a little ways behind me.

It seems I wait behind my pile of rocks for a couple of hours before I hears Ike and Howard and the other riders yelling as they push a dozen or so antelopes between the rows of rock piles. I can see them running, and they don't seem to want to come towards me, so I stays hidden. Almost before I knows it the antelopes are past the rock piles and between the rows of dead trees. Howard and Ike keeps yelling as they pushes the antelopes ahead of them. I hurry back to my horse, mount up, and follow. By the times I catches up, the antelopes is in the big corral, and two of the Goshutes has made a gate out of dead trees to keep them inside. The men spaces themselves around the outside of the corral so the antelopes will want to stay in the middle.

After Howard and Ike hold a meeting, Howard shoots the first antelope, a big buck. Then Ike shoots another buck. Then some of the Injuns with bows and arrows kills more bucks, until all the boy antelopes is dead on the ground. Some of the girl antelopes have big bellies, which means they is going to have babies. These the Injuns let out the gate so there will be more antelopes to kill the next year. The little ones, and the females without big bellies are let out too. Then all the Injuns goes inside the corral and starts cleaning and skinning the six dead bucks on the ground.

One of the hunters has a tin cup so they can gather up some of the blood as they slits the throats. They take turns drinking the cup empty whenever it gets filled up. They take big, happy bites out of livers and lungs, even kidneys. But they don't eat the brains, which Howard tells me they are saving to help tan the hides as soon as the brains get all soft and rotten.

Two of the men brung up skins of water from the spring so we can have plenty to drink while we feasts on the antelopes. We stay there all night, getting the meat skinned and cut up so's we can carry it back to the main camp where the women and children is waiting. We ties the meat and skins on the horses, so some of us has to walk back to camp, leading our horses.

As we make our way back to the main camp, I asks Howard to tell me everything he can about Peggy. He says Peggy and Mary just showed up one day asking him to take them to Sacramento. They knew he worked for President Young, so they were careful not to tell him very much, but he suspected they were running from polygamy. He said it was very unusual for pretty women like these to want to leave the territory. He guessed something was wrong when they didn't have letters from church leaders approving their departure. He warn't able to spend much time talking to them because a bunch of soldiers and government contractors showed up about the same time, also wanting him to guide them to Sacramento. He said the soldiers paid plenty of attention to Peggy and Mary. He said Peggy appeared to be in good health, and seemed to have a wisdom beyond her years. She did not seem very happy. He said Mary could not have made the trip without Peggy to shore her up, and help with the little boy.

While the men was out hunting antelopes, the women moved the camp closer to the steep mountains, underneath some rock ledges where there was plenty of shade from the sun which seemed to be getting warmer each day. Upon our arrival the women and children gathers around, excited to see all the meat and skins the men has obtained. While the men drops to the ground to rest from the exertions of their hunt, the women goes to work drying the meat and tanning the skins. One man had brung back a large intestine from one of the antelopes, which he cuts into foot-long sections, giving one to each of the children who run out to play, hitting someone with their intestine one minute, chewing on it the next.

Late in the afternoon while the men was still resting under the ledges, four riders appears at the far side of the sagebrush flat, not far from where the children is playing.

My first thought is that the riders is Egan's cowboys, coming to look for us. Ike and me is the first ones to see them, but while I'm thinking they is cowboys, Ike rolls to the back of the ledge, and grabs a rifle and two spears. Jim is already on his feet as Ike hands him a spear. As far as I could tell no words is exchanged between them, but Jim, seeing Ike's reaction to an unknown danger, is ready to do whatever it is Ike wants him to do.

Before I could say dad fetch it the two black giants is racing towards the sagebrush flat. Three of the Goshute braves joins them, but soon fall far behind, not able to keep up with the two powerful black men.

I looks over at Egan to see if he can tell me what is happening. He says Ike knowed immediately that the four riders was not cowboys, but Ute raiders, come to steal Goshute children. This explanation is confirmed as we once again looks across the sagebrush flat. The four riders is spread out and circling the frightened children who is now scampering towards the ledges. The Utes seems unaware of the two black men and Goshute warriors racing towards them.

The children is nearly surrounded by the Utes when a shot was fired from Ike's rifle. One of the riders falls out of the saddle. The other riders turns their horses around and tries to get away, but Jim and Ike was upon them. As one of the Utes attempts to cross a deep gully, Ike pulls him from the saddle as his horse struggles to make it up the steep bank on the far side. Before Ike can wrassle the Ute to the ground, Jim grabs him from behind and holds him while Ike twists his head until his neck is broken. The two horses of the fallen men joins their companions as they races to safety.

I looks back at Egan who was making no effort to join the fight, or to stop the killing. Seeing my face, he explains that their warn't very many Goshutes because the Utes, who has horses and is better fighters, is constantly stealing the children. He says if these four Utes had showed up a day earlier, while the men was out hunting antelope, they would have taken some of the women and children away. He says they sells the children to the Navajos, or trades them for horses.

A half hour later Ike and Jim returns to camp, each carrying a blood-soaked scalp. Jim looks fierce and defiant, his head high, just like Ike. Jim never looked that way before. He warn't the same man who used to rinse out bed pans for Miss Watson and the Widow Douglas, and peel potatoes for the soldiers. I is happy for him, and not even a little bit surprised the next morning when he tells me that he is not going with us to California, that he has decided to stay in Utah.

When we arrive in Ibapah, Egan tells me about our upcoming trip to Sacramento. He tells of the many killings of white settlers, freighters and mail carriers along the Humboldt River valley. The Shoshones has grown increasingly hostile since the gold seekers had come through their lands in 1849 and 1850, destroying the grass, killing the game, and plundering the Indians who lived there. Now no white man was safe along the course of the Humboldt River.

Two things would ensure a safe crossing. Large numbers of fighting men, like when the soldiers and freighters crossed with Peggy a month or so earlier; strength in numbers kept the Shoshones away. When adequate protection was not available the best insurance for safe passage was fast travel. Egan said that when there were small groups carrying the mail, the men would ride twenty hours a day at a fast single foot or trot. Horses couldn't maintain that kind of pace day after day, so mules was used. After twenty hours of riding, the men took an hour to prepare the one cooked meal of the day, then was allowed three hours of sleep before doing it all over again. The mail could move at a pace of about sixty-two miles a day. Indians would see the mail party go by, but by the time they put on war paint, gather up their weapons, ketched horses and got organized with their friends, it was impossible to catch up. Skinny Injun ponies couldn't keep up with the grain-fed mules.

Egan says Tom and me has to trade our horses for mules, and that we would trade in our worn out animals for fresh ones two or three times at his relay stations along the way. He says we should be prepared to spend twenty hours in the saddle, every day, ten days in a row. If we didn't think we could do that, we shouldn't come with him. If we wore out after a few days, and he had to leave us behind, the Shoshones would kill us for sure. I began to wish I had stayed behind with Jim and Ike, and Tom wished he were back in Great Salt Lake with Hickman and Rockwell.

Tom says ketchin' Peggy ain't worth what we has to go through to do it. He says things about her being defiled, running away from Forest, deserting little Flaxy. I can see what is happening. He don't want to ride six hundred miles in ten days on ugly old mules, wondering what Injuns might be a waiting at the next bend in the trail to take our scalps. He'd heard about Ike and Jim with their new scalps, and don't want other Injuns to do that to him. He's convinced himself that Peggy warn't worth it.

I didn't argue with him none. I says it is fine with me if he saddles up and goes back to Great Salt Lake. He can keep reading the Mormon Bible, let Porter Rockwell baptize him, and maybe even study law like Bill Hickman, or be a missionary in Germany or Norway. All of that was better'n havin' your hair lifted by a no good Shoshone. He agrees totally, and announces that is exactly what he is going to do.

But Tom is surprised when I tells him I ain't going with him. He asks me why I thinks I has to go to Sacramento. I say Peggy is worried about what happened to Flaxy. She don't know that Flaxy is safe in Iowa. I has to tell Peggy this so she can stop worrying.

Tom says there is more than one way to skin a cat, that I don't have to risk my life to tell Peggy about Flaxy. He drags me over to Howard Egan's splendid library where he fetches a piece of paper and a quill. He sits down at a desk with an ink well, and writes Dear Peggy: on the top of the paper.

"What do you want to say to her?" he asks.

"What do you mean?" I asks.

"I's writing her a letter for you. You can tell her all about Flaxy in a letter which we can send with Howard, then you don't have to go and risk getting scalped," Tom explains.

"I don't want to write her a letter. I want to go see her," I says.

"No," he argues. "You want to write her a letter so you won't get scalped." He don't wait for me to tell him what to say anymore. He just writes it himself.

Dear Peggy:

I hope this letter finds you safe in California, and happy too, even though you has been defiled and violated by Indians and trappers. Flaxy made it to Iowa with some soldiers, and is at your uncle's house. When you gets settled you can write to her and she will write back. Me and Tom are staying in Great Salt Lake City where we might become Mormons.

Your Friend
Huck Finn

When Tom hands me the letter I rolls it up in a ball and drops it in a waste basket, turns around and walks out. I ain't really mad at Tom. He just don't understand what's going on inside of me, and I cain't explain it to him. I has to go, that's all there is.

The next morning we is on our way before daylight. There's five of us, all riding nice fat mules, and we are leading three pack mules. One is carrying the mail, one is carrying grain for the mules, and the other is carrying our food, cooking pans and sleeping blankets. The other men carry rifles in scabbards on their saddles. I gots my Navy Colt and two extra cylinders in my pockets, giving me eighteen shots if I needs them.

I tells Egan that if I has to run from mean Injuns I'd rather be on a horse than a mule because a horse runs faster. He says he's used horses and mules on these mail expeditions, and mules is better because they can go sixty miles a day four days in a row. No horse can keep up with that, especially not those Indian ponies who don't get fed any grain. He says a mule don't need to eat as much as a horse, and can get by on sticks, leaves and buffalo chips if he has too. He says a mule don't trip as much as a horse when he gets tired, don't need shoes, and ain't so rough on the man who rides him. And with those big ears a mule will hear an approaching Injun pony a long time before a horse will know somebody's a coming.

Egan says if Injuns sees us in the morning or middle of the day, by the time they gets their war paint on, gets their guns and bows, and collects all their friends, we is so far ahead they can never ketch up. If they sees us in the evening just before we stops, it is dark by the time they gets ready to attack, so they waits until morning, but we leaves after three hours sleep in the middle of the night, so by the time it gets light we are so far away they can never ketch up. He says the men gets real tired, but they gets to keep their hair.

The very first night out, just after we has cooked our supper, we sees two Injuns walking across the desert to our camp. Egan ain't worried because they don't have rifles or horses, and we is still a long way from the Humboldt River country. As the Injuns gets close we can see they is naked except for loin cloths. They don't have no shirts or moccasins. It looks like their heads are bigger than bushel baskets, but it is their hair sticking straight like Ike's does, that makes them look that way. One of them is carrying a big, limp thing in his hand that looks about like the arm of a dead man.

They walks right into our camp and asks, in an Injun tongue that only Egan understands, if they can use the coals from our fire to cook their supper. That's when I see that the big limp thing the one Injun is carrying is not a man's arm, but a big snake, a rattle snake, and it is still wiggling. I has picked up plenty of mean snakes, and I knows how to do it, that you grabs it right behind the head so it can't reach out and bite you. But this Injun is holding this big old rattler by the tail, and it's wide big head is swinging back and forth past the Injun's bare ankle. Why it don't bite him, I cain't begin to guess. Egan says they can use our fire.

The fire ain't burning no more, but there is a big pile of hot coals, and the Injuns seems plenty happy about that. The one with the snake walks up to the edge of the coals, and drops the big snake. That's when we knows it was really alive because it starts to crawl away. The Injun picks it up and drops it in the middle of the coals a second time. This time it don't crawl out, but dies right there, and starts to smoke, and ketch on fire, and turn black.

I am surprised that these Injuns ain't more civilized in how they cooks a snake. They should have kilt it first, slipped out the entrails, maybe even skinned it, at least cut off the head where all the poison is kept. But no, they just throws it in whole.

Well, that old snake he just smokes and sizzles for about twenty minutes, then one of the Injuns, using only his bare foot, kicks the smoking snake away from the coals onto cool ground.

They waits a few minutes for it to cool a bit, then breaks off pieces and starts eating like they was enjoying a big carrot. They just eats from one end to the other--bones, entrails and skin along with the meat. The only thing they throws away is the head and the rattles. They licks their hands and arms until they are perfectly clean, then rolls up on the ground by the fire and goes to sleep. Five minutes later all the white men is rolled up in their blankets and sleeping too.

I swear I hasn't slept fifteen minutes before Egan is kicking me, telling me to get up and saddle the mules. By the second day I learns to sleep in the saddle. I grab the saddle horn with both hands, lock my elbows, drop my chin on my chest, and close my eyes. I sleep five or ten minutes at a time this way. The other men do it too, especially in the afternoons when the sun makes us extra warm.

At the end of the third day we is in the Humboldt River country, and has seen Injuns watching us a couple of times. Our guns are primed and ready as we approach our camp site. No one is napping. We hain't seen any Injuns for a few hours, so we reckon we is safe to camp. But when we gets there the spring that Egan says has been running all winter, is now dried up. Egan says we'll camp there anyhow because it is a hard place for Injuns to sneak up on us. While we is cooking supper, Egan sends one of the men to look for a spring along the edge of some hills. The mules have to drink, and we don't want to go down by the river where Injuns could see us.

An hour later, after we has finished eating, the man still hasn't come back. Egan is pacing back and forth, worrying that Injuns has ketched our man. Instead of unsaddling the mules and going to bed, we all mounts up and goes looking for our man, fearing he no longer has his hair.

We finds him, all right, and he still gots his scalp, and he has found a spring too, a nice clear one surrounded by a big patch of green grass. The man dismounted to let his mule graze a little bit, and was standing by it, his arm hooked around the saddle horn. He laid his head against the saddle to rest, and before he knowed it he were sound asleep, and that's how we finds him, sleeping like a baby, standing straight up like a soldier at the palace door, his face against his saddle. We let our mules drink and graze for a few minutes before we waked him up and headed back to camp.

We kept up that pace for ten days, and I reckon in the end I was getting used to only three hours sleep a night. I don't know how Egan waked himself up first so he could wake up the rest of us. He never seemed to be as tired as the other men. He would nudge us with his foot, but never kick a man hard for not waking up right away. I never heard him yell or swear at a man, but he did get real mad at his mule a time or two.

Chapter 24

As we gets close Sacramento it is like we is riding into paradise. We ride through fields of corn and beans and onions and potatoes. There's peach and plum orchards. We see splendid log cabins, and homes made from mud bricks called adobe, and when we gets real close to the city we see big houses made from boards and rocks. We see women in silk dresses, men in black coats with tall hats, and the biggest dogs I ever seen walking behind beautiful women as they santers up and down the board sidewalks. It is eight years since they found the gold, and Sacramento has become a splendid place.

After dropping off the mail at the post office, we leave our mules at a stable. Egan gives each of the men, even me, a ten-dollar gold piece, then checks into the Stanaslas Hotel. He gives us a stern warning, saying he will shoot any man who knocks on his door in the next forty eight hours. He intends to sleep for two days, and he don't want to be disturbed. His last words to me about Peggy and Mary are that he had dropped them off at the post office when he delivered the mail, and had not seen them since.

The rest of the men hurries to a place where they wash and sleep and drink and gamble, but I strike out on my own. I find a Chinese bath house and laundry where an old woman washes my clothes while I soaks in a hot bath, and all I gotta pay is a quarter. I soaks in the soapy water until the skin on my hands and feet is wrinkled and about to fall off, then I rolls up in a wool blanket and sleeps until my clothes are dry. After filling my belly with the biggest T-bone steak I has ever seed, I feel like a new man. With my Navy Colt strapped firmly to my side, I set out to find Peggy.

I walks back to the post office, where Howard said he last seen her. The postmaster says he don't remember anyone fitting Peggy's description, or Mary's either. I askes him where two women would go who didn't have very much money. He points to the whorehouse across the street. I tells him Peggy and Mary wouldn't go to a place like that. Then he points to a Catholic church down the street, saying sometimes women goes there when they needs a place to stay. So I decides to go there next.

As I walks along the street I am surprised to see so many soldiers. I reckon the government is so determined to put the Mormons in their place and put a new governor on the throne that it is sending in soldiers from every direction. The Mormons will have to go along even if they don't like it.

When I gets to the church a young nun greets me out in the front yard. I describes Peggy and asks the nun if she has seen such a person.

"Was there a woman with her who has a little boy?" she asks, and I nods that there was.

She says the two women and the boy stayed at the church two or three nights, about a month earlier, but had moved on after the nuns told them where was a wonderful business opportunity for anyone who wanted to open a home to take care of children while their parents worked in the city. Sometimes such parents needed a place to drop off a child before going to work every day, or when they went on a trip out of town. The nuns said if the two women wanted to open such a business the church could send them some children too. Peggy and Mary seemed excited about the possibilities, but the nuns had not seen them since.

I didn't know where to look now, so I just wanders down the street, wondering how I might find Peggy and Mary. It gets dark, and I starts looking where I might spend the night. I don't want to spend money on a hotel, but don't care to sleep outside, neither, because I don't have a blanket with me. I finally decides to go back to the stable where the mules were staying and see if they will let me sleep in the hay.

As I turns around I thinks I heard the cry of a frightened child, kind of a muffled cry, then nothing at all. I looked back down the street in time to see the bulk of a big man disappearing between two stores. It looks like he might be dragging something, perhaps a child. Quickly, I walks in that direction. Maybe a father was punishing a little boy for being bad, but maybe it was something more than that.

When I reaches the opening between the two buildings, I hears the child cry out again, then the gruff voice of a man telling the child to shut up. That man's voice is familiar. I has heard it before. Out on the plain. There had been the sound of crying children then too. This man is Captain Peabody. I am sure of it. I hurries into the alley, drawing my Navy Colt from its holster, and cocking back the hammer.

Some light from windows allows me to see. Peabody is so busy trying to get his dirty hand over the child's mouth to shut him up that he don't see me coming. I don't say nothing or make any noise reckoning I might have a better advantage if I get real close. The first Peabody knows about me being there is when I pokes the barrel of my gun hard against his ribs.

"Whoa," he yells like a man who has been scared by a ghost.

"Let go the child," I says, real soft, "or I'll shoot a hole in you big enough to stuff in an ear of corn, maybe two."

He lets go the child, and I takes a step back. A little Injun boy runs over to me and throws his arms around my leg. He is wearing long pants, but no shirt and no shoes or moccasins. I reckon he ain't no Goshute or Ute from Utah Territory, probably one of the California Injuns, maybe a Shoshone from the Humboldt River country. I steps back some more. The boy don't let go of my leg. Peabody turns around and gets a better look at me.

"He's mine," Peabody growls. "Paid fair and square for him."

"Far as I knows, California ain't no slave territory," I says.

"But he's just an Injun, no a'count." Peabody takes a step towards me.

"In my book you're the no a'count here, Mr. Peabody, sergeant, sir," I says, and by the look on his face I knows he is real surprised that I knows his name. He squints his eyes, and looks real close, trying like the devil to figure who is pointing a gun at him. Finally he says:

"Huck Finn, the lost boy I found naked in the road, unconscious. I saved your life. Now this, you ungrateful . . ." He starts towards me again. I waves the pistol so he is sure to see it, but he keeps coming.

"You're just a boy. You don't know how to use that thing."

I surprises myself by starting to laugh, and have a big smile on my face. Peabody stops.

"Bill Hickman spent all winter teaching me to use this thing. He and Porter Rockwell would be laughing with me if they saw a man bet his life thinking I cain't use it."

Peabody knowed who Bill Hickman was, Porter Rockwell too. I keep backing up until I gets to the street. Peabody stays where he is this time. I grabs the boy's little hand and starts running to the middle of town. Every time I look back, I cain't see no sign of Peabody.

When I talks to the boy, he just looks at me. Sometimes he answers in a tongue I cain't understand. He don't seem to understand what I says either. I don't know where to take him, and he don't seem to want to take me nowhere neither. His hair is long, and his feet are tough enough to walk on rocks. I don't know what to do with him, but the way he is hanging onto my hand, I knows I cain't send him away.

As we walks past some saloons I sees a big bear of a man with a metal star on his chest, a badge of some kind. I reckon he is a sheriff or marshal here. He is wearing the bushiest and thickest brown beard I has ever seed on a man. I walks up to him and tells him how I took this little Injun boy away from a mean Army man who was hurting him, but now I have made him safe, I don't know what to do with him. He don't speak no English.

Without saying anything back at me the big law man drops down on one knee so's he can look straight into the boy's face. When he reaches out with a big paw of a hand to pet the little feller on the head, the boys backs up some, still holding onto my hand. Seeing the boy is afraid of him the sheriff withdraws his paw and slips it in his coat pocket where he grabs a big slab of beef or buffalo jerky which he offers to the boy. This time the boy don't back away. He grabs the piece of meat out of the sheriff's hand and shoves one end of it into his little mouth. The meat is dry and hard, and it takes him a minute to bite off a chunk. The sheriff gets back on his feet, telling me he knows just the place to take the little feller.

"Follow me," he says.

We walks past a bunch of businesses and houses, maybe fifteen minutes. The boy is still chewing on the slab of meat, and I gets to thinking he might eat too much and get sick, so I reaches down to take it away from him. He won't let me do it, hanging on with all his might. He growls like a dog every time I tries to pull on it. I never heard a boy growl before, not like this. I finally gives up and lets him keep chewing on the meat. The sheriff just keeps on walking ahead of us, slow and deliberate, like he knows exactly where he is going, but ain't in no hurry to get there.

Finally he stops in front of a little green house surrounded by a fence made of empty flour barrels all tied together with long pieces of rope. There are lights in all the windows so we knows these folks ain't in bed yet. The sheriff moves one of the barrels so we can get inside the yard, and we follows him up to the front door. I feels my heart pounding in my chest, and don't know why it is doing that, until the front door opens, and there is Peggy standing right in front of us, wearing a clean white dress that is glowing in the light, like an angel from heaven. I just stares, my mouth open like a catfish about to suck in a worm.

When Peggy sees me she pushes past the sheriff and throws her splendid, white, sweet-smelling arms around me. I can feel her hands on my back, her hair in my face, her lips on my cheek as she kisses me. It all feels so good and my heart is pounding so hard, I fear I might just die. But I don't.

Finally she pushes away, looking down at the boy for the first time. He knows her because he lets go of my hand and pushes into the front of her dress. Her hand is on the back of his head, holding him against her.

"Where's Flaxy?" she asks. "I knew you'd find me, and hoped Flaxy might come with you."

"When I got to Laramie, she had already gone to Iowa," I says. "She's with your aunts and uncles. You can write to her, and she will write back."

The sheriff speaks up now, telling Peggy he brung her another boy to care for. She bends over and takes the boy into her arms, hugging and kissing him like she done to me. The boy don't push away neither because he knows her. When Peggy takes the boy in the house, the sheriff is ready to go. I ain't sure what to do. I don't want to leave Peggy. But pretty soon she comes back to the open doorway, thanks the sheriff for bringing the boy, and tells me that I cain't leave, that I have to stay right here with her and Mary, and tell them everything that's happened to me since they last seen me in Utah Territory. That's fine with me. After shaking hands with the sheriff I goes into the house.

It ain't no ordinary house. It's full of children, boys and girls: white children, Injun children, and Chinese children. There are beds and mattresses around the walls where the children sleeps, and a big table where they all eats. Mary is on the far side of the room cooking something on a big stove. She says hello to me.

Peggy explains real fast that when they got to Sacramento, and found this house to rent, that the sheriff came by to ask if they would take care of two children whose parents had been killed in a mine explosion. Then some lost children were brought to them, then people who worked in some of the downtown businesses began dropping off children on the way to work. Even the Army was paying them to care for lost Injun children until they could be returned to their native villages. The two women were taking in about $5 a day and there were so many children that they was looking for a bigger house to rent, and some other women to help.

When Peggy asks how long I is going to stay in California I says I had come to bring her news of Flaxy, and beyond that I got no plans. She insists I stay with them. There is plenty of chores to do and errands to run. They would share the income with me.

I don't know why I didn't get real excited about helping them take care of the children. I guess I had hoped something more might happen between me and Peggy, that she would want to marry me and we would go off together and start a new life. Maybe she needed the children to help her forget what had happened with Blue Fox and the trappers. Maybe the children helped her forget her own baby that she had lost. Maybe she warn't ready to get married, and having all the children around gave her something to do until she was ready. And maybe she just didn't want me, that she ran away from Utah to get away from me too, and now the children gave her a way to put me off. But still I loves her, and would stay and help, if that's what she wants.

They gives me a place to sleep, in a back room with some older boys. There is no beds, we just sleep on pads on the floor. I stops feeling sorry for myself when the little Injun boy insists on coming with me to the back bedroom. After I saved him from Peabody he warn't letting me out of his sight. By now his jerky was finished, and his face needs a good washing. While Peggy is cleaning him up, she warned me about being careless with my gun. She says the boys will want to play with it, and she don't want no one getting shot. She says the little boy had stayed here before but she don't know his name.

As we is going to sleep I decides what I will call him. Because he growled over the piece of meat, I decides to call him Wolf. Not Gray Wolf, Yellow Wolf or Brown Wolf, just Wolf. I finds out the next day that the younger children have a hard time saying Wolf. Most of them just calls him Woof, and by the end of the week that is what everybody calls him. At mealtimes he earns his name again and again by growling when-ever anyone gets near his plate of food. I wonders what could make a child growl like an animal over his food. I also notices at mealtimes that Woof ate twice as much as other children his same size. I can only reckon that regular and plentiful food had not been there for this boy as he growed up.

Those women keep me real busy. Wood gots to be chopped for the stove, and they don't trust the older boys with the axe, so that duty falls to me. There is leaks in the roof that needs mending and a new hole needs to be digged for a second outhouse. Once or twice a day they sends me to the store to get supplies. I warn't used to working like this, and don't like it at all, except when I can be around Peggy. The work they makes me do warn't as hard as straddling a trotting mule for twenty hours trying to keep up with Howard Egan, but that warn't work, even though it was hard to do. One time I starts showing the older boys my fast draw, and Peggy makes me stop. She says people will stop bringing their children to us if they knew we was playing with guns. She makes me take the cylinder out of the gun and keep it in my pocket.

It seems I just cain't have any fun at all, and Peggy is too busy to spend much time with me. I feels like an old hound with his tongue hanging down, waiting by the table for Peggy to brush a few crumbs my way. I keeps telling myself I has to be patient. Something is bound to happen, and it finally does.

Chapter 25

Three or four days later I had just come home from the store with a big gunny sack full of food when I notice that Woof ain't around to see what I brung home. I had never seen a child so interested in food, and it warn't like him not to be there. When I asks where he is, Peggy said the Army come and fetched him so they can take him back to his mother. I don't know why these words makes the hair on my neck stand up.

"What do you mean when you says the Army fetched him up?" I asks.

"The sergeant came by, the one who has picked up children before."

"Was they all boys?" I asks.

She nods.

"Did all of them not want to go with him?'

She nods, but says, "It is only natural for children to be afraid of big men in uniforms."

"Did the sergeant tell you his name?" I asks.

"Sergeant Peabody."

I never thought I could ever get mad at Peggy because she was so perfect and splendid in every way, but I was mad now. How could she be so stupid? I tells her that Peabody ain't the Army, that he likes to sleep with little boys and makes them cry the whole night long, that he is the mean man I took Woof from in the first place, and now she gives him back. As far as I knows, Woof might be dead.

Peggy starts to cry, and now I feels even worse, but this ain't a time to be concerned with feelings. I takes my Navy Colt out of the holster and puts the cylinder back in. Peggy keeps on crying, but I cain't do nothing for her. I turns and runs down the street, towards the place where I saved Woof from Peabody the first time.

It's middle of the day and there are wagons and plenty of people riding horses up and down the street. I just keeps loping along, hoping I will be lucky enough to ketch up with Peabody and Woof, if they went this way and not down some other street.

For once in my life, true luck is on my side. I sees both of them, walking down the middle of the street, their backs to me. Woof is holding back, but he is so little that Peabody just drags him along without any work in it.

I sneaks up behind them real quiet, then grabs Woof's little arm and jerks it free of Peabody's big paw, then steps back. Peabody didn't have a gun the first time I took Woof away from him, but this time he does, and as he spins around to see why the boy was pulled away, he pulls a pistol out from under his vest, and before I knows what has happened, he is pointing it right in my face. By this time I have let go of Woof, but he has wrapped his little arms around my leg and is holding on tight, afraid Peabody might try to pull him away.

"I hopes you is ready to die, Huck Finn," Sergeant Peabody hisses. "You have taken this boy from me one too many times." He cocks back the hammer on his pistol.

"The boy ain't going with you," I says.

"You got a lot of guts for a boy who is about to die," he says.

I don't like him calling me a boy. I figures I am a man now, after all I been through and all I have learnt. I think it's finally time for me to prove it, at least to Sergeant Peabody. I have to prove it to myself too. And I don't have much time. Peabody might pull the trigger any second. I don't know why he ain't done it already. It worries me that Woof is hanging on my leg. He might get hit by a stray bullet. I see Peabody's finger moving. He's getting ready to kill me. No time left for thinking and wondering, so I says:

"Sheriff, please take this man's gun before he shoots me." As I speaks I am looking at the building behind Peabody's shoulder. Their ain't no sheriff anywhere near, but the sergeant don't know that. He turns his head and looks away like he believes I am talking to a real sheriff. My time is here. I remembers how my hand wouldn't move when Hog had the drop on me. It better move now.

I draws and shoots, not once but three times. Peabody falls over backwards and hits the ground hard, like a sack of oats falling from a wagon. There's three holes in the middle of his chest. His gun didn't even go off, and falls harmlessly on the ground beside him. People starts yelling and running towards us. I feel a strong hand pull the gun out of my hand, and I don't fight against it. Some people drags me to jail, and some others takes Woof back to Peggy's house.

After they throws me in a cell surrounded by iron bars, they leaves me to myself. I am glad Sergeant Peabody will never hurt another little boy. I am glad I put to good use what Bill Hickman had learned me. I am glad Woof is back with Peggy. I am glad Peabody pulled out his gun first. I have shot him in self defense, and pretty soon they should let me go. There were other people in the street who saw it real good, it being the middle of the day and all with the sun shining.

The first person to visit me is the big bear of a sheriff who took me to Peggy's house with Woof, the first time I took him away from the sergeant. The sheriff tells me I am in serious trouble because I have shot a sergeant in the United States Army. I tells him it was self defense. He says the lawyers will argue I killed him in cold blood because I put three bullets in his heart before he could even pull the trigger. I says the sergeant had been hurting little boys and deserved to die. He says that was a matter for the courts to decide, not Huck Finn. He says I was going to hang if I didn't find a real good lawyer, real fast. His words were not nice, but I felt like he cared about me, and wanted to help. I tells him he could help me by fetching Howard Egan at the Stanaslaus Hotel.

Howard comes by that evening, saying he is heading back to Utah the next morning, that he would report what had happened to Bill Hickman and Porter Rockwell, and ask them to find a lawyer for me. He informs the big sheriff that a lawyer is coming, and that the trial must not begin until my lawyer arrives. The sheriff promises to tell the judge what was happening.

After that life fell into a quiet routine. I is alone in the cell, being fed two meals every day. The sheriff sleeps a lot, and sometimes playes cards with me through the bars. His name is John Henry Bean, and seems like a good man, though he warn't very good at cards. Sometimes I pester him to find out what was happening with my trial. He always said the judge is just waiting for my lawyer to arrive. He guesses they would wait a month or two, then go ahead with the trial anyway. He says two witnesses saw me shoot three bullets into Peabody who didn't shoot back at me, not once. Both witnesses says they saw a gun in Peabody's hand, but they warn't sure if he reached for his gun before or after I started shooting. Things don't look good, but there ain't nothing I can do except sit and wait—unless I wants to escape, and I thinks a lot about that, seeing where John Henry kept the keys, and knowing when he goes to lunch, how long he is usually gone, and things like that. I wishes Tom Sawyer was here. As smart as he is, he could figure a way to get me free.

On the second day, John Henry tells me the persecuting attorney is coming to see me, and I better be careful what I tells him because he is trying to convince the judge to stop waiting for my lawyer to get here, and to begin the trial right away. An hour later a skinny, clean-shaven fellow in a black suit with a bald head comes to the front of my cell door, saying he wants to ask me a few questions. He says the questions ain't important, that he just wants to get to know me a little bit before the trial. He says his name is Ebenezer Jenkins. After what the sheriff warned me about, I don't trust this lawyer none, not even a little bit, and am determined not to tell him anything.

After heming and hawing a little bit he asks how old I am. I told Peggy I was nineteen, but I remembers Bill Hickman telling me that if I got in trouble with the law it is best to be under eighteen. I am about to tell Jenkins I am seventeen, then decides to keep him guessing, so I tells him if he wants to know my age he better ask my lawyer. He don't like that. He asks if I am a Mormon, since I come from Utah. I tells him my lawyer knows the answer to that question too. He asks where I got the Navy Colt. I tells him I didn't steal it. When he asks how many other men I have kilt I says nothing.

On the third day Peggy comes to see me. She is wearing the same white dress she wore when the sheriff took me to her house, the one I thought was an angel dress. The sheriff must have thought that too, and he was so pleased that she come to visit his jail, like the president himself has come. The marshal brings a chair over to my cell so she can be real comfortable when she talks to me. He gives her a dish of candy so she can have a snack while she talks to me. She gives him a funny look when he tells her not to get real close to the bars because I might be dangerous.

Peggy is real sad, more sad it seems than when she was violated by the Injuns and trappers, and not because I am in jail. She says Woof is real happy and eating a lot of food, but she also says that before I came to Sacramento she gave two other Injun boys to the sergeant when he said the Army wanted him to take them home. She says she blames herself for the horrible things that might have happened to those boys.

I am surprised that she is worried more about them boys than about me. She asks why they are keeping me in jail so long and when they are going to let me go. When I tells her they wants to hang me for killing a sergeant in the United States Army, she throws her hands over her face and pushes her chair back. Then she says this is her fault too, because none of this would have happened if she hadn't given Woof to the sergeant.

When I tells her to stop blaming herself, I realize that things is different between me and Peggy. Before I always thought she knowed everything and was perfect in every way. She always knowed best what to do and say. Now I see that she ain't as smart as I thought. For once I knowed more about something than she did. I knowed it warn't her fault I killed the sergeant. It warn't her fault she gave him the Injun boys because she didn't know what he did with them. None of it was her fault. I tells her to be quiet and stop crying while I tells her what I been thinking.

"If he was a bad man and you were saving Woof, why do they want to hang you?" she asks. I tells her they think I just gunned him down like a helpless dog. They don't believe he drawed on me first and was going to kill me. The witnesses say they saw me shooting balls into his chest, but they don't know if the sergeant pointed a gun at me first.

The next day Peggy brings me some fresh gingerbread. The day after that she brings a roasted chicken. We share the food with the marshal, and he is grateful for that. He cleans the jail and office so it will be nice and neat when Peggy comes. Sometimes she helps him move things around and put them in the right place. He is a single man without a family, and it is as clear as spring water that he has fallen in love with Peggy too. She stops and talks to him when she comes and when she goes, and after she leaves his cheeks is red and he is bouncing around like a little boy at Christmas. I think that after they hang me, Peggy will marry the marshal. Maybe she will marry him even if they don't hang me. I am jealous but not able to do anything about it. I cain't tell Peggy to stop coming.

Then one day when I am feeling so jealous I can hardly stand it, Peggy slips her hand between the bars and takes hold of my hand. My cheeks turns red, chills go up and down my back, my stomach twists up in a knot, and my hand starts to get real wet. Then I feels there is something wrong with her hand. There's a hard, narrow, cold thing in it. I looks down. It's a key, maybe a key to my cell. I takes it from her and tucks it behind my belt. She whispers how she borrowed the sheriff's keys, and had the blacksmith make a spare cell key, the one she just gave me. Then she tells me she has my mule and saddle behind her house, and a gunny sack full of supplies. She cain't get my gun because it is in the judge's safe, but she will steal another from the sheriff real soon.

I cain't believe what she has done for me while I thought she was crying and wringing her hands over lost Injun boys. I tells her I will get out as soon as the sheriff goes to sleep, and come and fetch my mule. She tells me not to do it.

She says if I try to escape they will think I am guilty for sure. So I asks her why she brung me the key. She said I should wait, and only use the key if I am sure they are going to hang me. The best thing for me is for my lawyer to win in court, then I won't be an outlaw. I should only use the key if the trial goes against me. What she says makes sense. Once again I believe she is the smartest woman alive, as well as the most beautiful. But I am Huck Finn, and I been free my whole life, and I been in this jail too long already. I knows that key is going to burn a hole in me if I don't use it, but I don't tell Peggy. She asks me to promise not to use the key unless they is going to hang me, so I makes the promise, but I don't know if I can keep it.

Peggy keeps a comin', every day, bringing good things to eat, and the sheriff is as happy as a pig with his front feet in the trough, but I ain't. I killed a man who had it coming. Now they aim to hang me. I can feel it in the way people looks at me, the way people talks to me. It don't matter what's fair and right. They know I am going to die. The sheriff tries to make me happy like a fat steer, so I won't see it a coming, but inside I am sick. I don't want to die.

As days turn into weeks I begins to worry that maybe Howard Egan ain't sending a lawyer back. Maybe he cain't find one. Maybe the Shoshones along the Humboldt River scalped him so he can't even get my message to Hickman and Rockwell. Even the sheriff seems more nervous around me, like there's something he ain't telling me.

And I ain't real happy the way things is going with Peggy. She brings me food. She tells me about the children she is taking care of, and what Woof is doing. Sometimes she reminds me that I ain't supposed to try to escape. We talk about California, Utah, the Mormons, and Tom Sawyer and Bill Hickman, and Flaxy and Jim. She never talks about Blue Fox and the trappers, and neither do I. We never talks about us neither, and what we is going to do if I ever gets out of this mess. Almost never does she look at my eyes. She looks at my hands, my feet, my chest, the bars, the window, the floor, but she avoids my eyes, and I don't know why, unless she just don't like me. Sometimes I feels like the only reason she comes to see me is her feeling guilty about giving Woof to Peabody. She thinks it is her fault there was a gunfight where I killed him.

I don't know where I got the courage to do it, but one day I just up and asks her if she ever thinks she might want to marry me if I gets out of this mess. Suddenly she is looking into my eyes like she never has done before. She don't say anything at first, and neither do I. Finally she reaches out and takes my hand, pulling it between the bars. She starts kissing it. I can feel her wet tears on my hand. I cain't talk, cain't hardly breathe, and feels like my knees is about to give out. Then she says:

"After Blue Fox and the trappers I didn't think a good man like you would ever want me."

My mind is spinning like a whirlpool behind a big snag on a river bank. All the time I been thinking I ain't good enough for her, she been thinking she ain't good enough for me. And she calls me a good man. I realizes she ain't near as smart as I thought she was. I ain't no good man.

I can count the times I been to church on the fingers of one hand, and the number of times I have prayed ain't any more. I helped a slave run away, I stole a horse, I learned to gunfight, I killed a man, and telled more lies than I can count. Never had a job more than a week or two, and I ain't read a whole page in the Bible, not ever. And this Peggy thinks I am a good man. I want to crow like a rooster.

I knows I should say something about how the thing with Blue Fox and the trappers don't matter, at least not to me, because there warn't a dad fetch'n thing she could do about it. It warn't her fault, but no sound will come out of my mouth. I just keeps looking into them beautiful eyes, and feeling them tears on my hand.

Finally she reaches through the bars and pulls my face up against them. Then she kisses me on the lips. I never done that before, I mean being kissed by a woman on the mouth. I never knowed a body could feel the way I feels right now. Nobody ever told me about this, not even Tom Sawyer, but maybe he don't know about such things. Hot surges is going up and down my arms and legs, back and forth in my chest and stomach, up my neck and into my head and back down, down, down.

After Peggy leaves I cain't eat my second meal for the day, just shoves it back under the bars to the sheriff. And I cain't sleep all that night. I never had any extra flesh on my bones, and there's even less now. I just ain't hungry or sleepy no more. I just lays there thinking about Peggy, hearing birds singing and music playing when nobody else can hear them things.

Now the sheriff, he ain't too happy with what's happening between me and Peggy. He was hoping he might be the one, but now it's clear she has chosen me. He don't talk to me no more, and ain't so happy about letting Peggy spend so much time with his prisoner. He don't tell me no more what's going on at the courthouse. That makes me real nervous. I didn't want to die before the change in Peggy, but now the idea of hanging makes me frantic. I starts feeling that key more and more. I got to get out. I can't wait for the trial.

Three nights after Peggy starts loving me, I lets myself out of the jail. It's the middle of the night, and the sheriff is sound asleep. I hurries over to Peggy's. All the lanterns is out. I saddles my mule and hangs the sack of food over the horn. Then I hurries over to the house and taps on Peggy's window. As soon as she sees me she lights a lantern and lets me in.

At first she says I have to go back to the jail. She says we won't have a good life if the law is chasing me. I don't agree. I tell her my plan, since I don't know anything about California, is to go back over the mountains and back to Utah, but not along the Humboldt River where all the mean Injuns live. I'll go south and east, from mountain range to mountain range where I know I can find water. The Mormons have settlements all the way to San Diego. When I strike the settlements, I'll go north then back to Howard Egan's at Ibapah. She should join up with a group of Mormons or soldiers and go to Ibapah as soon as she can.

She thinks about my plan for a minute or two, then agrees to meet me at Ibapah. Then she opens a box and hands me a Navy Colt, in a new holster. I don't know where she got it, and she won't tell me. Then she starts kissing me. It's time for me to go, but I don't have the strength to push away from a kiss from Peggy, and don't know if I ever will.

Just when I thinks I will never get away, the door behind me swings open, and there stands the sheriff. He is pointing a gun at me and orders me to raise my hands. I have already strapped the Navy Colt on my hip, but I didn't check to see if it was loaded. I don't want to kill the sheriff anyway. He is a good man even if he wants to take Peggy away from me. Slowly I raises my hands as I turns to face him. Peggy puts her hands over her face and starts to cry.

"It won't look good for you if you try to escape," the sheriff says.

Then he hands me the key, the one Peggy had made at the blacksmith's. I don't know why he is doing this. He says.

"You might need this if they decides to hang you, but I am taking you back for now." I am thinking this sheriff might be my friend after all as I puts the key back in my pocket. He says if we hurry back, nobody will know I tried to get away, not even the judge.

I gives the gun and holster back to Peggy and goes with him. After he locks me back in my cell, he asks if he can see the key again. I don't know why he wants to see it. It don't make sense. He asks me a second time. I pulls the key out of my pocket and shows it to him. He grabs it away from me and takes it back to his desk. He don't explain.

I feels more scared than ever before. I knows this sheriff is going to help them hang me. I think now he just gave me the key so I would trust him and come back easy, and not try to get away. This sheriff is smart like a weasel. From now on I will be more careful. But the key is gone, and it won't be easy now for Peggy to get another. I feel more scared than before. If they decide to hang me tomorrow I will be helpless to do anything about it.

I lick my lips tasting the scent of Peggy's lips. She makes me more happy than I ever thought a person can be, and at the same time I am more scared than I had ever been before. Sleep warn't something that came easy, not anymore.

Chapter 26

The next afternoon I am visited by Bill Hickman, Howard Egan and Tom Sawyer. My three best friends in the world, except Peggy and Jim, have come to see me. Bill says he is going to be my lawyer. The reason they took so long in coming was that Howard had to go all the way back to Great Salt Lake City to find Bill. Before they left to come to Sacramento, Tom had found two of the boys who had driven wagons for Peabody in Wyoming, and they come along so they could tell the judge and jury what Peabody had done to them and other boys.

Two days later the sheriff takes me over to the courthouse for the first part of my trial. I am surprised to see the courtroom is full. There are a lot of soldiers who knowed Peabody, and this makes me nervous. The judge has a mean look on his face, like all he wants is to get the trial over with so they can hang me. The jury is a bunch of men who acts like they don't even care what happens, but every one knows there ain't nothing like a good hanging to give a man an excuse to quit work and get drunk. It seems everybody knowed Peabody, and nobody knows me, except Peggy and Mary and my friends from Utah.

I am scared, but Bill acts like he is doing business as usual. When I asks him how many men he has saved before, he says this is his first court trial, but he will do his best to win it. He says if he don't win, he and Porter Rockwell, expected to arrive in a day or two, will break me out of jail and sneak me back to Utah. He winks after he says this. I wishes he is more serious.

In his opening statement Ebenezer Jenkins says I am a cold-blooded murderer who killed a sergeant in the United States Army, a man who had been sent to Sacramento to protect its residents. He said I was reckless and hotheaded, and gave the sergeant no opportunity to explain why he had taken the boy in custody. I just walked up to the sergeant and murdered him in cold blood, and might do the same to anyone else in the room if they decided to discipline a child in public. The only thing that could prevent a person like me from killing again was the end of a rope.

When it was Bill's turn to make his opening remarks, he walks over to the jury, smiling like he is going to sell them something. He says when he first met me out in Wyoming, when I was driving a wagon for the United States Army, I asked him why Sergeant Peabody made little boys go to bed with him, and why he made them cry so much. He paused and let the jury think about this, then he says that when I saw the sergeant dragging a little boy to his bed in Sacramento, I decided to save the boy. When I tried to pull the boy away, the sergeant drew his gun and said he was going to kill me. I fired back in self defense, to save myself and a helpless child. The town of Sacramento ought to be ashamed of itself for throwing me in jail. They should have pinned a badge on me, given me the key to the city, and had a hero's welcome for the young man from Missouri who dared stand up to a wicked and evil man who deserved to die.

I feels a little better now, but there is no cheers when Bill finishes his speech. Nobody takes off my handcuffs. Bill's first witnesses was the two boys they had brung with them from Great Salt Lake City. When the first boy starts to tell what Peabody had done to him, Jenkins objects, saying Huck Finn is on trial here, not Sergeant Peabody. The judge makes him sit down, and let the boys tell their stories.

Jenkin's witnesses was the two men who saw me shoot the sergeant. Both of them says they saw me fire three times, smooth and fast like a man who had been born with a gun in my hand. The sergeant never had a chance to defend himself, even though he got his gun out of its holster. He didn't fire a single ball, while I was in the process of emptying my gun, when one bullet would have been enough. They didn't believe my story that the sergeant had pulled out his gun first. Jenkins argues that if that were the case the sergeant would have been able to defend himself, not just stand there like a helpless child while three balls entered his chest.

When the witnesses was done, Bill asks the judge for permission to do a demonstration to show the court how it was not only possible, but likely, that the sergeant had drawn his gun first. Bill nods to the back of the room. Tom Sawyer comes forward, carrying two holsters and belts, each carrying a Navy Colt revolver. Bill shows the guns to the judge, who confirms that neither gun is loaded. Then Bill tosses one of the gun belts to Jenkins, ordering him to strap it on. When the lawyer hesitates, the judge orders him to do it. Then Bill tosses the second gun belt over to me, telling the sheriff to remove my handcuffs so I could do a demonstration for the court. After getting a nod from the judge the sheriff does it. I straps on the gun.

Bill guides me to the middle of the room, facing Ebenezer Jenkins. He tells Ebeneezer to draw his pistol, point it at me, and cock back the hammer. Everyone laughs when he says he wishes the gun was loaded so he could spare the city of Sacramento the expense of a hanging.

Bill is in no hurry to get this over with. He tells the jury to take a good look at what is happening, and pretend for a moment that Ebenezer Jenkins is Sergeant Peabody, who has drawn his gun because Huck Finn has just stolen away his prisoner, the little boy. He tells Jenkins to order Huck Finn to let go of the prisoner, or be shot. Bill tells Jenkins to watch Huck Finn, to pull his trigger if Huck doesn't obey, or if Huck goes for his gun.

Bill tells Jenkins to cock back the hammer on the pistol he is pointing at me. Then Bill tells him that if I do the wrong thing and go for my gun he should pull the trigger and kill me as if the gun ain't empty. He tells the jury to watch Jenkins' gun real careful, and Huck Finn's too, so they will know which one shoots first. Then Bill tells me to draw and shoot whenever I wants to. I have played this game ten thousand times, and knows what to do.

"But, what if . . ." I says, looking over at Bill like maybe I don't understand everything. Then I draws and shoots. Jenkins don't see it coming. My gun clicks a full second before his and the whole jury knows it.

"I wasn't ready," Jenkins says. "Let's do it again." He is surprised when Bill don't have a problem with that. I puts my gun back in the holster. Jenkins cocks his again, and points it at me, this time holding it with both hands, and looking real serious. I reaches around with my left hand to scratch my fanny while some of the men starts to laugh, then draws and shoots. Again I am faster. Jenkins is mad and wants to do it again. This time as soon as he cocks back the hammer, I draws and shoots him. I beat him three times. Jenkins wants to do it again, but the judge says that is enough. The marshall takes away my gun and puts the handcuffs back on.

Then Bill says he has one more witness, a boy named Woof, the little boy who saw it all right up front. Jenkins objects, saying the boy doesn't understand or speak English. Bill says that don't change the fact that he was there, and saw what happened better than anybody else. The back door comes open and Peggy marches forward, holding tight onto Woof's little arm, dragging him behind her. He don't want to come. He is afraid of all the people, all the big men. He is pulling back as hard as he can, trying to bite Peggy's hand, yelling in protest, but nobody can understand what he says.

Peggy drags him right up to the witness chair, throws him in it, and holds him tight while he continues to squirm. I am surprised that Peggy don't try to calm him, hold him to her bosom, cooing kind little words so he will know it is all right. She is a mean washer woman, holding him in the chair like she is holding a goose so someone else can chop its head off. I starts to get up and go to the boy. He sees me for the first time, and tries to come to me, but Peggy holds him fast. The sheriff pulls me back and makes me sit down again.

"Let him go," Bill says to Peggy, when he knows everybody in the room is watching. She does it.

Woof flies off the chair, over the railing, and before I knows it he has latched onto my leg, and he ain't about to let go, even if they tries to kill him. Bill tells everybody to look at Woof, then reminds the jury that Woof is the court's best eye witness because he was right there, being pulled back and forth between Huck Finn and Sergeant Peabody when the shooting started. Then he says:

"When the shooting was over this little Indian boy didn't throw his arms around Sergeant Peabody and start crying. No, he was hanging onto Huck's leg just like he is doing now. We all know the boy can't speak or understand English, so we have to figure out what he would want to tell us, if he could."

Jenkins tried to object, but the judge told him to shut up and sit down.

"Do the boy's actions agree with the prosecution's claim that Huck Finn is a mean-hearted outlaw who would gun down an innocent person without cause? This boy was in the middle of a gun fight to the death. He saw both men, and what they did, before and after the fight began. So who does the boy trust more than any other man in this room? The defendant is this boy's hero, the man who saved him from the clutches of an evil and wicked man. If we could ask this boy if he is in favor of hanging Huck Finn, or letting him go, we all know what the boy would say. How can the court ignore the honesty of an innocent and frightened child? I think the court knows what to do, so let's do it."

Peggy goes back to her seat, but the judge lets the boy stay with me. Bill is pleased because the jury would see Woof right up to the end. There is a few more closing comments, then the jury goes out to talk about what had happened in the courtroom. They ain't gone very long, maybe half an hour, and when they returns they told the judge they decided I was innocent. The next thing I knowed I am being hugged by Woof, Peggy, Bill and Tom, all at once while the sheriff is trying to take off my handcuffs. I is the happiest boy alive.

The next day Peggy and me goes to see that sour-faced old judge and asks him if he wants to have a wedding since he can't have a hanging. He says he does. Tom is the best man, and Mary is the best woman. Woof holds the ring, and eats half the wedding cake all by himself.

A few days later Peggy, me and Woof gathers up our things for our journey back to Ibapah, the paradise in the desert. Howard, Bill and Tom get ready to go with us.

Peggy and me have a plan. We are going back to Iowa Territory and see how little Flaxy is getting along, then I want to float down the river some, show Peggy my favorite places where I growed up. Just lazy around some, ketch a mess of catfish, swim in the river, play some at night and sleep when the sun shines. Maybe we can figure out where we want to live and what we wants to do with the rest of our lives. I don't rightly care what we decides, as long as we do it together.

As for Tom, he says he is coming with us, but he don't seem real happy to go home. He liked his adventures with the Army and the Mormons, once we got away from Blue Fox, but he says real private like that he misses Becky Thatcher and wants to see her, but he is sure he will come west again, maybe to live forever.

When I asks Howard Egan if he thinks Jim will want to go home with us, he says Jim doesn't want to go back to a place where white folks bosses him around and calls him *boy* and *nigger*. Howard tells me Jim has joined Ike as co-chief of their little Goshute band, and has even found himself a new squaw. Jim won't want to be leaving anytime soon. Especially he don't want to go through country where the United States Army might see him and make him be a cook again, or shoot him for running away.

When we say goodby to Mary and the children, the sheriff is there fixing a broken window. She has invited him to stay for supper. We rides right through the Humboldt River country where I learns that book honeymoons and real honeymoons ain't the same, but Peggy and me are too happy to care about that.

The End

Other Western Adventures
by Lee Nelson

Storm Testament I
Storm Testament II
Storm Testament III
Storm Testament IV
Storm Testament V
Rockwell
Walkara
Cassidy
Storm Gold
Black Hawk Journey
Moriah Confession
Ephraim Chronicles
Wasatch Savage

More information on these and other Lee Nelson titles is available by calling 1-800-SKYBOOK or by visiting **www.cedarfort.com**

9 26575 76801 8